Russell Celyn Jones is the author of *Soldiers and Innocents* (which won the David Higham prize), *Small Times*, *An Interference of Light* and *The Eros Hunter*. He has taught at universities in England, the USA and South Africa. He lives in London and is a regular book reviewer for *The Times*.

SURFACE
TENSION

Russell Celyn Jones

An *Abacus* Book

First published in Great Britain by Abacus in 2001

Copyright © Russell Celyn Jones, 2001

A CIP catalogue record for this book
is available from the British Library.

ISBN 0 349 11311 4

Typeset in Cheltenham by M Rules

Printed and bound in Great Britain
by Creative Print and Design (Wales) Ebbw Vale

Abacus
A division of
Little, Brown and Company (UK)
Brettenham House
Lancaster Place
London WC2E 7EN

For my children
Rebecca, Rachel and Ben

PART ONE

'Eyes and ears are false witnesses if I do not know the language.'

— HERACLITUS

SYNAPSES

Whenever I think of a hospital I always think of it as a woman. Those sweetheart impulses governing the place are why I work here and why I never want to work anywhere else. Institutions shackle the imagination and make a stone of the heart, but this one is inspirational. It has made my luck. It's also been my longest relationship, the one anatomy I've remained faithful to, along with the women who manage my schedule: like Mavis, the control clerk who just now informs me that patient Jackson in Cardio is awaiting a ride to Surgery One.

As I wheel a large chair out of the mess Mavis hands me a love note to deliver to the male nurse she's sweet on in Cardio. Then she starts coughing, hacking away like a plumber splitting floorboards. Sooner or later Mavis's sixty-a-day habit is going to put her on the other side of the Front Line, I keep telling her.

From the neutrality of the porters' mess I enter the roaring thoroughfare of the hospital corridor, enter the stream of traumatics. Motes of dust float like spindrift in the shafts of early evening light.

In Cardio I ask the duty sister for Jackson. Without looking up from her desk she points to the far end of the ward of occupied beds, and I am as astonished by the sight of this homogenous community of the sick as on the first day I started working here, seven years ago. How it must shake you down, to be one moment pickling apricots, studying the racing form, reading an aerogramme from a prodigal child, then in the next waking up in here without use of limbs, an IV in your arm, feeding tubes up your nose, surrounded by strangers in starched white gowns. The confusion still registers on their faces.

We know them only when they are sick, but it never escapes me that these men and women, until they lost their way, have led full lives. Many of the stroke victims have lost their voices and cannot tell us these stories. So it is a matter of courtesy that they be treated with respect, as they stand naked in backless gowns, lifted on to a commode, with a raw hurt burning in their eyes. Any good medic knows to take this holistic approach – like the male nurse who helps me lift Jackson from her bed on to the chair.

I slip him Mavis's love note and can't help feeling sorry for her. Unrequited love is an illness too, with no known cure. The erotic cathexis of a hospital extends only so far. It's a doctor and nurse affair that does not engulf the auxiliary staff. On account of their quotidian contact with naked flesh, medics' desire builds throughout the day like electrons picked up by a generator. On the out, in mufti, they fall for each other. But they never fall for me, or Mavis or anyone else in the porters' mess. We are low caste, the untouchables.

The only women to fall for me have all been patients. Such as the tall Texan with psoriasis; the north London Jewish girl with diabetes; the African-American lesbian with gynaecological complications; the Irish fiddle player with cancer (God rest her soul). All these women I have had time with, but couldn't settle with any of them. They complained of me being distant, cold even. Perhaps the truth is I don't like to give out. I don't enjoy losing control, allowing someone to push me around like the steel balls in a pinball machine. I have only ever truly belonged to one woman – my sister Geena. But that's another story I shall come to.

Patient Jackson is black, in her sixties, eighteen stones on the scales and terrified. She wears a gossamer veil over her thinning hair. On her feet are slippers with little pink tassels. As I wheel her through the ward the other patients watch our progress. They can't speak and they can't raise their arms to offer her a send-off to Surgery, but I sense the goodwill in their stony silence. And gratitude in their eyes that it isn't them going under the knife.

On the way to Surgery I ask my patient what op she's having, but she doesn't reply. So I ramble on about how nice the surgeon on duty today is, which is an out-and-out lie. The surgeon's perfectly competent, but he's a racist and I know she wouldn't want to hear that. But whatever I say is lost on her. She can't speak a word of English.

In Surgery I leave the patient in a bay and go looking for a nurse. On the slab in theatre is a young woman under anaesthetic. She is having a tonsillectomy, so the surgeon really has no business peeling the sheet down to her ankles. What he is staring at with such lewd fascination is her tattoo. Her pubic bush constitutes the body of a black widow spider, its legs tattooed down her thighs. 'Can you imagine going down on *that*?' the surgeon says to me. 'One of these days some guy's going to take a two-by-four to that thing.' When I fail to reply the surgeon looks up at me, sees that I am only a porter and his eyes glaze over.

I've never wanted to be a doctor. They may perform miracles but their personalities are a disease. Men of medical science whose ambition is aimed squarely at gaining power in the institution are lost to the good world. They seek promotion, then spend their lives in politics.

I've never wanted to be a nurse either, not even a paramedic.

5

I am happy with my place in the scheme of things. I know my Re-sus ABC, how to treat wounds, recognise dinner-fork fractures, cerebral vacuolar attacks, coronary thrombosis. These things I have picked up along the way. But I don't perform miracles. I help those who do, content in the routine that hardly changes from day to day, week to week, year to year.

Normally eight porters on each shift, we are two down today, throwing what we call a duvet-day on the busiest end of the hospital week. Which is why I am now running from Surgery into Neo-Natal, Chest, Heart, Liver & Kidney with a sackful of blood and urine samples for the Path-Lab. I am running but nurses hardly notice me. They do not care to know who I am, what I know.

The only nurses who engage with me for longer than a couple of seconds and about something other than urine samples are the West Indian mothers-of-five. They tease me in the canteen during my dinner break for having a book open on the table beside my plate. The closest they come to making a direct statement is to call me a dreamer, and then throw their heads back in peals of laughter. But in such a place as this, to be a dreamer is the only way to fly.

If nurses hardly notice me then doctors don't even see me. So it comes as something of a surprise when a junior doctor sitting at my table, who has been watching me for some time with my head in my book, leans across the Formica and asks why I don't try to do something more with my life. (He is a New Zealander . . . does that explain anything?)

What is more? I ask.

He points to my book. More would be taking a degree course in care management.

I say, When you refuse all power no one will ever be afraid of you.

The junior doctor laughs and asks why I read if not to advance myself.

I tell him, What I read and what I do for a living move in opposite directions.

The junior doctor admits that he has no time for reading, on call one hundred hours per week. I tell him how my lowly, dead-end job gives me not just the time but the space to absorb what I read. The job is not who I am.

Then who are you? he wants to know.

All I know for sure is that I am a reader and that literature is as real as any hospital.

He seems to think about that for a second, then replies, Work is a defence against despair.

I say, What is your defence against work?

The junior doctor gives up on me and leaves the canteen and I am able to return to my book, *All Quiet on the Western Front*, that does not flinch from describing the wounded and the dead. The characters are teenage recruits who, unlike the patients in Cardio, have not had a chance to settle into an adult life before finding themselves face-down in the earth as the darkness rocks and rages around them, as whole woods are lifted into the air and smashed to pieces. They feel a thousand years old applying emergency first aid to their school friends dying in meadows tossed like storm seas, as bayonets of even younger recruits pierce the mist of poison gas that wriggles into the trenches like jellyfish. Coffins are ripped out of a cemetery and the sky rains corpses – the dead who provide cover for the living, trying to survive someone else's bad idea.

The control clerk calls me on the shortwave and tells me to go to Thorogood Ward and take a Purple-Plus to the Mortuary. This is not as contradictory as it seems (what I read and what I do move in opposite directions, etc.). As many people come here to die as to be cured. Nonetheless, Mavis feels the need to warn me in advance that the Purple-Plus is a girl of nine, a victim of meningitis.

I can hear the wailing from outside the ward. As I enter

7

Thorogood I see the commotion created by the mother who lays across the bed and won't allow anyone to take her child away. But there are patients waiting for this bed and two nurses are gently trying to prize the mother's hands from the body. It is very upsetting for everyone.

I suggest that I take the mother as well to the Mortuary. So she sits in my wheelchair, this poor distressed woman, and the nurses lay the corpse, wrapped in a starched white sheet, in her lap.

Outside the ward the movement of the chair seems to comfort her. There is a sense of optimism that comes from motion, as though time is somehow being reversed. She is even able to talk with me, explaining how her daughter was at a birthday party when she was taken ill. Then her grief is fully reprieved as we enter the elevator. Two other persons, laughing as we step into the lift, are immediately silenced by the tangle of bodies on my wheelchair, by the sight of five fingernails painted orange protruding from the sheet and a flash of red hair flecked with silver glitter that the mother holds in her hand.

Mavis finds me on the shortwave again while I'm still in the Mortuary. She saves me from my morbid feelings with a detail designed to give me a lift. She tells me to go and deliver a couple of oxygen cylinders to Maternity.

Maternity is the only wing of a hospital where no one is actually ill. In pain maybe, but very different to the pain in, say, Cancer or A&E. Maternity is upbeat, a goldrush town where every panhandler walks away with something precious. Five, maybe ten times a shift I go into Maternity and witness at least one child being born into the world. And sure enough, as I arrive, a girl (eight pounds, six ounces) is delivered to a bricklayer's wife, as he stands weeping with joy over her bed, raising the flag in the memory cells of the infant's brain. Synapses bring out the very best in human nature. Love is a biological imperative and such intense moments of it that I see may never be achieved again. But that's the thing about Maternity, you get to see truth and beauty at its peak. So whenever my control clerk sends me to the Delivery Suite, it's free air miles to me.

DARK SIDE OF THE MOON

I track down my sister Geena by ringing her mobile phone. She tells me she's in the Royal Mail on Upper Street and can she crash at my place tonight. My parents have been putting the thumbscrews on her again: telling her to find a job. Whenever this happens she pitches up at my flat and stays for a week or so, making the pilgrimage along the disused railway line from where they live in Finsbury Park to where I live in Highgate Hill, carrying all her CDs and videos in a Virgin Megastore carrier bag. She has her own set of keys to my flat but tells me she's lost them . . . again. Geena has gone through five sets of my keys in as many years. I start to ponder the obvious implications of how she's going to get in when I'm asleep, etc. If I go home now she'll only wake me by ringing the bell in the early hours. So I decide I may as well join her in the Royal Mail.

In an eight-hour shift I must put in twenty miles of footwork. But those miles are never as arduous as this slog down the Holloway Road, which links Highgate to Upper Street, a junk-yard of second-hand furniture stores, off-licences, theme pubs, kebabs, import-export, Hal-Al butchers, curry emporiums. If I were a tourist and pitched up here on my travels I'd think, *Whoa!* Take me back to Kansas! This arterial road (A1!) has long been colonised by the immigrant poor as a stepping stone into Greater London and I don't really know what it means; I cannot speak the language, it is a foreign fiction.

Twenty minutes later I'm penetrating a crowd of students, office workers, rude boys and raggas wearing gold chains and gold teeth, black girls with blue weaves in their hair in the Royal Mail. This ecumenical gathering is catching a football game on the big screen. When the ball flies into the roof of a net they all raise their arms as though in a revivalist meeting. I spot Geena at the back of the room and push my way to the bar and buy two Budweisers.

I hand her one of the beers and her eyes smile at me from down at my chest. I often wonder how such a discrepancy in height could occur when both my mother and father are tall. It's like that rusty hue in her blond hair, which she prefers to wear in a French plait, that no one else has got in the family. There's a bit of the red squirrel in her.

Geena is four years older than I am. Thirty-two and no job, no pressing reason to get out of bed. She lives exactly as she did at eighteen: carefree, uncommitted, hanging-out, living for the day, as if she fears getting too far away from youth, as though there are questions about youth that she still has to solve before she can move on. I often think that something about the adult world has failed Geena, but don't know what. The adult world is a malign shadow in the beautiful picture of childhood, from which she has never woken.

She and her posse are debating whether or not to go on to a club. Everyone has to be in the mood for a club. They start late and cost proper coin. Eight quid to get in, ten quid for E, five quid for some skunk and another fifteen for drinks. The no's win the debate. So no club then, but one thing's for sure, they can't stay here. The Royal Mail is not working for them.

11

Mobile phones are firing off every few seconds as their owners stay in constant communication with other members of their herd, travelling up and down the Essex Road in cars, drinking in the Salmon and Compass in Chapel Market, playing pool in a Turkish shebeen in Dalston. I sense these separate cells getting closer to a single pasture when Geena says on her mobile: 'We'll wait ten minutes. But if you come and we aren't here, we've gone back to Efes. If it's not happening in Efes, I'll give you another call and tell you where we are.'

A courting couple in the group announce they're throwing in the towel. They are giving up altogether in search of the crack, to go home and watch *Peggy Sue Got Married* on the VCR. This simple change of heart, this almost imperceptible shift in aspirations, puts a downer on the others. It is a nail in the coffin as far as they are concerned. It reeks of maturation. Mortality. The bell tolls for thee. Two young hipsters are growing up and the survivors start to smell the smoke in the air.

We leave the Royal Mail for Efes. But as soon as we are out on the street the destination is changed. We're going to the Dark Side of the Moon instead. The mobiles are all fired up again and the herd moves on, getting closer to a single field.

Wandering down Upper Street I keep my distance from Geena, so as not to cramp her style among her friends. 'Friends' may be an elaboration of the truth. The truth is they mock her. She is ten years older than the oldest of them. The prejudice of these young bloods is to regard anyone over twenty-five as through, *kaput*, sad fucks, particularly those like Geena who try to muscle in on their action. So she plays the percentage game, working hard to avoid amorous attentions from the boys, which would alienate the girls, and never venturing out in the midday sun with them. Sunlight is more discriminatory on age than the gloaming of a pub where she met them in the first place.

12

One of the reasons why I think she still lives at our parents' home is to emulate her friends, who are all living at home too. Ditto: adorning her body with permanent mutilations; an abstract expressionist tattoo on her left arm, diamond in her nose, a navel ring. She wears hundred-pound trainers with long dresses. The paint job – foundation, mascara, lipstick – takes her an hour to apply.

But there are differences. Out on Upper Street I overhear some of them talking of college, career paths. Certainly they all have jobs, as shop assistants, lifeguards, office juniors; while in ten years Geena has put in three and a half weeks paid employment at Prêt à Manger in Piccadilly Circus, and four and a half days as a filing clerk at Murphy's Construction. I was eighteen at the time, studying for my A levels at the kitchen table when she would drag in at six, a fine grey dust of cement cascading off her narrow shoulders. Her bright eyes were dimmed and she smelled of compressors, grease, steel . . . masculine odours. Red diesel rimmed the cuffs of her white blouse. She even picked up an Irish accent that made her sound harsh and comic at the same time.

One Friday I went to meet her at the construction site high up on the Westway flyover. Elevated position, sublunary work. She walked out of a Portakabin to meet me, through a gauntlet of labourers driving their shovels into piles of sand, using the inside of their knees to propel the shafts – flesh, wood, steel, all one nexus. I shivered, thinking of Geena logging them in, logging them out, making their teas, the brunt of their violent sex fantasies. It was me this time who encouraged her to hand in her notice.

She signed on a few days later, and the DHS insisted she take another job or enrol on a skills course. So she stopped signing on. She disappeared from registers, paid no poll tax, forfeited her right to vote, lost her banking privileges and began to live off windfalls from me and my parents. Ever since she has floated over the world as though in a glass-bottom boat, where the sharks, currents and cold can't get to her.

We reach the Dark Side of the Moon, which is so packed the bouncer (black, built) won't let us through. He does however allow me in on my own to get a round to bring back to the posse (they don't deign to talk to me but they drink my beer; my money's good as anyone's).

Outside we are forced to stand inside a cordon, behind a red line painted on the pavement. Clutching my plastic glass to my chest I'm reminded of the tube in rush hour. That's hard work, but this is meant to be fun, and optional. I am crushed against strangers, inhaling their cheap colognes and bedsit odours, but I can't talk to them because they're all in their late teens, early twenties and therefore too cool. I start to envy the couple who drifted off earlier to watch *Peggy Sue Got Married* and distractedly slip a foot over the edge of the red line. The bouncer appears in my face ordering me back inside the line. I am so staggered by the penal conditions I let out a loud sigh which sings to another like-soul in the crowd. The woman smiles at me. I give myself just enough time as is decent, or cool, to take a measure of this button-lipped, watery-eyed brunette in ellesse combats and bell top, but take it no further. I would if I could, but don't know the terms of engagement.

The terms of engagement are pretty atavistic. A young girl in a tight mini-skirt is refused entry into the bar to use the toilets. She disappears behind a parked car, rolls up her skirt and squats. Moments later she returns, smoothing down her skirt. Two young guys who've been throwing glances at her, wander casually behind the same parked car and silently inspect her pool of urine.

Geena and her friends' opinion of the Dark Side of the Moon tonight oscillates back and forth, the criteria too subtle for my eyes and ears. Some of it has to do with the music on the PA.

Manufactured bands make them feel down, and formerly cool artists who have become manufactured, like Whitney Houston.

'Whitney's gone cheesy, man, trying to be Anita Baker.'

The music changes. Things look up again.

Geena declares, 'Lauren Hill, she's safe.'

'Nah, she's too right on.'

'No she ain't,' Geena, the elder, protests. 'What did she say the other day, she said she'd rather have a baby die than a white person listening to her music.'

'But that's not what she meant at all.'

'That's a direct quote.'

The music moves on. Drum and Bass.

'Alex, man! Alex Reece is seriously safer than Goldie.'

And so it goes. One band is up and the other down, changing status in the space of a week. I can see now why Geena fears taking a few days out. She would be in serious risk of getting behind, going cheesy on them. There are no classics in this world, nothing is stable.

I suffer all this for the sake of a set of keys. I promise myself that tomorrow I'll get a spare set cut, for Geena to lose again. In the meantime all I have to meditate on is the traffic, passing by in an endless procession. The windows of the cars are so dark they appear auto-piloted. The same old Mercedes convertible loops around for a second time, circling our punitive settlement like a meteor around a planet. On its third orbit there are two guys in the back seat who weren't there before. They are smoking huge reefers and looking us over. I watch the convertible pull over a few yards up the road and the two guys in the back get out. The driver U-turns in the middle of Upper Street and cruises past, stopping a few yards further down from the Dark Side of the Moon.

I feel that woman's eyes on me again, the woman in the ellesse combats. My moment has come to say something to

15

her. It's do or die. I misquote something I've read recently. 'I have the feeling that all these cars are gathering for a special reason that I don't understand.'

'Do you have a car?' she asks.

'No.'

'I do,' she replies.

The conversation stalls. I sense this relationship hitting the rocks already.

But then she tries again, with better results.

'It's like the government building roads to ease congestion. Four lanes, eight lanes, sixteen lanes . . . it never makes any difference.'

'Because the more roads you build the more traffic you create.'

'Exactly. My name's Natasha.'

'Mark,' I say and we shake hands.

'Are you two going to talk about cars all night?' Geena breaks in, a keen set of ears, particularly for her brother's business. As she speaks she steps outside the cordon, one foot beyond the red line. In the next instant she is bowled over by two blokes wearing hoods. For a moment I feel unable to cross the line as though a more substantial barrier exists. But then I do go beyond it, the first out, followed by her friends, who are all clucking away behind my back as I pick Geena to her feet. Her bag has gone, changed hands, raced down Upper Street with the steamers. I see them jump into the Mercedes convertible and the car pulls away at speed.

I look at Geena again and see beads of sweat forming on her face. Her eyes are bulging and she makes a gargling noise in her throat. She lists to one side and I just manage to catch her from falling on to the pavement.

As she comes round, she says, 'I just heard the sea; I could see that.'

It signals an early end to the night.

I take Geena back to my place in a taxi. The motion of the cab brings her round. 'Did those guys hurt you?' I ask.

'All I remember is seeing the sea . . . talking.'

'What do you mean talking, the sea talking?'

'I heard voices and then the sea lit up like a spotlight was shone on it.'

I throw back my head. 'I don't know how you can afford to get drunk, I really don't.'

'I'm not drunk. I was hallucinating.'

'What are you on?'

'I'm not on anything.'

'Then what's happening, Geena?'

'What's happening? The most extraordinary thing is happening, that's what's happening. Two times now I've had, felt this, my shoulder joint shrinking. I get pins and needles in my hands. I see a big black space with white spots around it; I see that. I hear voices. The voices are like camera flashes and then I see other things.' She talks with a powerful conviction and such strangeness in her voice that it worries me.

'What things?'

'There's this woman; I've seen her. I feel a bit desolate when she goes.'

'What does she look like?'

'Don't know. It's always too brief to tell.'

I sigh. 'And you've lost your bag.'

'My phone was in my bag. Now I don't know where everyone's going.'

My colleagues in the porters' unit prefer to live way out in the sticks – Epping, Eltham, Enfield – where a two- or three-bedroom flat is affordable. The downside is the hour and a half it takes them to travel to work. I rent a bedsit up the road from the hospital and walk in. Someone's attic for storing junk once upon a time, it is now partitioned into a living room, kitchen and bathroom and filled with cheap furniture. My books are all down one wall.

When Geena and I arrive there we hit the sack. We fall asleep in each other's arms, and the relief goes all around the world.

I can't just say that and leave it there, so let me declare right now: Geena's body does not articulate carnality to me. The natural borders are always present. It's a childhood thing, sharing the same bed, a privilege my parents withdrew when Geena reached puberty. They'd shut my door and keep hers open. Not that it stopped her roaming back into my room after they'd gone to bed. By torchlight under the sheet we'd play gin rummy and talk of death and running away from home – which basically is the same thing when you are eight and twelve. At dawn she'd go back to her own room.

Some people sleep with their cats or their dogs. I sleep with Geena. End of story.

I know of some brothers and sisters who are devoted without sharing their griefs and intimacies. Their private lives remain private. Geena and I just don't follow that pattern at all. I am the first and last person she talks to about her dreams and failures. And no one comes near to the relationship I have with her. This has always been the case. If I was bullied at school, she would be my only confidant for such a humiliating experience. I stole from sweet shops, I shared the caramel cup with her. I made pipe bombs filled with weedkiller and sugar and set them off in garages, wanting only to impress her with my pyrotechnics. I wrecked garden sheds purely to secure her love. If I fancy someone I take an account of the woman to Geena; she imparts her advice. Guys she goes out with all come to me in the end for information. Not that I tell them anything. 'Oh, she's an enigma,' I say. Not so, not to me. Sometimes she says, 'Mark, how am I ever going to find a man who'll mean as much to me as you? Who'll understand me as well as you do? You know what I'm thinking before I've thought it.'

We are so empathetic it sparks off premonitions. I've been sitting at home at my parents' flat and suddenly got out of the chair and walked three blocks until I found Geena crawling on her hands and knees on a grass verge after some monumental piss-up. Another time when we were ten and fourteen we were ambling along Stroud Green Road together when a couple drove past on a Lambretta scooter. We both clocked them pointing and laughing at an old Vespa parked outside the butcher, and simultaneously started running after them. There were two factors pushing us forward. One: that Vespa belonged to the butcher's son, whom we had known all our lives and liked. Two: we knew they were going to crash. And sure enough they took a left turn, disappeared from view, and then we heard a sound of steel screaming and glass smashing. Seconds later we found them spilled onto the road, their scooter smoking and broken beside them. They'd skidded on black ice.

We have recalled that event many times. Just how did we know? After they'd laughed at the Vespa, did we set off together, or was there a split second interval between her reaction and mine? In other words, had it been Geena's premonition and I followed? I think maybe it was, but the event has become fused in our minds as synchronous. The agency of love is two instincts working in the same direction like that. It's definitely claustrophobic, but preferable to living in parallel emotional universes. In all our lives we have never been apart for more than twenty-four hours. From the moment we go our separate ways in the day we start to feel the pinch and begin making mental preparations to end the separation.

In the middle of the night Geena wakes me when she rises from the sofa bed and drags her feet, pigeon-toed, to the door. I turn on the bedside lamp – an illuminated medieval Globe – and see her looking out into the kitchen. She wears the green plaid pajamas I bought her one Christmas. Her arms hang to the side, her eyes engrossed in what lay beyond the door.

'What's wrong?' I ask. 'Can't you sleep?'

In that glazed and alien voice I'd first heard in the taxi and which seems to come from another place, she describes what she's just seen. 'There was a very large room; I saw that. And voices coming from inside, the same voices I heard before. I don't know whose, but they brightened that room.'

'You're sleepwalking,' I suggest.

'No, I'm awake.' She returns to bed. 'And that room seemed awfully familiar, Mark.' She clenches her hand into a fist and worries her mouth with it.

The hallucination had carried such a high voltage she is too frightened to close her eyes. A door slamming in the flat below makes her jump. She says it 'feels' like someone's gone mad.

Geena does finally fall asleep sucking her thumb, but I am not so lucky. These things she suffers have an atrophying effect on me. I stay up for another hour reading a collection of Freud's essays. I am struck by one in which Freud relates the tale of a boy who calls out to his aunt to speak to him, because he is frightened of the dark. His aunt says, 'What good would that do? You can't see me.' And the boy answers, 'That does not matter. If anyone speaks it gets light.'

WHITE CHRISTMAS

Geena's new best friend is Natasha, the woman I talked to outside the Dark Side of the Moon. They met there again and have gone out together every night consecutively, drinking, clubbing . . . who knows what exactly. I'm more sanguine about this new friend than all her others. Natasha is crowding thirty for one thing.

On Thursday afternoon, with an hour left of my shift I am manning the phone in the porters' mess while Mavis is having a fag outside the non-smoking building when Natasha telephones. I don't realise it's her at first.

She asks for me by name. 'This is he,' I say.

'Oh hi, this is Natasha . . . we met outside the Moon the night your sister got mugged?'

'Sure, I remember you. Geena's told me—'

'Geena gave me your number.'

Natasha doesn't mess around. She asks straight up if we could meet – to talk about Geena. About this she is specific.

I don't quite know how to read the signs, but this is not the first time I've been subpoenaed by a new friend of my sister to give a character reference. Geena raises more questions than answers: the thirty-two-year-old who acts like a teenager, the VCR archivist of soap operas who's never had a proper job, and so on. People convince themselves that Geena is hiding something, like a history of mental illness in the family. My job is to reassure them with my presence, the sane younger brother with a proper job.

'I don't mind meeting up, but can I bring Geena along too?' I say.

There is a pause. 'That kind of defeats the purpose really.'

A background noise travels down my receiver of men shouting, phones ringing, keyboards clicking. Natasha is a busy girl in a busy life.

'I'll only tell her whatever we discuss, you know.'

'Okay bring her. I don't care.'

'I hate it when people say I don't care, when what they mean is I don't mind.'

'I don't mind and I don't care. Come round to my place tonight. Geena has the address.'

The moment I put down the phone the two West Indian women who coordinate the hospital cleaners from the same mess start to make assumptions. 'Markie has a girlfriend!'

'She's not a girlfriend.'

'Our Markie's got himself a pretty little girl,' the one called Angela breathes on the words.

Ginger and BJ, two porters taking five in the mess join in with the chorus. 'Way to go, Mark. Slip her a crippler.'

I don't bother to reply, for what can you say to grown men who have nothing in the world to trade on other than their unskilled labour, who live for a decade in the hope of hearing some doctor commend them, then spend the next decade rolling those couple of words around in their heads like a song. Ginger and BJ are empty carapaces.

Mavis comes back into the mess in the middle of all this. The phone rings, she records the information in the daily worksheet, then says to me, 'Urgent samples in Meyrick for the Path-Lab. On your bike, lover boy.'

Early evening, Geena and I travel to west London in a mini-cab. She is so morbidly self-absorbed I pass the time staring out of the window. I snatch glimpses of the defunct Regent's canal under the Westway flyover and the vast lunar industrial desert behind Paddington station. For that moment all the trouble is outside there and not in here and allows me space to meditate, to consider how decommissioned industrial sites attract me like street hookers. They bring out lewd impulses that leave me feeling disorientated. Perhaps it is in human nature to feel drawn by ruins because they reflect our fallen nature. Buildings coming down are more inspiring than build-ings going up.

Out there amongst the rubble and beside the polluted canal nature has taken over again. Flowers and trees and shrubs push through the broken concrete and the rusting steel. Urban deserts like these can be a respite from metropolitan intensities. Like the disused railway line Geena and I spent so much of our childhood playing on. Yet I don't like the country at all, where there is only nature. Nature is not nice, it needs architecture to defend us from it. The other reason why I like cities and not the country is cities evolve over centuries of time, and are what we remember. They are dreams made man-ifest.

I wish to share my insights with Geena. 'Modern cities may not be objects of art, as are ancient cities, nor are they expen-sive to build, as say, Rome and Jerusalem, but all cities, ancient and modern, exist because we wish them to exist. They're choices of will. While mountains, rivers and seas were made before our time, and in a few minutes of violence.'

'They all come to an end though, don't they – cities,' she says. 'But not mountains, not the sea . . . God's country.'

'God's country, but can you speak the language?'

'I read a poem the other day. Want to hear it?'

'You learned it off by heart?'

'It's not long.'

'Go ahead, please.'

'"I sought my soul – but my soul I could not see;

'"I sought my God – but my God eluded me:

'"I sought my brother – and found all three."'

I felt a blush kindling my cheek. 'So what do you want me to tell Natasha when we get there? That you're MI5? An RAF pilot?'

'Tell her anything you like.'

'It would be useful to know in advance, so I don't embarrass you.'

'I haven't told her any lies. I don't think.'

'What have you done together?'

'We've been to the pictures.'

'What film did you see?'

'I think it was, *The Invention of Love.*'

'That's a play, not a film.'

'Yes, sorry. Half of it was in Latin. We walked out in the interval.'

'What else have you done?'

Before she can answer the mini-cab swings violently to avoid a motorcycle courier and I'm thrown on top of her. I feel the chassis of this old Peugeot swinging on its suspension, hear the exhaust pipe rattling. We turn into Westbourne Park Road before I manage to climb off.

Geena's face is taut with anxiety and perspiring heavily. 'I heard someone singing "White Christmas"; I heard that. Those two words.'

'Who was singing?'

'I don't know. And I saw a pale sheet or canvas. Like the sails of a boat.'

24

Through his rearview mirror I spot the African driver's big watery eyes studying us in the back of his cab.

'That's number six. The fifth I dumped on Mum and Dad last night. The fourth I had during that play, which is why I remembered it as a film. It's as if someone's trying to reach me, Mark. Like a message in a bottle.'

'Mum and Dad, how did they react?'

'A bit frightened.'

'So am I.' I tap her forehead with my fingers. 'What's going on up there?'

'I don't know. Nothing lasts more than a few seconds.'

'See a doctor.'

'No,' she says tenderly. 'No doctors.'

By the time we reach Ladbroke Grove Geena is becalmed. The driver is still looking at us in his rearview mirror as we alight onto the pavement. I hand a £10 note across to him but he won't take the money. 'Is my money no good to you?'

'Don't put a jinni on me, man,' he says in some West African accent. 'Keep your monies.'

My initial impression of Natasha the first time I'd met her outside the pub was that she seemed eager to get on your wavelength before you tried to get on hers. In her own home I can feel that insecurity again. From the moment we arrive she is asking me what music I want to hear. I haven't come to hear music.

'I don't mind. Whatever.'

'Garage? Hard House?' She looks a little crestfallen when I don't respond. 'I suppose you have to go clubbing to appreciate it.' Then she brightens. 'Do you go clubbing?'

'Afraid not,' say I. 'That's Geena's department.'

She wears clothes from the sixties, when she was born: flared yellow needle corduroys, silver platform-sole boots, a skin-tight bell top with Che Guevara emblazoned on the chest, her pierced navel exposed. She's cropped all her hair since we last met into a boy's number three haircut, with a tuft in the front. On her arm is a Kama Sutra tattoo. Her complexion is desperately white.

In her flat clothes spill out of wicker baskets, cross-pollinating with bowls of cat food. There are toothbrushes in the lounge, CDs on the bathroom floor. Upon a high-backed sofa two long-haired cats sleep. Then I start noticing other things, like original paintings hidden behind rubber plants and seminal texts on the shelves: *Ulysses*, *Moby Dick* and a few titles that I don't recognise: *Liar's Poker. The Black-Scholes Model.*

She paces around in a flat-footed sort of way on those platform soles. She pours us a warm chardonnay but drinks mineral water herself. Moreover she seems to be suffering at the spectacle of me and Geena putting it away, staring intensely at our glasses as though trying to remember a dream. Her face is serious, until she smiles, then beams a generosity previously held on ice. She is not what you could call promiscuous with that smile.

Geena makes herself at home, lying on the sofa with her trainers up on the Indian coffee table, heels hooked over the edge, like she is settling in for a night of TV. Except Natasha doesn't seem to have one, at least not in view. Geena's louche presence affronts the cats, who take themselves off.

The flat is on the ground floor of a four-storey house. Cobwebs hang from the high ornate ceiling. French windows are open to a large communal garden. As she is explaining that the house belongs to her parents, Geena hauls herself off the sofa, picks up her wine and wanders out into the garden.

'So,' Natasha begins, 'Geena tells me you're a doctor.'

'Is that what she said!'

'Yes.'

'I work in a hospital. What do you do?'

'I work for a merchant bank, as a derivatives originator.'

'Derivatives? What are they?'

'Futures, options, swaps, Ginnie Maes, gilts, bonds, butter-flies, caps, collars and floors.'

I laugh. 'If that's not a found poem, then what is.'

'Yeah, but the kind of poem that makes money.' Natasha looks out the French windows to see where Geena has gone. Her eyes fall away like stars. 'She's like Edmund, isn't she, wandering around Narnia looking for the fawn.'

'Little hills up and little hills down.'

Natasha smiles. An awkward silence ensues.

'She's been erratic lately,' I say. 'Geena.'

'Why does she still live at home, with your parents?'

'Economic reasons. Why do you live with yours?'

She laughs, rather bitterly I'd say. 'Oh, they just live upstairs. But I don't have much to do with them, ever since they sent me to boarding school. Did you go to boarding school?'

'Comprehensive.'

'What's wrong with Geena?'

We have reached the purpose of my visit.

'What do you mean?'

'She's hallucinating.'

'Yes. Seems so.' I inhale for the next question. 'Are you sleeping with her?'

Natasha guffaws. 'That's none of your business.'

'Geena sometimes sleeps with men and sometimes she sleeps with women. But she's heterosexual.'

'Surely you mean bisexual.'

'No I don't. Women are halfway there already, is my point. You don't see straight guys hugging and kissing or walking down the street arm in arm like women do. You don't have to cross such a wide avenue to be intimate with one another, do you?'

'There was a time in my life when I thought I was lesbian,' Natasha confesses candidly. 'Men just want to beat their meat when they fuck. Male and female orgasms are parallel experiences. Women don't need orgasm to procreate. In fact it can hinder conception since the thrust is a downwards one. It pushes semen out of the vaginal canal.'

'I didn't know that,' I shudder.

'And what do men know about the transcendental orgasm? Two women can come and come again, while a guy drifts off to sleep in a foetal position as soon as he's finished. With his back to you. If there's a moment of doubt I have about the naturalness of heterosexuality, it's then. Lesbianism may be the primal instinct.'

I collapse back into the sofa. 'Maybe,' I say. 'But I don't think homosexuality is the primal instinct. I don't think sodomy is the flagship of the species somehow.'

Natasha is still laughing at that as Geena comes indoors. She dumps herself on to the sofa next to me. 'I've just had another one,' she says and sneezes violently.

'Another what?' Natasha asks. 'Hallucination?'

Geena's eyes are still bewildered from whatever burst of light and sound she'd been subjected to. She comforts herself by stroking the cats, until the cats move from the arm of the sofa on to the table to lay on top of a pile of newspapers. Natasha pads over and now she comforts herself on their fur, stroking them contemplatively under the chin. No one says anything. The silence hangs like a knife in the room. It hurts when I swallow.

Natasha walks out of the room and stays out. Geena and I look at one another. A minute later and she returns wearing an olive green leather jacket and red lipstick. 'I want to buy you both a drink in Hammersmith,' she announces.

We drive in her car to Hammersmith via Shepherd's Bush, sheering off Goldhawk Road down a side street. She pulls into a bus stop and points to a Victorian pub on the other side of the road.

'Is this where we're going?' Geena asks. 'That dump?'

'I just want to look at it for a second. A few years ago I was on my way to Jackie Rotherham's when my father was in the hospital, dying basically, and I didn't feel right about going to Jackie's, who was a friend of my father, twice my age and we'd been having this secret affair for two years. So I went across the road to that pub and had a drink, to think. I came back to the car parked in this bus stop and called the hospital on my cell phone. I was leaning against that lamppost there when the duty sister told me Dad had died about fifteen minutes earlier . . . Let's drive.'

Less than an hour ago her father was alive and kicking, living above her. Maybe she's having hallucinations too. Sitting in a car with these two I feel short of a few maladjustments.

We shunt down Paddenswick Road to Hammersmith, ending up at the Dove on the river west of the bridge. Natasha goes to the bar, leaving Geena and I gazing out the window at the last of the daylight skimming the surface of the river. She returns clutching two half-pints of Fullers and a coke, and proceeds to tell us more about Jackie Rotherham. I don't really know why.

'He always wore a kilt but wasn't Scottish. He thought women were sexist, and wore this kilt to get up their noses. And it's true, some would say things like, "Nice pair of tits on him." Jackie would shout back: "Aye, lassie, but not as big as your balls." He looked for an ally in me for his misogyny.'

'And did he?' Geena asks. 'Find an ally?'

'I didn't much like myself at the time.'

'Was this before or after you thought you were a lesbian?' I ask.

Geena looks at me, she looks at Natasha. Natasha looks at both of us, but refrains from answering my question. 'That's another story,' she says. 'I haven't finished this one. About a year after we broke up Jackie was dying of lung cancer and wanted to see me. But I didn't go. And now he's dead. That's

29

something I have to live with for the rest of my life.' She takes a long pull on the coke. 'That's my confession. Now you show me yours.'

'Show you what?' I say.

'Come on, you know what people call you in the Dark Side of the Moon.'

'What?'

'The weird siblings.'

'Do they?' Geena seems surprised.

'You told me you're a doctor, Mark, but I don't think you are.'

'I never told you I was a doctor. I told you I worked in a hospital. I'm a hospital porter, as my father was before me.'

'Have you got something against career advancement?'

'Not particularly.'

'You're just not ambitious.'

'It's in my blood to be a carer.'

'Doctors are carers too.'

'Not the ones I know. They may start that way, but they never ever finish that way.'

'What else do they say about me in the Moon?' Geena asks.

'Truth?'

'Truth.'

'They say that you and Mark are, you know, incestuous.'

Geena leans across to me. 'Are we, Mark? Incestuous?'

I feel my anger rising. 'You shouldn't believe all you hear in the Dark Side of the Moon, or wherever. What do nineteen-year-olds know?'

'My friends aren't nineteen,' Natasha says.

'My friends are,' Geena says. 'Some of them.'

'What about these hallucinations? What's that all about?'

'That's something new,' Geena says. 'I get those.'

Natasha tries another tack. 'I don't give a fuck what people say. I want to be your friend. Both of your friend.'

'Fine,' I say. 'Okay with you, Geena?'
'Depends.'
'Depends on what?' Natasha asks.
'Who's the best: DJ Levi or DJ Cool?'
'Levi.'
'Okay,' Geena says, 'you're in.'

MACHINE WITH WINGS

I don't quite trust that American-style intimacy Natasha is dispensing and decline her invitation to spend a weekend at her country cottage in Suffolk. Geena goes on her own. I go to work on the three-to-eleven.

Around midnight I am back at home, reading Melville's *The Encantadas*, a fiction camouflaged as cartography. Based on his knowledge of the Galapagos Islands encountered while serving on an American whaler, Melville layers upon these volcanic rocks an inverted Old Testament prophecy. One of the sketches subtitled *A Pisgah View from the Rock*, for instance, alludes to the summit from where Moses saw the Promised Land. But in this promised land ten million spiders writhe and crawl inside the charred craters. The islands on the outer rim are inhabited, but the primordial evil enchants all who live there. Pirates replace a democracy with a riotocracy; a widow spends her entire life waiting to give her husband a Christian burial; a hermit lures sailors to his shores and makes them slaves.

Hilarious stuff. Actually it is more terrifying than gloomy, and Melville does have a supervisory humour guiding the whole thing along.

As I am drifting off to sleep my doorbell rings. I open up to find Geena, clutching her stomach with both arms, accompanied by Natasha as pale as snow.

'She walked in front of a car,' Natasha explains.

My arms outstretch towards my sister. 'Are you all right?'

Geena doesn't answer, so Natasha acts again as her proxy. 'One minute I'm talking to her outside the Moon, then she suddenly walks into the road.' (She crossed that fucking red line!) 'The car wasn't travelling very fast, thank God.'

'Where do you feel pain?' Geena pats her stomach. 'You may need an X-ray.' To Natasha I ask, 'I thought you two were in the country?'

'We came back early. It didn't work out.'

I get dressed and another minute later we are driving down the hill in Natasha's car to the hospital.

I leave them sitting in the waiting room of the A&E and wander off to find an assessment nurse. Nurses will give priority to employees' relatives if they are not busy, but tonight they are busy, and the nurse tells me she'll get to Geena as soon as possible.

The A&E porters are one short and the action is hotting up as the night progresses. While we wait for the assessment nurse I help them out. In the following half-hour I bring in a priority-two, who is too drunk to walk, from a taxi; assist a girl cut with flying glass who requires leg elevation; hold down a teenager with a knife sticking out of his thigh while a nurse sedates him. I have vomit on my shirt and blood on my shoes as a dozen pub brawlers arrive, bringing their fight into the waiting room. The receptionist puts in a Zebra-Zebra Situation call on the radio telephone and minutes later four security guys charge in to separate the tribes.

Yes indeed, the A&E is a different story to the wards. Here you can gauge the temperature of the city outside, in the tail-end of round-the-clock violence. It is always in here that the

33

hurt merchants end their ritual, along with their quarry – the mugged, steamed, rolled, the broken and the pillaged citizens. A war goes off in the city every night and this is only one local A&E. The song is just as plaintive in St Mary's, Guys, UCH.

Geena sits like a sparrow with a broken wing through all this heavy weather. A bird I want to see fly. But not out of the open window, not out of my life. She may fly into dangers. What is dangerous? I'll tell you what is dangerous. A world without primal love.

Love is a bird cage. Love is protection.

A psychiatric patient is brought in for treatment after slashing his chest with a serrated kitchen knife. He has four attendants standing sentinel around his chair. Psychiatric patients are in a league of their own. Medics and porters alike are afraid of them, for there is no way of knowing who they really are, and so you can never know what they are capable of doing.

I am becoming afraid for Geena for similar reasons.

'Why did you wander into the road?' I try again.

'I saw a machine with wings. I went to look at it.'

'A machine with wings?' My voice trails off hopelessly.

Natasha stares keenly at the psychiatric patient, and makes me wonder about her, why this wealthy originator of derivative instruments would pursue a friendship with a hospital porter and his unstable sister. Among some successful women insanity is a status symbol. But Natasha isn't altogether on her trolley either. She lied about her father still being alive, she is an alcoholic, and has affairs with misogynists.

But I can't solve her problems. I only want to solve Geena's. Something I read about hallucination related it to absence, a substitute for an object, a wish fulfillment – and that seems about right in Geena's case. In one of her lucid moments she described the people who appear to her as negative images, unidentifiable, yet which hold her in rapture. What she sees and hears are very real to her, yet belong as much to the imagination. It is a light out of nowhere. For those few brief seconds her brain operates independently and penetrates scenes of such primitiveness that she has no way of understanding them.

'Geena, you have to see a doctor,' I blurt out.

'I'm waiting, aren't I?'

'A neurologist.'

She is alarmed by what I've said. 'I don't want to see a neurologist,' she whines and hangs her head on my shoulder.

In the next two hours I think of how I've been doing this for years, waiting around for Geena. Things haven't progressed much since that day when we were children and I was running with a posse of boys who said Geena could only come along if she kept up. She couldn't keep up and I waited for her, incurring the censure of my friends. My friends were friends no more. They come and go still, and for similar reasons.

Perhaps it would be better for her if we spent more time apart. But the thought doesn't survive. I think of Geena drifting away from me on a neurological tide, and slay the idea before it is fully born.

Around 2.15 a.m. Geena goes in alone to see the doctor. I wander over to the Croissant Shop and buy two cappuccinos. On that winter night the girl serving is languorous and wistful, in the hours before she goes off duty at seven. 'How's your sister?' she asks. We all know each other's business in here, the news travelling by word of mouth.

'I think she'll be all right. She's in with the doctor now.'

'You wear too much denim,' Natasha remarks as I return with the cappuccino. 'Makes me wonder about the music you listen to. Crosby, Stills and Nash? Joni Mitchell?'

She spins her pink feather boa around her neck. I clock what else she is wearing. PVC trousers and trainers. A black leather jacket hangs from the back of her chair. 'I'm not sure what you mean?' I say.

'Too much denim for a guy with blue eyes.'

'So what goes with blue eyes?'

'I don't trust men with blue eyes. There's something dishonest about them.'

'I don't think I'm dishonest.'

'Geena's got hazel eyes.'

'Natasha, I don't really give a damn. But there are some things I want to ask you. Like what happened at your cottage? You were meant to be spending the whole weekend there.'

'She started to panic the moment we set foot in the place. Said she was convinced she's going to die there.'

'She said *what?*'

'I'm going to die here.'

'What's your cottage like?'

'Nothing life threatening. A simple cottage next to the sea.'

'These hallucinations she'd been having, there's often a house by the sea in them.'

'We turned round and came back to London. It wasn't going to work.'

'This is your own cottage, right?'

'My father left it to me in his will.'

I have my cue. 'When we first came to your home you told me your father was still alive. Why did you lie about that?'

'Why did I lie? Why does anyone lie? Because when the truth is ugly only lies are beautiful.' She blows on her cappuccino, moving the froth along. 'Since we're on the subject – my mother's dead too. She died when I was eleven. My father's sensitive response to that was to pack me off to boarding school. As far as I was concerned they were both of them dead.' She throws back her head and moans, and as though needing to impress me further, informs me about getting pregnant at eighteen. 'I wanted an abortion, but Daddy threatened to litigate if I tried. So I married the kid's father. Two years later I had another one.'

36

'You have two children!' I am stunned. It seems implausible.

I don't know if I want to hear any more, but she tells me anyway.

'My kids are eight and ten, boy and girl. But I don't see them. I left them with their father.' Then she adds: 'I did abort them after all. Ten years after the fact.'

'That is a terrible thing to say.'

'I'm banking on you having an open mind, Mark.'

'Don't you ever want to see them sometimes?'

'Sometimes. But my children don't want to see me.'

'Is that why you have a drink problem?'

'Had . . .' she says. 'It's not as though I threw them into an orphanage or anything. They're well looked after by their father. Some women aren't cut out to be mothers. Some men are better at it. I pay maintenance.'

All this is hard for me to digest. The information is lumpy going down. 'It sounds to me like you've lost your faith in love.'

'Why do you think I studied maths at university? I craved certainty in the way others crave religious faith.' She put her hand on mine. 'What's the probability of us two making out?'

'Us? Don't you mean Geena?'

'No.'

'I don't see a future for us, Natasha.'

'Why not?'

'Wrong chemistry.'

'Perhaps if you came clean about your relationship with Geena it might help the chemical reaction.'

I pulled my hand away from hers. 'What do you know!'

'What do I know? I know the price of a share if I know the price of an option. I know when to cover my ass by hedging in the opposite direction. I know that maths is in nature and that the markets are a force of nature. I know that if God exists it's because mathematics is consistent, and I know that if the devil exists it's because we can't prove it. A few years ago when

Yeltsin woke up with a hangover and declared that Russia won't pay back their debts to the West, he fucked the maths. People like Scholes lost half a billion dollars of investors' money on that single day. So now I know to use instinct as well as maths. That's what I know. And I have an instinct about you. That you have an elaborate defence against reality. That you take precautions.'

'I read a lot of fiction, is my defence.'

'I'm a native speaker of Algebra – that's mine.' She smiles her generous smile that is like bad weather clearing. Then she leans across and kisses me on the lips.

Geena emerges with a clean bill of health, nothing broken, just a few bruises. She asks to be taken home to Finsbury Park, into the cradle of my parents. At 4.30 a.m. I leave her settled in an armchair with a Star Trek video, the episode when Spock gets his brain surgically removed, then Natasha drives me to my bedsit. We sit in the car in silence, while a fierce wind shakes the vehicle. Hailstones pound the windscreen. Electrical storms break open the dawn skies, doing the talking for us.

CLEMENT McLUHAN

Saturday afternoon I walk to my parents' flat via the disused railway line: the urban gash, London's parting, the city's Red Sea. I breathe oxygen straight out of the trees. This private strip in a public city is a snug for people like me who have something that doesn't correspond exactly with dominant concerns, who prefer attics and basements over rooms with a view. Some days I even read as I walk, with nothing to run into but the odd gay hustler looking for dancing partners.

I find Geena prone on the sofa, watching TV. On the coffee table are the remnants of her breakfast, lunch and afternoon snacks. In a stack beside the TV is her video collection: *The Girlie Show*, *Eastenders*, *Friends*, *Neighbours*, *Cheers*, Feltz, Springer and Oprah. Geena records all these programmes, including such numinous events as Jarvis Cocker gatecrashing Michael Jackson's set at the Brit Awards ('Jarvis is *safe*, man!') to replay during *Newsnight*, during the barren hours.

'Where's Mum and Dad?' I ask.

'Out and about. Shopping 'suspect.'

'What have you been watching?'

'I watched Wednesday's Richard and Judy; I watched them. They are so unhip they've become hip. I watched the omnibus edition of *Eastenders*; I watched that. Grant and Phil are getting like Richard and Judy. Too mainstream. Beppe and Gianni are much cooler.'

'Who run the Italian restaurant?'

'Yeah . . . they're the new Grant and Phil.'

Geena watches TV with so much dedication that actors have become as real to her as me or Mum and Dad. Sometimes she even talks to them as though they're in the room with her. One time we were watching *Emmerdale* and suddenly she blurts out, 'Make some tea for us, Mark, and for these poor farmers standing out in the rain.'

Her devotion to the haunted fishtank in the corner of the room is not as bad as it sounds. Her passivity has gravitas. Doing nothing is an activity requiring great skill. If I am a media teetotaler idling away my leisure time with books that have an ever diminishing readership, she claims to be psychically tuning in to the wider universe. 'TV is the new Stonehenge,' she once remarked. 'Mark Lamarr, Jonathan Ross, Matthew Kelly are like, druids. If you ask me, *Stars in Their Eyes* emits electronic pulses that connects the viewer with the rest of the world.'

After the Brit Awards débâcle, Jarvis Cocker was front page news the next day, so maybe she has a point.

I think she watches so much television to have an edge down the pub. TV soap is the lingua franca at the Salmon and Compass, Bar Lorca and other such haunts.

My parents arrive home from Sainsbury's in an irritable mood. I can guess the reason why. The way my mother shops for food is executed like a military campaign. She goes in on point and forms a bridgehead. Then she pours over every item looking for special offers, digging in the back of the dairy produce to get a better sell-by-date. My father comes up the rear with a trolley, biting her heels, making reprimands for taking too long. They are both restless souls, and that seeps into their marriage as petty irritation.

My folks were born in South Africa, of Scottish and Welsh descent. They emigrated to England when Geena was three years old, and I was born the following year. Migrants are never quite at home in their adopted nations and South Africans are among the most restless. Nor do white South Africans inspire much affection in the democratic world.

No sooner are they in when they part company. My father vanishes behind a book on the failed conquest of Everest by Malory and Irvine in 1924. He likes that kind of tragic romanticism, of young men risking everything for a belief. His bookshelves are lined with such accounts of epic tests of every kind of faith. Yet it is my mother alone who has religious faith. He is too sceptical for that, too sceptical even for works of fiction.

As he reads about Chomolungma, the Goddess Mother of the World, my mother starts preparing tea in the kitchen.

From whatever points on the London map we happen to be on a Saturday afternoon, Geena and I never miss her evening tea. This is not to suggest my mother's Prue Leith. On the contrary. For instance, today we are having tomato soup, baked beans & chips, fruit and custard – a three-course meal from cans. In two and a half decades the week's menu has varied little. Sunday: roast joint with all the trimmings; Monday: leftovers with chips cooked in dripping; Tuesday: fried egg, tinned ham and baked beans; Wednesday: shepherd's pie, tinned carrots, tinned peas . . .

Thirty-some years ago they were eating Dutch melktart and sosaties, Huguenot pickles and fig preserves, Malaysian chili and coconut dishes, sweet and spicy Indian curries. I once asked Dad if we could try some of the old country's cuisine, and in a mood of suppressed rage, he said, 'What good would that do? South Africa's a closed chapter. We are an English family now.' An English family with English gastronomic bad taste. Although I admit that when I am crazed from work or an unrequited flame for someone, a slab of my mum's canned pineapple quilted with warm custard usually bucks me up.

My mother attempts to lay the table around Dad, who is leaning his great arms across the yellow Formica, his book split open in front of him. The sleeves of his white shirt are rolled halfway up his biceps, exposing his ancient blue tattoos. When we were children he used to lift Geena and me up at the same time, like weights in his powerful arms. His arms was all he had to keep the wolf from the door, he liked to boast. His physical strength kept the family alive, that alone. He was his own instrument. Very Lawrentian. Before they emigrated to England Dad was a porter in Groote Schuur hospital in the Cape Town suburbs which, being a job out of the rain – into a well-heated space as all hospitals are – was considered an advancement over his Scottish ancestors who built the dock basin in Cape Town in the days when stone arrived from the quarries on broad-gauge railways and the only automated power was steam driven. They weren't treated much better than the convicts the job was originally earmarked for, nor the blacks they laboured alongside. Shortly after the completion of the Victoria and Alfred docks (named after King Alfred presumably, the ninth-century King of Wessex and overlord of England who defeated the Danes and encouraged learning and writing in English. Or it could just be a mistake: Alfred instead of Albert. The Cape Colony was a confused place at the turn of the century) diamonds and gold were discovered in South Africa and a lot of colonists got rich. But not my ancestors.

'There's honour in that. Our family has never profited from the misfortunes of others,' Dad would boast. 'It is not prestigious to be wealthy in a country where everyone is poor.'

After the fall of the old regime it was hard for me to know whether he was pleased or not. Whenever I asked if he was tempted to return to the new South Africa, he just blushed. Why blush? Tourists were flocking into South Africa but he remained politically agnostic. He seemed to know before anyone else about Mandela's Faustian power-sharing deal with the architects of apartheid in exchange for amnesty and regarded the Truth and Reconciliation hearings a travesty of justice. 'Reconciliation without reparations! How can that ever work? It goes against human nature to give away so many concessions.'

Geena eats with her head hovering over the plate. Stoking the furnace. Her arms are elevated as she cuts with her knife and fork, elbows at right angles to the body; a deformity of etiquette from all her years eating TV dinners, with a plate on her lap. My mother tries to get a conversation going, irritating my father who prefers to eat and go. Eating is a chore to him, like mowing the lawn. But my mother can't tell stories and when you can't tell stories you ask questions. Which is another reason why Dad objects, I think. He doesn't like questions. But boy, does he listen to our answers. I often wonder if he doesn't submit a few questions to my mother on the sly, before we arrive, and whether her solicitude is his also.

Mum asks Geena: 'What have you been doing today, dear?'

We all know it's a rhetorical question. What Geena has been doing today she did yesterday and all the days that preceded it.

'I watched *Kilroy*, *Eastenders*; I watched all those.'

'I don't know how you can bear it,' Mum says.

I can tell what is coming up next.

'Unemployment figures are down ten per cent this month,' Mum says. 'That's something you should take encouragement from.'

Geena replies with something quite novel. 'I'm thinking about going to college.' This was news. 'I thought I'd like to study psychology.'

'Since when have you been interested in psychology?' Dad asks.

43

'This family's taught me a lot about psychology.'

'You'll have to read a lot of difficult texts,' I caution.

'You think that's beyond me?'

'Why psychology?' Dad persists.

'Why not?'

'Psychologists are like doctors, they try to make a science out of the uncertainties of mind and body. It was a doctor who told your mother that it was "impossible" for her to get pregnant.' He glances a look off me. 'Lucky for us he was wrong. But how many other women did he tell that lie to? How many women are now living with wholly inappropriate men because of their children who they never imagined they'd have when they made love without contraception?'

I have to smile in admiration for my father. His cynicism is a gift, like music is a gift to others.

Mum turns to me for advice. I am enrolled on a part-time degree course in literature at North London University. 'Do you think it a good idea our Geena goes to college?'

I don't believe for one second that Geena is being serious, but play along anyway. 'Why not. It's three years' security.'

My father guffaws. 'Security . . . what security?'

I think I know what this is about. In the 1950s my father was a geology student at the University of Cape Town, but dropped out several months before he was due to graduate. Had he obtained his degree, a lucrative career in the gold and diamond mining industries would have been his for the asking. The political contradictions were too much for him, so he baled out early and sought the kind of lowly job that most white South Africans would call 'kaffir work'.

'What about education for education's sake? I thought you believed in self-improvement.'

'That was a different age,' he says.

Geena breaks in. 'You don't want me to have a vocation? Fine, I'll continue doing nothing. I'd rather do nothing anyway

44

than run around a hospital pushing a wheelchair.' Dad flinches at her remark as though she'd snapped a wet tea towel against the back of his legs.

Before he retired my father was head porter in the Hospital for Neurology and Neurosurgery in Queen Square, which meant, for Geena and me, that money was always tight. He handed his wages over to my mum, who made sure there were no material caprices in our home. But we were happy enough without money, as they always liked to remind us.

Were we happy? Is a kid driven to school in the rain happier than one who has to walk? We did have a structured childhood, I suppose, I owe them that. Structure is a form of love. And we were fed. Out of cans.

We also got an annual vacation; one week in August, always to the same place, pitching up at Hastings on the East Sussex coast. To see Mum and Dad sitting in rented deck-chairs on the cold, windswept shingle actively resisting the attentions of other parents trying to engage them in conversation marked the tenor of those holidays.

If my folks are isolates now, in Cape Town they had been gregarious. Among the photographs of them in South Africa I've found, buried deep in the attic, they looked happy enough, with their arms around each other and around many friends on the top of Table Mountain – all dressed in comically tilted hats, their white teeth set against black or suntanned skin.

I once pressed one of these photographs into Dad's hands, seeking annotations. Who are these young, coloured, black folk with you? But instead of answering me, he just left the kitchen table, left it for my mother to explain. 'Everyone in that photograph is dead,' she said. 'Even though I am old now I still remember them as young.' I asked her how they'd died and she just sighed, 'No, I just can't get them out of my head at all.'

It was on holiday that Geena and I first forged our tight convergence. To ward off their doldrums we wandered barefoot along the water's edge, avoiding other children, doing our time, like the beach ponies dead on their feet going up and down the drenched sand. I can still picture us in swimming costumes and woolly sweaters, arms behind our backs, climbing over groynes and sewerage pipes, weaving between family cricket matches, the din of voices coagulating in the air. For fun we'd stare up at the sky, then at the ponies, transferring an image of the sun onto their motley hides.

Or we'd take our chances on the promenade, dodging the posses of skinheads who made Hastings their pilgrimage objective in those days. We'd get our photo taken with a parrot on our shoulder on the boardwalk of the pier and watch the fishing trawlers being launched off the beach. Geena was always drawn to these boats more than I was. In my view the sea was all right, but trawlers smelled of rotting fish. 'When I grow up,' Geena would say, 'I'm going to have a boat of my own. When the sea is white all I'll have to do is touch it with my boat and the water will turn blue again. I'm going to live on it, that's what I'll do, catch fish for my dinner and sail to Cape Town.' The forbidden city.

Taking us to Hastings was a deliberate attempt to indoctrinate us. Why else would they insist that we take the West Hill lift together every year to visit the same 1066 story in pictures and words, where I learned things like the Battle of Hastings was all over in less than six hours. 'Imagine that,' I'd say to my sister, 'the birth of England took less time than Mum was in labour with me.' Hastings might have been endemically English to others but it was an endurance test to me and I had to wonder why William of Normandy ever bothered to conquer it.

If it rained, Geena would go to the amusement arcades and I'd be allowed to return to our guest house and read. In those cold wet days in Hastings, I started a process that continues to this day – of constructing a character for myself out of fictional ones *who do not exist*. What I know of myself I know only in the unity of a 'true' fictional universe. Like the sculptor Christo who wrapped a cliff face in 92,900 square metres of fabric one year when we were in Hastings, I have always been intrigued by the relationship of nature to ordnance. As Christo's sheet increases awareness of the cliff – its mass and shape, the very fact of its existence – a similar thing happens with text and reality. Text is navigation over an amorphous map.

Hours of solid unbroken reading later, I'd put down my book to stare through the window at the rain making an imperceptible sound falling on the sea. This sealed image always depicted death to me, which immediately brought me upright, worrying about Geena out there somewhere, slipping coins into slot machines, an arcade penny hustler caught in a time bend, her character devolving gradually in a formless world.

After tea we sit in the living room and watch television – *Gladiators*, *Blind Date*, *Family Fortunes* in series until my jaw drops from ennui. And it is still just eight o'clock. In the commercial break Mum wheels in four mugs of strong gunpowder tea on a trolley. As she slides doilies under the mugs on the glass-top coffee table, Dad's knee knocks the edge and spills one of the mugs of tea on the carpet. We watch him and wait. After years of feeling trapped, every statement one makes, however trivial, is an indirect reckoning on life. So when Dad complains to my mother: 'I don't know why you make tea all the bloody time anyway,' I know what the real problem is. Seconds pass and he comes closer to the truth. 'I've got to get back to work again.'

'You're too old,' my mother admonishes. 'Can't you just enjoy your retirement?'

'I watch any more of that TV my head'll explode!' He comes to his feet, and says, 'I'm going for my walk. You coming, Mark?'

We look at him. Why me? It's not as if this were a routine. But then with my father we have always had to try and guess what he's feeling.

He seems to be burning with a desire to talk to me, but does not know how to begin. I realise this is why he's invited me on his constitutional to Victoria Park. Out there we'd have something else to concentrate on other than one another's faces across a table. And walking helps to work things through; linear motion shuffles thoughts, however tumultuous, into a deck.

We put on our shoes and coats and step out into the night.

As much as he wants to talk to me, I want to talk to him. Like why does he continue to impose a curfew on the events of the first half of his life from entering the second half of his life? Am I not old enough to be trusted to know the reasons? Freud once said that of all his patients, those who could tell stories about their lives had it more or less sussed. Stories are all we have to save us getting shredded in time and space.

But Dad won't tell stories, he doesn't have it sussed. And I can't help him. All I manage to say as we walk in the dark through the avenue of oak trees is: 'How many hospital managers does it take to perform an open-heart operation?'

'Is this a joke, Mark?'

'Yes.'

'Then tell me.'

'Fifteen, trying to save on the surgeon's fees.'

He doesn't laugh, doesn't even smile.

Maybe he has a lover tucked away on the other side of the world. Maybe that twinkle in his eye – the keyhole in a locked door – is reserved for her. Our parents can have secrets we never account for.

I'd be interested even if he had a lover tucked away on the other side of Victoria Park.

By and by he says, 'The London Broncos beat Wigan on Thursday.'

'The London Broncos are ninety per cent Australian. You might as well support the Brisbane Broncos.'

'They still did well to beat Wigan. Good game too.'

At that time of night the park is empty apart from a few winos staggering half-blind through the trees. Being his only transit these winos shake him down. He makes a few more false starts and then he does manage to say what ails him. 'Geena seems a bit off colour. Your mother's very concerned. The other day . . .' he tails off. He cannot bring himself to describe her distress. Or maybe he just doesn't have the vocabulary. 'What's happening to the girl?'

'Well, one of the problems is, that girl is thirty-two.'

'I'm not talking about that. Something's gone wrong inside her head.'

This was always going to be difficult, explaining the quick vicissitudes of Geena's hallucinations, but I try. 'Her brain's behaving like a radio, tuning from frequency to frequency. She glimpses things that are very familiar, possibly out of the past.'

'Like what?'

'People, houses, the sea.'

My father stops walking to hold on to a tree. 'It's a neurological condition, then?'

'Yes, it's a neurological condition.'

'I could get her an appointment with a consultant. I haven't worked all those years for nothing. I know some neurologists. Maybe they'd let her jump the queue.'

'Geena won't see a neurologist.'

'You make her see reason then, Mark.'

'She's not in any real pain, Dad.'

'She might not be, but your mother and I are.'

This is the first time he's ever articulated to me any anxiety about Geena and it hits me hard. All these past years he has silently tolerated her peccadillos, her unemployment, flights into eternal youth, boyfriends creeping out of her room at eleven in the morning. Now a hallucination of strangers by the sea from out of the past undoes all that. I feel his concern coming over strongly, the blunt pain of a parent who discovers he has not finished the job.

ROSE McLUHAN

Last night I did something I've not done in years: slept in my old bedroom next to the kitchen. I dreamed that I'd found all the answers to the mysteries of the world stored on a single video, then spent the rest of the dream looking for a TV and VCR to play it.

Around eight I wander into the kitchen to find Geena eating cereal. Nothing odd about that, except for the time of day.

'How come you're up so early?'

'I think we should buy a car,' she says suddenly.

'You can't drive.'

'But you can.'

'I don't need a car for where I go.'

'I wish I had a car and I'd go somewhere far away. I might never come back home, if I had a car.'

'You don't need a car to do that.'

'Then I'll catch a train; that's what I'll do. Sit on a train right to the end of the track until I get everything sussed in my head.'

'Geena, you're sounding drunk.'

'I have a hangover. I went out last night after you went to bed and had a shedful.'

'Why would you want to go away?' I feel wounded. 'Why all this talk of leaving and never coming back?'

'Because I'm frightened.'

'Frightened of what?' I reach out for her hand.

She pulls back. 'Frightened of you.'

'Me? Jesus Christ.'

Raised voices from the living room distract us. My parents are rowing. Big deal maybe, but we have never heard them argue so loudly and it feels awkward being in earshot, voyeuristic. I go in there to referee. What I see is comforting. My father has a brand-new Aiwa radio cassette machine on his lap and is reading without his spectacles from an instruction book. He's bought the cassette player for Mum so she can copy tapes of choir singing on loan from her church.

He reads with his arms at full stretch. '"To go to dubbing . . ."'

My father is short sighted and she is short of hearing. 'Dublin?' she says. 'I'm too old to be traipsing off to Dublin.'

'DUBBING! woman.' In frustration he depresses all the buttons. Red and green lights fire off the casing. 'There,' he says sitting back, 'now that's recording.'

'Wind-up gramophones were never this much trouble,' my mother says. 'Remember old Moses Dkeni, Clement? Every Sunday Moses came home with a bellyful of beer and sat in the street listening to his Caruso records. He'd wake up when the record stopped, wind it up again and go back to sleep.'

This is the closest to a South African story I've ever heard her tell.

In the 1850s my mother's grandmother was sent to the Cape Colony by the English Fund for Promoting Female Emigration. She worked as a domestic servant until she died. But that's all I know about her, and that she was parentless. Her choice of destination, I imagine, was arbitrary, a sleight of hand, as was the case with my father's ancestors. They could just as easily have ended up in America.

Of my mother's time in South Africa I know that in Cape Town she worked as a sales assistant, in Garlicks & Stuttafords department store. On arriving in London she waltzed into an identical job, at Peter Jones on Holloway Road.

Geena and I used to meet her there every day after school, waiting for her to finish at five so we could walk home together. In the haberdashery department where she worked, she looked a study of the condition of exile, smiling at all her customers until her face began to craze like an egg. Whenever she talked to customers, her South African voice would sound like a plaintive song. In Peter Jones more than anywhere else it was apparent to me that her home was somewhere other than London. I would look up into her eyes under the bright shop lights and fancy that I could see foaming seas and herons in her spectacles.

My mother still attends the same crumbling Presbyterian chapel on Seven Sisters Road where Geena and I endured Sunday school. We avoid church when we can, but there are certain times, like today, when we find ourselves in the wrong place at the wrong time and get roped in to going along. Oddly enough, Geena seems quite keen. But then she has always claimed to feel religious with a hangover.

I take to church Isaac Babel's stories of the Red Cavalry to read under my prayer book, but in the event listen to the minister, who is new and says some things that interest me.

'Why does God allow us, his most cherished creation, to die?' he begins. 'For the authors of the Old Testament death is the ultimate evil. Eden is the metaphorical centre of the Old Testament, the Tree of Life a specific against disease and death. It is a fountain of youth. When God showed Adam this tree he failed to warn of the consequences of temptation. But did God really fail? For that would suggest a human fallibility. If he failed then God is not all-powerful. If intentional then God is not all-good. This paradox is as old as religion itself. There are no answers to it from the heavens, only frost falling from the sky.

'If God had foreseen the Fall, why then does he not take responsibility for the evil in the world? Or is the loss of inno-cence a price worth paying for the knowledge of good and evil – the condition of humanity itself?

'Life without death remains one of our most cherished fan-tasies. It has engendered the heroic quest intended to search out all the secrets of the universe in the time that we have in it. Meanwhile the only kind of immortality allowed us is the enter-prise of children.'

Geena sleeps in the pew beside me, her head on my shoul-der. *I am frightened of you.* What could she possibly mean? Maybe she didn't quite mean what she said. But the words are out now, they exist and float freely in my head, unwelcome and hurtful. Words are stones that start avalanches. I am losing her, the slide has begun. These are wild thoughts! Maybe she's having some kind of maternal pang, a girl thing, making her sensitive in ways hitherto unfelt. The enterprise of children. But we are our own children. If she had a kid how would I feel? Friends, lovers, they come and go, but children don't. Well, Natasha's might. If Geena had a baby we'd have something that exists between us that would outlive us. We would gain our immortal status.

Fucking hell!

As we are leaving chapel the minister stands on the thresh-old to greet his congregation. I hold back while Mum introduces him first to Geena. Mum still holds out hope that Geena might be drawn into her religion, while she regards me (and Dad) as a lost cause. She and Geena already share a con-cept of faith in a way. Mum's faith is rooted in the past, as all religious doctrines are historical, and Geena's faith is rooted in the future; that everything will turn out all right. I seem to share my father's agnosticism. We are the only ones in the family who continued education beyond high school, and the rationality of the texts we consult makes having faith more difficult for us. This means I do not understand my mother from the inside as well as I'd like to.

When it is my turn to be introduced to the minister, I shake his hand and say, 'I enjoyed your sermon. Have you read Melville by any chance?'

'Indeed I have,' he replies. 'The Calvinistic view of Man as totally depraved sits nicely with Melville's view.'

'So do you think God is terrible?'

'God is not terrible, only inscrutable.'

Back home my mother invites us to listen to the tape Dad recorded earlier. Geena and I sit on the sofa as she turns on the tape. But there is no singing. There is no music at all. Somehow Dad has managed to record Mum's story about Moses Dkeni playing his Caruso 78s in a Cape Town street.

MEN AND SHEEP

Natasha just won't quit on us, this girl. She has now invited Geena to her cottage for the second time, insisting I come too, as insurance against Geena going pear-shaped. I don't know what she wants from us. I don't know what Geena wants from her. I sure as hell don't know what I want from her. For so long what I want has been inextricably linked to what Geena wants and it's a difficult concept to grasp that we could one day be wiring up our circuitry to a virtual stranger. Natasha brings out a lot of feelings I've been happy to leave untouched for decades, and it's not an altogether comfortable sensation. Perhaps her plan is to differentiate and separate us. Some mathematics is Machiavellian.

Natasha suggests I meet her at her City bank and then we can pick up Geena on the way out of town in her car. For a mathematician her logic is not so sound. It would be easier for her to pick us both up from here. But maybe I'm missing the point, maybe the equation is she just wants to spend a few hours with me alone.

After finishing my Friday shift at the hospital I take a tube from Highgate into the City. By 4.15 p.m. I am standing in the foyer of Goldstein Wolff's, watching all the bankers go by. Like hospital staff they also wear uniform around here: grey suits drift through a grey marble coliseum. At 4.30 Natasha comes down in the lift. She is completely transformed since the last time I saw her, now dressed in a short black skirt, black lycra tights, white blouse and metal-framed glasses on her face. She looks five years older. She looks her real age.

We take the lift up to Equities & Derivatives on the third floor. Each door we pass through she opens with a swipe card. Close-circuit cameras kept us under constant surveillance.

There are four thousand employees at the bank, she tells me, three hundred of which are beavering away at computer screens in Equities & Derivatives, in rows of partitioned desks. Traders are all under thirty-five. Several are taking early supper at their desks, off paper plates, prepared in the refectory on the ground floor where no one has time to sit and eat. Breakfast, lunch and dinner to go.

Natasha leads me through the causeway between desks, past customised screen savers: naked women; log cabins; surfboarders. Dreams of leaving.

A woman cloned as Natasha, in black skirt and white blouse, makes a cryptic announcement over the PA. Some 'hot money' has just floated on to the market and gets everyone going. Researchers shout to salespersons and salespersons shout to traders over the top of their desks. If they are making vast sums of money I can't see the colour of it on the electronic airwaves.

At her desk she pauses to drink out of a bottle of mineral water while I study what looks like calculus equations on a pad.

She indicates to the pad. 'That's an algorithm. For predicting volatility in the market.'

'Right,' I say. 'Uh-huh.'

'If you can read this then you'll have a better idea of when to sell, when to hedge and when to dump plain vanilla into a

Footsie basket.' She holds out her arm, holding the room in the palm of her hand, and refers to the derivatives market as a casino.

I try to read her e-mails on one of the two Dell PCs on her desk, but she slides her ass on to the desk and covers the screens. 'What else can I show you, Mark?' she says, then opens her legs to let me see she is wearing stockings and suspender belt, and no knickers.

This sight of her hot, hairy, jumping nexus shocks me. Natasha is making me an offer but I don't believe it. When a woman offers her sex it is an act of faith. But so is love an act of faith, existing only as belief shared by two people. It cannot be seen any more than electronic money. But love grows over time, whereas Natasha's offer is based on nothing, is borne on thin air. It could be a trick, fool's gold to trap me.

Am I being too churlish? Am I looking a gift horse in the mouth?

I press her legs closed. 'Did you choose this job or did the job choose you?' I ask.

'I don't know. But we were made for one another.'

It is dark by the time we arrive at Natasha's cottage. There are no streetlights and Natasha leaves her headlights on for Geena, who runs from the car, leaving the door swinging on its hinges, and retrieves the key from under a pot. If she was terrified of dying on her last visit there is no evidence of it now. Her excitement is like a child's.

I help Natasha unload the bags and groceries from the boot as Geena lets herself in and turns on the lights. As we carry the bags into the kitchen I can hear Geena's feet shuffling around upstairs above the low ceiling.

She reappears as we are stocking the fridge. 'There's no TV,' she complains. Natasha confirms it is so. 'So what are we going to do?'

We decide to go out into the night to take a look at the sea.

A new moon in its first quarter is suspended over the water. We stare at the combination for a long time, at the moon tugging at the tide. Natasha breaks the silence, telling us that astronomers are using ever more powerful digital telescopes on different continents, linked together to see objects receding further and further away in intergalactic space, and are getting closer to observing the moment of the Big Bang itself, the moment when maths was created.

'I saw a ghost yesterday,' Geena says, apropos of nothing.

Natasha laughs. 'That sounds good.'

'And I knew her too.'

'This was a woman?'

'She used to bully me at school. Andie Burley; it was her. She threw my satchel out of the bus. She even set my hair on fire once. When she died of a brain tumour I was ecstatic.'

'Where did you see the ghost?'

'On Chalk Farm Road. Her eyes were like headlights.'

'Chalk Farm Road, in Camden?'

'Yeah. She followed me down the road, so I nipped into a McDonald's. Since I was there I thought I might as well get a hamburger.'

As I laugh I feel Natasha's arm reach around my back. The air is cold on my skin.

'There was an offer of a free slush cup with every Big Mac and fries. But the girl wouldn't give me one because I hadn't bought any fries. I got into an argument with her. You know, like, what's the big deal? McDonald's not going to go bankrupt over a slush cup.' Geena's face is blacked-out and there is not enough moonlight to read her by. 'When I left the ghost had gone. I went home and there she was, sitting on the doorstep waiting for me.'

I squander the next five minutes trying to think if there is a McDonald's in Camden and whether the fries don't come free.

We return to the cottage and I go to bed, having been up since 5 a.m. I climb the narrow staircase that leads into one of the two bedrooms. From the small window I try to glimpse the sea, but a heavy fog is now running, covering both sea and sky.

I dig around in my holdall for my washbag and enter the bathroom. There is a second door to the bathroom from the other bedroom and as I am cleaning my teeth Geena comes in by that door. Natasha follows seconds later. She rests her back against the wall and folds her arms. 'Well,' she begins. 'You two seemed to have claimed the bedrooms. Where am I to sleep?'

I have my mouth full of toothpaste, so Geena answers. 'I can go in with Mark. We usually sleep together.'

'The plot thickens,' Natasha says.

'No, not really,' I say. 'Why don't you and Geena sleep together.'

'And tomorrow I get to sleep with you?'

I have difficulty getting to sleep. The bed is soft and new to me. The background noises of the city are noticeably absent. But I think if I'm honest it's the knowledge of Geena and Natasha in bed on the other side of the bathroom that plays on my mind. It races through my head the whole time that I've never been so proximate to Geena when she is in bed with someone else. Before we'd all said goodnight I saw Natasha briefly in her black silk pajamas, and with her hair as short as it is, she looked like a boy.

I wake sometime before dawn and smell Geena lying next to me. She's sneaked in as though we were children again, breaking our parents' law. Back in London when she comes to bed I can always smell where she's been . . . an Indian restaurant, a pub. By morning those smells would all be gone, replaced by her organic odour; a fragrance that retains something of her youth. At night I smell the present, by morning the past. Freud calls the pleasure intense smell gives 'reichlust'. Geena gives me a lot of reichlust.

But tonight there is something I can't work out. Geena never wears perfumes, scents of any kind. Yet that is what I smell on her. I inhale again and recognise Natasha's Lancôme regenerating night cream. I can smell the other woman on Geena and grow painfully erect. I have to get out of bed not to embarrass myself.

In the pale blue light just before dawn I wander downstairs with that erection inside my pajamas and find Natasha in the kitchen in her underwear, making toast and brewing espresso. Rain falls softly outside the house. She gives me a long carnal look. The toast catches fire under the grill and the coffee starts to percolate. Natasha throws her hands up and shouts in amusement: 'The coffee's burning with glee! It's slapping!'

After breakfast we take our first walk out into the rain, leaving Geena to sleep in, and the rain clears for us. The clouds stay low and soggy. We walk beside a river estuary and follow its course inland. Wooden jetties and wharfs are spectral on a low tide and upon black groynes cormorants are perched. Fishing nets tumble down the steps of wooden sheds. Primary coloured trawlers bleed into the sepia. Everything smells of pitch, asphalt, turpentine, petrol – anally erotic odours.

We are the only excursionists in this homemade world. Natasha puts her arm inside mine and says, 'My kids love this river.'

'Your kids,' I repeat. 'The ones you don't see any more.'

'I don't have any other kind,' she snaps back. She removes her arm and, in a rapid change of tone, declares, 'If you measured this river as the crow flies, and again along its true length, you'll get a ratio of three to fourteen, Pi. What Pythagoras called an evil number.'

'Any river?'

'Any river; the ratio between order and chaos.'

'How can a number be evil?'

'If evil is primordial then so are some numbers. Pythagoras tried to prove the existence of God in terms of perfect numbers, then his student discovered Pi, the evil one, and Pythagoras had him drowned. In a river.'

'Your children. Can I meet them one day?'

'Maybe.' She drifts away, bending down by the river bank to stare at a trout coming up to feed on the insects stuck in the meniscus of the water. 'Why didn't you want to sleep with me last night?'

'Did I say I didn't want to sleep with you?' She looks at me, and waits. 'Geena and I have never shared a friend before, let alone a lover.'

'I know you're close, but how close is that?'

'It is what it is. I go to work. That's my life.'

'Go to work where everyone is sick.'

'I go to work at a place of safety. Like your mathematical universe at the bank. Where the children can't gnaw away at you.'

'I admit to that. The bank's a place of safety.'

'Except my work is no longer distracting me. These hallucinations are worrying. Geena's very fragile at the moment. I hope you appreciate that. You haven't known her long.'

'You think she's going to break?'

'She's going to break my heart. Your children . . .'

'Do they break my heart? I think about them every day. I don't even have to try. Their faces just pop into my head. But you *see* Geena every day. Perhaps a little distance might make you feel better about her. Brothers and sisters aren't meant to be so close.'

She's trying to separate us. 'I see nothing wrong in it.'

'But there is something dysfunctional about you two.'

'Geena may be dysfunctional, but me?'

'I think she's happier than you.'

'That's because she's naïve. She's led a sheltered life. Perhaps we should get back now. Geena'll be wondering where we are.'

In the cottage we cook the lemon sole we'd bought from a shed. The smell entices Geena out of bed. She pads into the kitchen, rubbing the sleep from her eyes as I am removing from the oven the potatoes and organic carrots roasted in sesame oil with whole cloves and coriander.

Geena leans against a worktop, her hands behind her back. 'I feel content here,' she says.

'That's a great improvement on your last visit,' Natasha replies.

'Last visit I could smell dead things.'

'Them maybe . . .' Natasha points to the double portrait over the kitchen table of her parents. The military father, lithe from years of self-discipline, stands over his wife, whose scrawny hands rest on her lap, barring all entry. The sole is so fresh and delicate to seem insubstantial. Natasha drinks mineral water and watches Geena and I down a bottle of South African sauvignon.

'Still miss it?' I ask. 'The drinking?'

'I missed my children. So I started drinking and I stopped missing them. But that had to end.'

'I think we should live here,' Geena says. 'Live here for ever and have children together.' She ponders the obvious implications. 'Well maybe not me. You and Natasha have children. I'll be Auntie Geena.'

'A symmetrical idea,' I say, 'but how do we pay for it?'

'I'm serious,' Geena adds. 'You and Natasha have a brood. I really feel at home here. By the sea and everything.'

Natasha refuses to be drawn into this fantasy of happy families, children. She's already been down that road.

I try to lighten the tone. 'We'd have to get a TV, I suppose.'

'I'll do without one,' Geena says. 'I won't need a TV.'

'Wait a minute here!' Natasha takes the plates to the sink. With her back to us she says, 'How about we take another walk. To sober up.'

The afternoon is bright and sunny with fresh winds from the north. It chills our skin as we walk along the edge of the sea, under great lolling clouds.

We go inland as the last of the light is receding over the sea. Geena pushes ahead and I sense her as being separate from us. It is not a comfortable feeling, not at all. Nor is walking along country roads. I don't know how I'm meant to relate to wheat fields. The critters in the hedgerows make me nervous. The roads are blood baths, covered with more dead birds, rabbits and hedgehogs than I've ever seen alive.

We reach our destination, a heritage village where the thatched roofs are combed, the lawns manicured, the pub sign painted by a local Picasso, the postbox polished and the wood-stacks all of equally sawn logs. I feel we should be wiping our feet before traipsing through.

Behind a row of fir trees I glimpse something odd going on in the courtyard of a medieval house. Nine women stand in box formation, three rows deep, dressed in identical full-length black coats. They are all young, attractive and well heeled on the evidence of the German cars parked in the courtyard. We hear a low chanting and then in one synchronised move the women start to release their shoulders from under their coats. Pale white skin is unveiled.

'What are they doing!' I ask.

'It's a centre for personal development,' Natasha replies.

'But what are they *doing*?'

'I've no idea. Therapy. Playing the fool.'

We walk into the Olde Tea Shoppe, a threshold that even Charles Dickens in his most generous mood would not have crossed, and sit at a window seat and order cream teas.

Mothers and daughters, husbands and wives avoid eye contact with each other and say nothing at all. Ours is the only conversation running, which these patrons tune in to with a hunger.

An elderly waitress in a starched gingham apron appears at our table. Unsmilingly she begins unloading scones, pots of cream, strawberry jam off her silver tray and onto the table. Natasha says loudly, articulating to every corner of the room: 'Withnail and I go into a tea shop just like this. And Withnail says, "Bring me your best wines! We're millionaires and I'm going to buy this place and install a juke box."'

She laughs and the waitress stares with extreme prejudice at her. Geena pushes back her chair, the legs screeching along the polished wooden floor. Natasha's laughter falls like coins to the floor the moment she catches sight of Geena's face. I turn to see what she has seen and discover that Geena has turned pale and is drenched in sweat.

Geena catapults out of her chair and darts around the room like a hen in an enclosure, shouting: 'There are men . . . and sheep with guns!' The customers hold their breath in that emblematic English way, as though smothering hiccups.

Natasha and I try to head her off. Three young-uns in leather trousers, jeans, trainers, shirts outside belts, pins through noses and navels – run amok in the Olde Tea Shoppe.

The waitress gives us a cold firm command. 'I'm going to have to ask you to leave.'

Outside in the street Geena moans softly. She has recovered, the possession has lifted. But it has left her more shaken and more frightened than ever before. A shoal of faces behind bevelled glass watch us, their eyes as beady and inscrutable as fish. Natasha puts her arm around Geena as the clouds fold over what is left of the blue sky.

The English countryside has become a place of peril. Geena stays insecure, in dread of the next fit. The joy has been knocked out of her. The good times are over. She is rebegot of absence, darkness; things that are not.

Late that night I am woken as my mattress depresses and a naked thigh beaches upon my leg like a large fish. I smell Geena very strongly and as I battle with the confused sensations occasioned by Geena *naked*, I realise it is Natasha who's come to my bed, straight from the arms of my sister. I can't bring myself to touch her. She's as desirable as any woman I know but there's a barrier I can't cross. It feels disloyal for one thing, as though I'm cheating on my sister, stepping out with her lover. The trinity just won't work here, it is negatively charged. Perhaps when the smell of Geena has worn off, maybe then it will be easier. Natasha is completely still with her head cradled in my neck and I sense with some relief her falling asleep. She just needs to be comforted.

For what must it be like to lose your children, your own blood, bones, hair and teeth? Some women would die from the grief, but not Natasha. She is very much alive and that is her great achievement, not to snatch at thin air, but embrace with all she's got that which has been left her. She will not be counted out.

Isn't this the pattern for most of us? Who really leads the life they thought they'd have when young? We are all three still young, but not so young that we have yet to fix our course. We are already on course. What we have is what we have. Compensation *is* the life: work, sex, friendship. This is the rule of survival.

Maybe Natasha has recognised the same quality in us. Maybe I've been wrong in my suspicions, a bad habit picked up from my parents. As I begin to feel compassion for her, I also begin to feel desire.

I consider briefly Geena sleeping alone and place my hand between Natasha's thighs, arousing her as she sleeps, arousing myself stealing pleasure in this way. She begins to get wet; wetter as her sleep thins. Her eyes spring open, her mouth opens and she rolls on top of me. Her breath smells brackish on my face as she guides me into her.

'You can come inside me.' This invitation to violate are the words all men like to hear. But I cannot accept it gracefully.

'Don't you have enough unwanted children?'

'It's a safe time in my month.'

And so I come, followed by a state of such crippling vulnerability that the whole world is renewed. Just for a moment it's as if I've never seen or felt anything before. This *jamais vu* is what Geena has immediately following a hallucination.

I dare not face Natasha in this state and so look out of the window at the sky full of stars. In the distance red and green lights move across the surface of the sea. White navigational lights flash coded messages, but I don't understand the language.

PART TWO

'Our dreams are a second life.'

— GERARD DE NERVAL

DREAMY STATES

'So let's shake the trees a little,' Mr Stein begins on a relaxed footing, running a Mont Blanc pen along his rack of smoker's pipes. 'What do you hallucinate?'

'Familiar things. But not so familiar,' Geena says.

'Is this one single hallucination recurring, or more than one?'

'More. But with the same people. One woman almost breaks out.'

'Breaks out?' repeats Stein, raising his eyebrows.

'I can't explain that. Breaks out is the best I can do.'

'What woman?'

'I don't know.'

'Where do you see her?'

'At a beach house, sometimes.'

'Do you have any loss of consciousness?'

'No. I keep on my feet. I don't go down.'

I add my contribution. 'She does *seem* to be out on her feet sometimes. She walked into the road and got . . .' I see Stein's eyes glaze over and I can't finish. The space I occupy in the consultancy room is an empty hole into which he pours his negative energies. I get the distinct impression that I am not welcome here and sit back resolving to say no more.

The neurologist looks as if he's stepped out of another century. His thin moustache is waxed, a suede tie hangs from his throat like an ox tongue and his tweed jacket is snagged in a thousand places as though he'd crawled through a thicket hedge on his way to work. My father arranged this appointment and I begin to wonder just how good an ex-porter's contacts can be.

'Do these turns happen at night, in the morning? When do they occur?'

'Night and morning.'

'What are the sensations you get, immediately before?'

'Like what do you mean?'

'Bad taste in the mouth, foul odours, a tightening of the throat.'

'Yeah, some of those. I get those. Pins and needles in the shoulder . . .'

Stein interrupts. 'Are you standing or sitting when it happens?'

'I'm usually just . . . hanging around.'

'But you don't fall, you say?'

'No.'

'And your body, does it stiffen?'

'I don't think so.'

I seek permission to speak, not quite with my hand raised, but almost. Stein's eyes still look hostile so I address him through Geena instead. 'Tell him how you went off that time after your bag was snatched. Outside the Dark Side of the Moon.'

'The dark side of the moon?' Stein repeats.

'It's a pub,' I explain.

But Geena ignores me too. 'Once I was sitting on a train looking out the window and this strong sunlight came

72

through a line of trees. Suddenly I'm on a boat. For all of two seconds.'

'When were you on a train?' I fight my way back in.

'Was the train moving?' Stein asks.

'Oh yeah. The Virgin line. The rock 'n' roll railway. I thought maybe some clever steward had put something in the tea.'

'Do you use hallucinogenic drugs? LSD, Ecstasy . . .'

'No.'

'Are you sure?'

'Well, I've done Ecstasy.'

'Ecstasy can stay in the bloodstream for weeks after use.'

'I haven't done Ecstasy for months. Can't afford it.'

The neurologist lays down his pen on top of the notepad and knits his fingers together.

It is show time.

'It sounds to me like you're suffering from simple partial epilepsy.' His voice is as clear as a church bell on a fine day.

Geena straightens in her chair. I reach out to touch her shoulder. She is stiff as a pillar of salt.

Mr Stein continues. 'You have cephalic sensations, followed by auras, premonitions. But not automatism.'

'Automatism?'

'When inhibitions disintegrate. You never suffer a complete loss of control, you say, which might mean you're not having seizures.'

Geena twists in her seat. 'Then I'm not epileptic, am I?'

'There are over forty types of seizures,' Stein explains. 'Some are wrongly diagnosed as epilepsy. What you may be experiencing is non-epileptic attacks. Or aborted seizures.'

'I don't get this,' Geena simpers. 'Either I am or I'm not.'

'Well, we don't understand either. The brain's still a mystery, like a fifteenth-century map of the world.'

Maybe that doesn't advance the diagnosis but it does help explain his wardrobe. When one's *métier* is a medieval cortex

I guess you miss out on all the fashions of this world.

He reads from his notes. 'Your seizures have been triggered by someone snatching a bag from you (he *has* been listening to me). By sunlight flashing through trees. These phenomena can cause electrical potentials to activate previous similar experiences held in the brain, filed under "snatching" or "sunlight through trees", so to speak, and brings on the hallucination. Each experience of "snatching" or "sunlight through trees" may differ but all link in the way they stimulate the original memory in the temporal lobe.'

Geena's face clouds over. My attention is drawn to a framed cartoon on the wall behind Stein's head, of two old men sitting in a nursing home surrounded by other wheelchair-bound inmates, falling out of their seats, drooling. The one says to the other: 'Imagine, we gave up smoking for this.'

Stein resumes. 'Excitation in the cortex activates the mechanism that recalls past experience. A re-experiencing of the past. Or it can be a false interpretation of the present.'

'You are losing me, Mr Stein,' I have to say. 'Sorry.'

To Geena he asks: 'You mentioned a woman . . .'

'She's like, a virtual woman. A hologram. Sometimes she appears and there's a car. Mountains, sea. I glimpse all those. In a house by the sea. But she is always eluding me. Giving me the slip.'

A light goes on behind Stein's eyes. 'Were you ever involved in a car crash, as a child?'

'I don't think so.'

The light goes off. 'You should check with your parents, anyway.'

'I don't have to. They can't drive.'

'Tossed by a horse, anything at all that may have resulted in temporal skull fracture. Such an accident can leave a deep imprint. The cortex is then conditioned, so that hallucinations are influenced by the original accident.'

'But why is this happening now?' I want to know. 'Geena is thirty-two years old.'

'That's not unprecedented. Another thing. Hallucinations can be closely linked with your wishes, anxieties, neurotic conflicts.'

'Oh. Right. *Fucking hell!*'

'Have you had infant meningitis, severe pneumonia or some febrile illness?'

'Not that I've been told.'

The neurologist returns to his notes. He is insatiable. 'Do you also have auditory hallucinations? Do you hear sounds?'

Geena points to her head. 'Buzzing and whistling, talking and singing.'

'Buzzing, whistling would appear in the temporal gyrus of Herschl. But Herschl doesn't produce speech. Speech is produced on the dominant side of the temporal lobe.' He raises his hand off the desk and looks us over, to see if we are still with him. 'I know this is a lot to take in.'

It sure is, I think.

'We can run tests. An MRI will help determine whether this is epilepsy. Or not.'

'I don't want tests,' Geena adds.

'Why not?' I ask.

I catch the neurologist smiling at Geena, his small grey eyes simpatico. Geena's illness has a poetic condition which he reads like a book. 'You find these hallucinations quite comforting?'

'Yes, I do,' Geena says, like she is exchanging marriage vows with Stein. 'But not the run-up to them.'

I am stunned by their sudden intimacy. Their eyes weld and hold a look I can never forget, like the eyes of star-crossed lovers. The bedrock of love is in recognising who the other person is.

'The run-up I don't like. But once I'm inside I feel all right. Peaceful, like I've gone home.'

'These hallucinations are what we call "dreamy states". There is still no better definition, in my mind.'

'I still don't understand whether Geena has epilepsy or not,' I complain. Earn your wages, lover boy.

'But that's all right, you see. Making a diagnosis of epilepsy in someone is to profoundly affect their social status.'

'Will I be able to hold down a job?' Geena looks sideways at me. 'Okay then, will it go away?'

'If it's epilepsy, no.'

'Will it get worse?'

'I don't think so.'

As we get up to leave Stein imparts the following information: epilepsy is far more common than most people think. One in two hundred is epileptic. One in twenty has a seizure at some time in their life. Children you see fluttering their eyelids all the time may actually be epileptic, suffering 'absences', or 'petit mals'. Then he tells Geena to go out and have a full and happy life.

We leave the hospital in altered states of mind. For a long time we sit in Queens Square Gardens, unsure of where next to lope off to. The iron railings surrounding us are as unyielding as the bars of a prison. The Imaging Centre, the National Institute for Neurology, the Royal Homeopathic Hospital snuggling up together around the Square seem for those few moments like a movie set. Even a statue in the garden, marooned between these institutions dedicated to the enigma of mind and body, has a duplicitous inscription: 'This statue thought in the nineteenth century to be of Queen Anne is now widely regarded as that erected in April 1775 to commemorate Queen Charlotte consort of King George II.' All the roses are still in bloom so late in the season and the air reeks of their perfume. It is a garden for the blind, I realise, when a man comes by pushing an empty supermarket trolley. He wears a crash helmet and his eyes are masked by sunglasses.

In the taxi going home we stare out of our windows, through a glass darkly. We don't talk. Everything outside the taxi has short-circuited. Black office buildings are stacked up like chimneys. From the sky a powder falls onto the pavements, welding pedestrians to the spot. Buses and cars and lorries fly past, their tyres on oily roads sounding like rivers tumbling over limestone shelves.

READING BETWEEN
THE LINES

Geena sits in Mum's kitchen with her eyes shut, trying to con-
jure up early childhood. She pads across to the window. The
plane trees clicking against heather-blue slates on red brick
Victorian buildings, the residents' bicycles chained to the
iron fence – all this familiar terrain she declares as a foreign
land.

'What do you mean, foreign?'

'I don't belong here. This is Mars.'

Mum and Dad wander in and out of the kitchen, almost
pathologically restless. Geena keeps asking them about her
infancy. Did I have meningitis? Did I suffer any skull fractures?
They reel from the questions as though they are accusations,
as though punches. They draw down the shutters, their coun-
tenances grow shifty.

Not getting what she wants from them, Geena begins searching the flat for clues. She climbs the aluminium stepladder into
the tiny loft as Mum and Dad sit in the kitchen with their hands
folded on their laps, heads bowed. Geena's illness has rocked
their belief in themselves, as if her mental condition was
indeed a result of reckless parenting, even though they have
never been involved with her in a car accident, dropped her on

her head as a baby, or any of the other things Stein said might have triggered her condition.

Geena comes down from the loft with a cardboard box full of Matchbox cars, potato guns, comic albums, dolls and teddies – all covered in insulation fibres and ceiling plaster. She seems quite pleased with her haul and holes up in her bedroom.

My parents both bow their heads. 'What's the matter with you two?' I ask. But they won't or can't answer me. Dad just closes his eyes and shuts out the world.

I leave them in their misery and to go attend my seminar on Dostoyevsky at the university. What else am I to do?

The lecturer tells the class that in Dostoyevsky, grave philosophical ideas are presented in a playful, half-joking way. The novelist does not take a single moral position but sets a variety of opposing discourses against each other. All dogma is hypothetical in his 'true' fiction.

The subject is lost on the twenty fresh-faced teenagers surrounding me. They may have their bums on seats but their heads are still in the student union bar of the night before. They only come round when he cross-pollinates Dostoyevsky with Madonna; *Crime and Punishment* with the video of *Like A Virgin*. Madonna's treatment of Catholic dogma, he insists, is performed with the same half-joking style as Dostoyevsky.

A year ago when I was deciding which university to attend I deliberately chose an inferior one. I thought I'd have more in common with ordinary students in an ordinary institution than with all those fencing champions at Oxford and Cambridge. The downside is the way this university sells courses like one would a used car; anything goes providing it increases student roles.

This is my second bid for a university education; my original attempt to enter the stream at eighteen was scuppered by Dad. Academia was anathema to him. While it is true that the

University of Cape Town politicised him, through the student ANC, his lecturers were meanwhile writing the theoretical scribes for apartheid (at nearby Stellenbosch University to be exact), and this meant the system was corrupt, the fountain of knowledge poisoned.

'But this is England, Dad,' I protested, 'not South Africa.'

'All academics have one weakness. They are physical cowards.' He described how lecturers in more recent times drove out to give their support to the ANC demonstrations. But if the demonstrations turned bloody, their white asses were nowhere to be seen. Some made agreements with the police to warn them beforehand if any teargas, water cannons, stoppers, dum-dum bullets or live ammunition were to be discharged into the crowd. The deal was, if the academics made no attempt to kill the police, the police would make no attempt to kill the academics. So they'd walk away from some shoot-out, giving the police far more freedom for repression than if they'd remained, and returned to their ivy-clad campus on the hill to speak to one another on the courtyard steps about building socialism in the country.

'Well, you left the country,' I said. 'Where's the moral courage in that?'

My father became ashen-faced as he said, 'South Africa was like a beautiful woman who men pursue in order to deface.'

He said nothing more. I was left confused by his simile. Yet he succeeded in his objective: I went into his line of work at eighteen.

But now I can pay the fees myself, I'm doing part-time what I wanted to do full-time ten years ago.

I return to my parents' flat around 5 p.m. I can't find Geena anywhere, but the raided cardboard box from the loft sitting on her unmade bed gives me a clue as to what she's been doing. In the box she seems to have struck gold: a locked diary she'd kept as a child lays on the bed, bent open at the spine. The lock has been broken with a screwdriver. Several pages have been torn out and scattered across the floor. I put together an entry written when she was thirteen, around the time Michael Jackson's second album *Thriller* was released.

I'm trying 2 pick up the courage 2 ask Dad if I can go to MJ day (again) in Hammersmith Palais with Emma. I'll say something like, 'Well Emma has never been.' Emma's worked in Disney Shop, McDonald's, Blockbuster, Burger King but got sacked 4 daydreaming. I don't know if he'll let me stand outside the Dorchester. I went to Oxford Street on Saturday. Mum is like my dad she doesn't like me spending money on MJ either. Shall I cut my hair? Just a little off the bottom and fringe. I wonder if I can persuade par to go out *avec* Mum tonight? It'll be cool 2-B home alone with Mark! But she's going to a church meeting and he hates those things. I have cut my hair loads of times. First it looked bad. Second time it looked good.

Dad has just said yes to MJ day! But I have to finish all my homework 4 the weekend tonight. Mark says he'll help me with my English, and he's only nine! Dad's gonna take me 2 Hammersmith Palais. That's the deal. Oh my giddy aunt! I'll B sooo embarrassed in front of my friends.

The second entry torn from her diary was written some years earlier.

Mummy and Daddy run off into the trees and left me behind. I am lost in the woods. I cant find Mummy and Daddy and its as dark like when I lay under the blankets. Birds are flying out of the trees I am frightening them. Im frightened that an animal is going to jump on my back.

Animals come out at night. Im running and then I fall over. I am crying. Theres a old black woman with no clothes on. Shes washing herself in the stream. She stops me and I cant understand what she is saying. She puts on an old sack. She holds my hand and takes me out of the woods to the house. The door is locked. She takes me round to where the sea is and looks through the window. Im looking through the windows with her. No one is home. Mummy and Daddy are not in there but theres a pot on the stove for dinner. Theres glasses of wine. I can hear them speaking. I can hear them they are calling my name. They sound like wind chimes. I cant see them. I am crying and the old black woman is wiping my face with her dirty hand. I can hear my own name being called but I cant see my Mummy or Daddy.

From the alleyway behind the block I hear a dull thump that draws my attention to the window. Outside I see Geena standing next to a dustbin and the dustbin is on fire. Barefoot and with her hair in pigtails she is throwing all her toys and dolls into the fire. Through a large tear in her jeans I can see a patch of bright yellow knickers. Her bare midriff folds gently over her belt. She looks like a child.

My mother beats me into the alley, where we stand together, united in our concern. Neither of us knows what to say to Geena, what questions to ask other than the obvious ones. She keeps shy of us, and with her back turned asks a less than obvious question of Mum.

'Why didn't you tell me I had a sister?'

'You don't have a sister.'

'I had a sister and she's dead.'

Mum bursts into tears. I put my hand on her shoulder. 'Okay, Geena, you quit this now.' But Geena holds fast, as unsympathetic as I've ever seen her.

'I had a sister. I can feel it.' She bangs her chest with her fist. 'In here. Maybe a twin, who died.'

'You don't have a sister,' Mum repeats. Then she takes a deep breath. 'You don't have a brother either.'

I take my hand off Mum's shoulder. 'What did you say?'

She takes several seconds to focus whatever is in her mind. 'I should have told you this a long time ago. There are exceptional circumstances why I didn't, but . . .'

'Tell me what?'

'You were adopted. We adopted you when you were three.'

Geena forces out a laugh, like a dog barking. She wears a pathetic smile, like a brave face at an execution.

My mother's words spin around in my head like rotary blades. I feel all my twenty-eight years being lifted off the ground, out of the alleyway, leaving only my heart behind. I can see it beating in the gloomy alley, a red brick in the wall.

No one moves. Geena begins to sweat and shiver, her eyes rolling around. She clutches her fists by her side. Then everyone moves. Mum and I try to reach out to Geena who backs right through the open doors of an empty lock-up. She hides in the shadows between hanging tyres and shouts out, 'I was in a car. There was a level crossing by the sea; I saw that. The gates came down and snapped the aerial off the roof.'

Mum and I look at each other across the yard; a canyon opens up between us. We can't go forward and we can't go back, so we stand in our chains, inhaling the toxic fumes of the burning plastic dustbin, serenaded by the weeping from inside the garage.

BOOK OF REVELATION

In a bare white room at a municipal office in Hackney, the social worker hands Geena her identity piecemeal. Every sentence in those records has the power to shock. They are dramatic epistles; revelations of a lost three years that get under the skin. Geena blinks hard as she reads down the pages, stunned by the speed in which three decades can be rewritten.

There is a well-oiled mechanism for tracking true parentage. The Children's Society acquired Geena's Adoption Order in Pretoria in such a casual, easy way that suggests they've known all along. All they were waiting for for the past twenty-nine years was her call. They arranged for her to pick up the papers at this local adoption agency. Her records could only be viewed providing she came in and submitted to . . . *counselling*.

We have come to the counselling session together, spoiling for a fight.

The social worker watches over us as we read through the records. The court that made the Adoption Order was Wynberg Magistrates Court in Cape Town. Her birth certificate was abridged in Pretoria in the name of her adopting parents. The original birth certificate can't be issued without the birth parents' permission, because it was a non-disclosed adoption.

In a non-disclosed adoption, the birth parents give their con-
sent never to try to contact their child at a later stage. Nor are
the records 'tagged' with biographical notes in the eventuality
that Geena would one day want to make contact with them. So
who they are, what they do, where they are, we know not. We
don't even know if they are still alive. The information gets
more shocking the deeper we read. On page seven is a copy of
the social services report. Geena, apparently, was placed under
a safety order and removed from her parents because of their
drug abuse.

'Drug abuse?' Geena slaps her palm on to the files. 'I'm a
drug abuser! Half the people I know are drug abusers! I lost my
parents because they liked to share a few chemicals?' She
throws herself back into the chair, claps her hands on the top
of her head and struggles to speak over her icy tears. 'Do my
adopted parents know this?'

'They could have been told by the adoption agency. Or by
your foster parents.'

'I had *foster* parents?'

'For three months.' Still nothing registers on the face of the
social worker. His voice is a trained monotone, colourless at
the very edges of despair. 'It might be useful if you start your
search with them. They might remember your birth parents.'

'They're in bloody South Africa!' Geena shouts.

'Your adopted parents can help you to find them.'

'I've had enough of their fucking help.' To me she adds: 'This
is why they never wanted to talk about South Africa. In case it
opened a can of worms.'

'Try not to hurt them,' the social worker says. 'Consider
their feelings too.'

What kind of counselling is this! Who's this guy, telling us
how to handle our folks? I am brimming over as I stare at his
M&S shirt, jacket and trousers, Clarke's docksiders, white
socks. He is in his early thirties and balding, and I don't trust

men who go prematurely bald. They always find ways to avenge themselves. How many innocents has he scalped in his twenty-year career?

'You've gone very pale,' he informs Geena.

'Of course she's fucking pale! Wouldn't you be?'

He takes everything I can throw at him on the chin. He isn't fazed at all, has seen and heard it all a thousand times. He offers her a drink of water; the glass and the bottle pushed along the table.

Like the neurologist Stein, the social worker has eyes only for Geena. He blanks me out as he warns her about the road ahead. Tracing parents is no solution to the day-to-day problems of being of unknown descent. He predicts the emotional trauma that a successful (or unsuccessful) search will create. It may take Geena twenty days or twenty years. Many adopted people develop fantasies about their birth parents, he says, which can go against the grain, can be very different to the reality. A search will stir up feelings of guilt and shame and anger. Birth parents are only a part of the story that makes up a person's identity.

Behind us in the queue the crowd of orphans is building. He moves fast towards his conclusion. 'If you go ahead with this, contact the Post-Adoption Centre in Cape Town. They will make a request in Pretoria for your original birth certificate. But remember, that will only be issued with your birth parents' permission. Which means they will know that you are trying to make contact. If they can be found, that is.'

From this moment on nothing will ever be the same again. We feel it walking out of the counselling session into the busy London street. We are like veterans returning home from war only to find ourselves alienated from that home. Lorries rolling by scramble my thoughts. Teenagers playing pool in a Cypriot café – indifferent to us an hour ago – stop playing to stare at us through the window. A crowd of Jamaicans give us a wide berth. We are strangers in our own flesh.

We are strangers to one another too; a cruel parting that has been occasioned by different reactions to the same trauma. I feel the guilt of a survivor, she feels bereaved. On the one hand she mourns for the lost three years of her life and on the other feels stripped of rank, now her biological rights to my parents have been excised. She has taken the rap for a misdemeanour she never committed. Because of that misdemeanour she is now less than me. What a single week can do to our souls.

I try telling her that our relationship will be the same as always but I'm kidding no one and she gets the hell out of my bed. She gets out of my bed at precisely the moment when it would be okay to stay. We could have comforted each other, acted on instinct, let legitimate desire grow. Now the past has been rewritten, it has set us free. But if there is an historical sexual attraction between us, Geena does not want it disturbed.

SQUARING THE CIRCLE

This is what I've believed my entire life: Mum and Dad are dull souls who have no friends and are always bloody moaning.

I never bothered to understand them. What was there to understand? All knowledge is filtered through your parents when you are young. What I or Geena knew is what they wanted us to know. Which was practically nothing. The way they could move from elation to mind-numbing depression in the space of fifteen seconds I put down to unfulfilled lives and occupations. To an overdose of bad TV. To Geena fucking around. Present dangers, never past ones.

But now that single truth has been liberated, it liberates many others. One out, all out, through the breach in the wall. Mum tells me and Geena that she and Dad had been activists in South Africa.

'You were *political*!' My parents! My *ain* folk!

'What does that mean, political?' My mother sounds angry. 'When your friends get into trouble, you do something about it. Like Miriam and Erasmus.'

'Dad's gone down the road,' Geena observes. 'He can't cope with this.'

We are standing in the kitchen, leaning against separate

walls, the space between us as unyielding as solid geometry. I try to remember if Mum or Dad had ever spoken the names of Miriam and Erasmus. Ruth First and Joe Slovo certainly, whispered to one another in this kitchen. I can remember Dad leaving one Saturday morning in the early eighties and asking him where he was going. To stand in a crowd outside the South African Embassy in Trafalgar Square, he said, with a nonchalance as though it were a football match. Something about the character of the London-based anti-apartheid movement made him feel uncomfortable. All those actresses and pop stars with their simple theology of good and evil he compared to the Irish Americans who have never stepped on Irish soil, giving their support and money to the IRA.

'So who are Miriam and Erasmus?' Geena asks.

'They were our best friends,' she says. 'I was maid of honour at their wedding. Then Erasmus was arrested for not carrying a pass. You know about passes? The police arrested him and sent him to work in a farm and Miriam started to hear his voice inside her head. When an African says that it means he's entered the spirit world.'

'Dead?'

'We went out to that farm in Kuilsrivier to see. What we saw, well that's another story too. There were men hoeing the field thin as scarecrows, shoeless, naked. They were being lashed with sjamboks. Slaves of the farmer, in 1967, not 1867. But we found Erasmus. His arms and legs were broken and he was being forced to work. We had to pay the farmer all our savings to let him go. All our lifetime's savings as compensation. I joined in the protests after that. I did that all right. You couldn't sit on the fence after that.'

My father was a porter by now and a very rare bird as an activist, as trade unions had a policy of non-co-operation with black workers as a means of restricting competition. Their two white faces among several thousand blacks were easily picked out by Security Police photographers. Not long afterwards they were paid a series of house visits, under the gaze of their neighbours, who started to call them 'kaffir lovers' through the windows of passing cars. Shopkeepers turned their 'closed' signs around as she approached their doors.

'So why keep this from us?' I ask. 'If you were on the right side?'

My mother hot-wires the connection to Geena for the first time. Mum had wanted children for years. But after receiving the gynaecologist's verdict ('It's impossible for you to get pregnant') they registered with an adoption agency.

'When we went to see you for the first time all we knew was how much we wanted a child in our home. We saw this three-year-old already walking, talking and the man from the adoption centre asked if we liked this one. "Yes, we like this one," we said. "We like her. We love her. We *will* love her." The man said adoption is like an arranged marriage, love is something that grows. What is of more concern are the lives of the adopting parents. It was more important to him that you went to a good family, to a safe home where you'd be protected. "South Africa is a terrible idea locked into a beautiful country," he said.

'It took us less than a month to go from liking to loving you. Then it became impossible to imagine life without you. You'd turned our lives around and we knew we couldn't stay. If the adoption agency were to run checks on us with the security police we'd have lost our claim on you. You'd have been an orphan again. We left Miriam and Erasmus and our other friends to fight for themselves and emigrated.' She sighs deeply. 'You cannot imagine how painful that was. But every time I felt like hanging myself from the nearest tree you always came along, begging for the rope to skip with.'

Their story then becomes a tale of two cities, two cities that could not co-exist, the roots of the old pushing up from below in the new. They internalised these afflictions and grew more and more depressed.

'It's difficult for me to understand how you loved that country, with all its unlovely violence, more than you ever loved this one. England is a temperate place, is it not?' I ask.

'I suppose it is, temperate, yes. But what is the point of it? We had no role to play, apart from raising you two. We don't know who we are, not here. We are South Africans, good South Africans. On the right side, as you called it. But that made it worse. You were damned if you stayed and damned if you left. But a little more damned if you left.'

'But you were safe,' Geena says.

'And that meant you were safe.'

I am moved by her testimony. She and Dad sacrificed everything they held dear – nationhood, political beliefs, profound friendships – for a child that wasn't even their own.

I am moved but Geena remains scornful. 'I still don't understand why you couldn't have told me I was adopted.'

'We were afraid you'd want to go back there to find your parents. We couldn't have gone with you.'

'You were selfish. You acted cowardly.'

'I'm sorry.'

'Not as sorry as I am,' says Geena.

She ups and puts on her coat to go to Natasha's place in west London, preferring the solicitude of a stranger than the solicitude of intimate strangers. I have to give her the money for the tube fare.

In her absence I counsel my mother. You are good folk, I say. You are blameless. Geena's situation is a product of happenstance. There's a great deal of calamity in the world that made her. Together we can see this thing through. Our hearts are strong, with enough throttle to handle the bends.

But she remains inconsolable. As an adoptive parent she is more tortured about Geena's unhappiness than if she had been born to her, as she has no excuse for Geena's troubles but her raising of her.

Nightfall softens the edges of the city but does nothing to soften Geena's mood. She lies on Natasha's sofa in knickers and T-shirt, downloading the new information about her origins. To be denied biological rights – the brain can only keep that classified for so long, and her eyes flicker on an ebbing current.

Natasha sits on the floor, her legs crossed in a yoga position, reading a book map of South Africa. She pours over place names in the Western Cape. 'Somerset West, Gloucester, Epping Forest, West Riding, Llandudno, Surrey, St James . . . do they mean anything to you?'

'How would I know?' Geena mumbles.

'They're all within twenty or so miles of each other.'

In the time before I arrived here, Natasha seems to have persuaded Geena that the only cure for her broken heart is to try to find her birth parents. It makes me so furious I want to smash her in the face.

'Let's go out,' Geena suggests. 'Before I lose my fucking mind altogether.'

We take a bus to Trafalgar Square. London is on the move around us, changing up in tempo from day to night. We sit on the top deck, lost in our own private thoughts.

In Trafalgar Square we walk in circles around the South African Embassy. Ridges of white cloud amass in the southern sky.

'What are we doing here? Geena's roots are not in Trafalgar Square.'

'There's a well-known saying in juggling,' Natasha remarks. 'The balls go where you throw them.'

'This is not a game.'

'It's all out there for her to find. The brain has the power to

92

solve its own mystery. Think about those hallucinations for a moment.'

'We're walking around in circles. All that'll get us is sore feet.'

So we start walking in a straight line along Pall Mall, with the wind in our hair, past the Horse Guards on Whitehall, Downing Street and onto the Thames at Westminster Bridge.

I look down at the river below. Under its compression, the dull countenance of the sky, the sluggish water looks like a swarthy man engaged in sex, its slow thighs rubbing against the muddy banks, the ruined wharves and docks.

A wave of nausea rises in my stomach. 'What are you going to find out anyway by tracing your parents? It was only three years of your life.'

'Yeah, but the first three,' Geena fences. 'I watched this TV programme. It said your character is set in stone in the first three years.'

I look up from the hard surface of the river to find myself eye to eye with Geena. I feel an overpowering sense of shyness. There is no virtue in shyness at the best of times, and this shyness is like a sin. But I can't look her in the eye any more.

Natasha says: 'Why are you trying to put her off the idea?'

'I'm not trying to put her off the idea. As her brother . . .'

Geena catches my mistake. 'You're not my brother.'

'That's hurtful,' I say.

'But true,' Natasha adds. 'We're all equals now. Three friends helping one another.'

'Wrong,' I say. 'You're not our equal.'

We trail along the towpath on the South Bank. No one says anything for a long time. I drift away from Geena and Natasha and hold onto a lamppost. St Paul's Cathedral emanates inside the honeycombed city of light, its reflection burning the waters of the Thames. What was it Natasha said about rivers? I can't remember. Then I do remember. Rivers engendered Pi, the evil number.

As we are crossing Waterloo Bridge I wonder how three *unrelated* people came to be walking across the Thames, over the battle between order and chaos. How has that come to pass? Natasha would say that probability has an element of instinct involved. But how apocryphal is instinct?

'Let's go back home, Geena,' I plead.

'What are you scared of, Mark?' Natasha asks.

I play it back. 'What are *you* scared of?'

Things Natasha is scared of: Feet under the table. The empty place beneath the bed. Life below the surface of the sea. Remaining still for too long. Movies in which characters talk without moving, like *My Dinner With André*. Ice-cream cornets. Squealing brakes. Trees rustling in the wind in Greenwich Park. Supermarkets on Saturday. Shoe shops. Magazine racks. Window displays in dress shops. Old Compton Street since it went gay. Children's bookstores. Egg shells. Bees in the house. Moths trapped in the curtains. Flying ants hatching behind the kitchen boiler. Splinters in the heel of your foot. Dogs of all kinds. Dirty people. Boiled eggs.

Things that I am scared of: Losing my sister.

ACCIDENTS CAN'T HAPPEN

Geena decides that she has to go alone to Cape Town. I try to persuade her to change her mind. For so long semi-detached and now detached, Geena is isolated, in a state of freefall with the ground still a long way off. She has not learned the skills to be free of her dependencies. Her desire has run ahead of the safety equipment. She has never left the country before. She hasn't the resources for coping alone in a strange place. She even has trouble lacing her own trainers.

But Geena's not for turning.

I offer to go with her. Natasha offers to go with her. My parents offer to go with her.

Geena says no to us all. She is going to Cape Town alone or not at all. What she does accept is Natasha's money to buy an airline ticket.

When the day comes we take her to the airport in Natasha's car. We leave late, far too late, an hour and a half before departure time. At this hour, rush hour, the M4 is fearful and pitiless, a chicken run, but the only artery to the airport, once committed to. The traffic is sickening in the way it keeps building, mysteriously slackening for no apparent reason, then building again. Where there is no rhythm there is always danger. There must be a hundred thousand cars on the road, a whole city stretched in a line between junctions one and four. I sit side-saddle in the front seat, keeping my eye on Geena in the back and the Ford Escort tailgating us. I can see the passengers inside laughing, paying little heed to the hazards around them. They keep slamming on their brakes each time Natasha is forced to slow down. We listen to hard-house on Kiss FM.

We are in the outside lane when a pheasant suddenly appears in front of us. Having successfully traversed a hard shoulder and two lanes of busy traffic, its tail is cocked bull-ishly as the central reservation comes within range. It might have made it all the way had it not been for Natasha. Unable to swerve Natasha hits the brakes hard, but runs down the bird anyway. I feel a lump going under the front wheel. A second later my body pitches forward as the Ford Escort slams into our rear, pushing us into the car in front. I hit my face against the windscreen. Natasha hits hers against the steering wheel and Geena ends up in the front with us, across the handbrake. A warm river runs through my sinuses. I put my hand over my head and wait for others to join us, but that is the end of the affair. A three-car pile up, three stones in a moving stream. Vehicles swish past, altering course to avoid our stationary cars, any involvement. They have destinations, they have engagements.

I look behind and see the Ford rolling backwards, in recoil. I have the time, all the time in the world it seems, to be amazed at how quickly a car's form can change. The body of the Ford has concertinaed, the engine exposed like bared teeth. The other sight I see is the spindrift of pheasant feathers rising into the air. But no bird, dead or alive. The pheasant has dis-appeared.

Geena hauls herself back to where she was before the acci-dent. For a second I am almost persuaded that nothing untoward has happened, as if the clock has turned back. I sit there for a while believing in this possibility until blood from my nose drips onto my shirt.

The driver of the first car motions to Natasha to pull over. All three cars limp on to the hard shoulder. The slip road to the exit is just there. As I get out a moving lorry shaves by, tugging my hair at the roots. Four young lads from the third car are leaning against the barriers. They make with the cigarettes, tooling up, cupping hands around lighters. They say sorry several times as their radiator leaks antifreeze on to the road. Geena, I notice, has elected to stay inside the car. My nose has cauterised in the bitter air. The driver of the first car, the blameless one, shivers in his shirt sleeves. Or is that the driver of the Ford? They all look the same.

The first dialogue evolves, about liability. Natasha fetches a sheet of notepaper from her bag and writes down her name and address. The boys follow her lead. She tries to get their registration but the plates have shattered. She has to guess at numbers, at the order of things. She can't remember her own registration number when one of the drivers asks for it. Then a police BMW swans over from the stream. The policeman gets out and says to Natasha: 'What caused this accident?'

'A bird,' I say.

'There's no such thing as an accident,' Natasha amends.

What does she mean, there's no such thing as an accident?

This is the first 'real' experience I've had in many years and my first instinct is to get out of there as fast as we can. And we don't wait around. Natasha drives up the slip road to a round-about. We have lost only ten, fifteen minutes at most and can make up the lost time if she can put her foot down. But Natasha's car sounds very troubled. The back end rattles. The engine fan grinds metal. To add to our troubles, where the slip road ends the roundabout is blocked. There's no way back onto the motorway, so Natasha starts reversing down the slip road. Lorries swerve around us, their blaring horns warping with the Doppler. A second police vehicle, this time a Landrover, drives up the slip, lights flashing. Both policemen jump out. They can't believe their luck, a fair cop so early in the evening. They appear at Natasha's window and I hear her say, 'I've just been in that accident and can't get back onto the motorway.'

'You're going to have another accident in a minute!'

'The first one wasn't my fault. I've got to get onto the M4.'

They tell her the name of some B road that joins the motorway at the next junction, and that is where we head. As we travel at 60mph through the autistic suburbs, the Peugeot rattling in both bow and stern, a smell of roasting pheasant seeps into the car through the air vents.

Geena checks in with ten minutes to spare, no time for long goodbyes, for which I am grateful. Maybe that car accident *was* no accident. Everything is planned in the bright and clear universe. It is all in the mathematics.

We watch Geena fumble with her virgin passport at passport control. She waves briefly over her shoulder before disappearing into the Moloch-like departure lounge.

Never before have we been parted and I feel rocks in my stomach.

In the multi-storey car park we inspect the damage to the car. I open the bonnet to see if the fan can somehow be wrested from the engine to stop the rattle, and discover where that pheasant disappeared to – or part of it. Welded to the manifold are two drumsticks, cooked very well-done.

A distressing scene begins to build just feet away. A woman in a navy blue pinstriped suit, stiletto heels, painted fingernails (probably fake judging by the length of them), her hair streaked blond and lacquered, gives her small son several sharp tugs on his jacket, half on, half off the boy's back. Like his mother, the boy is dressed in designer clothes, but the thing I notice more is how ghosted he looks. It seems to me quite reasonable if he is slightly fractious after being on some flight from the sun. But his mother shouts in his face in a voice that is full of winter. She shakes him like a cocktail. Natasha and I are equally alarmed by this spectacle, stalled before our own car. Then a man appears with a trolley loaded with four matching suitcases. He is suntanned, dressed in kid-leather jacket, brown corduroys, half-brogues. He abandons his trolley, walks over and whacks the kid so hard he falls to the ground. He picks up the child by the collar, feet off the ground, and whacks him again on the backside, the boy swinging like a pendulum. The father's calm, easy manner suggests this way he has with children is quotidian.

From my point of view it amounts to child abuse, and I let it be known. 'Leave him alone.' I hear my voice as separate from me.

The man turns round slowly. 'What did you say?'

'I said leave him alone.'

I begin to regret my intervention almost immediately. For now he comes bearing down on me. Three strides and his face is inches from mine. I can smell spearmint chewing gum on his breath. 'Don't you dare tell me what I should do to my kid.' Then a minor remorse: 'You don't know how much he puts my wife through.' End of remorse, and the beginning of real anger now, now he's been forced to confess something about his personal problems to a total stranger: 'I can smack my own kid any time I want.' The man's wife has disappeared somewhere with their son. I feel his paw on my chest, pressing with a thumb. 'I don't want to embarrass you in front of your wife . . .'

'Okay,' I say, 'I don't . . . I didn't . . .'

'Don't you *dare* tell me how to raise my kid,' he repeats. 'It's none of your business.'

Natasha appears at my side. 'Actually, it is our business. My children might play with yours. They might go to school together, as far as you know.'

The guy swivels round to face her. 'What did you fucking say?'

'You're just a big bully, aren't you,' Natasha returns.

How did I get into this situation? This guy is muscle, fighting class. I have crossed a border and lost my own identity momentarily on the wrong half of the social divide. I don't belong here in this altercation. I don't put scaffolding up around London, I don't pack weapons in the army or whatever it is he does. Whatever he does he does with his hands that hang at his side like a pair of shovels.

I scramble to get back onside. I try to negotiate. When that fails I simply turn and walk away, praying that Natasha is following. If this continues I know which one of us will be the recipient of a punch in the mouth.

There has been another witness to this scene, standing with his own two children a few metres away. As I am passing him he offers his condolences. 'You just can't get through to some people.'

'No, you can't.' I agree.

I hear a set of locks being sprung, a dull thump. Very cautiously I turn around to see the man opening the doors of a Land Cruiser, a fierce machine with tinted windows and cattle bars, its lights flashing for a second as the locks open. He catches my eye over the roofs of cars. 'You got anything else to say?'

'No.'

I start to worry that as soon as he's got his wife and kid and luggage stowed away he'll come back to floor me, just like he did his son. With this playing on my mind, the other father (dressed like me incidentally, in jeans, trainers, puffa jacket: a New Man) says: 'I should have backed you up, man. I'm kicking myself.'

'It's okay,' I say. 'He was fucking scary, let's face it.'

Natasha materialises and turns on the New Man. 'Oh right. Retrospective courage. Like hell you would.'

'If he'd started something I'd have been in there. I'm just sorry I didn't say something.'

'Oh sure. You'd have run a mile.'

'Natasha! Open the fucking car, damn it, so we can get out of here.'

It is raining hard as we head back to north London. The car is rattling and shrieking. Natasha nods off to sleep a couple of times while aquaplaning down the southbound carriageway of the motorway. I don't bother to talk to her, keep her awake. I don't care that other drivers are swerving to avoid us. For my own threshold of fear has been lowered. Nothing seems dangerous to me. I am like some climber caught above the snowline who thinks his body is warming up when in fact he is freezing to death.

On the A312 she mounts a kerb and it bucks her right back up.

'It wasn't me you wanted to sleep with at the cottage, was it?' she says out of nowhere.

'Oh, that old chestnut.'

'But no longer taboo.'

'The boundaries are still there.'

'You're not coming clean, Mark.'

'And you're drifting across two lanes.'

'Then you be straight with me!'

'I've told you no lies.'

'Who's talking about lies? You once described yourself as a carer by nature. But what if your nature is basically selfish? In caring you control. You've always had this sense of duty towards Geena. But that duty serves your own interests. Let her go. She's a free spirit.'

'Free to do what? Free from what?' I hear my raised voice in

101

the dark interior of the car. 'I'll tell you what free means, it means someone you don't know spots you a beer in some bar on the other side of the world. Geena's free, yeah, like some domestic rabbit you let out of its cage who hops into the woods and says, "Hi Mr Fox! Wanna play?" What's freedom anyway but another song you once believed in.'

'She's going to South Africa to get away from you.'

'She's going to South Africa to find her parents.'

'Finding them is only the first step. In order to belong to them, Mark, she has to be free of you.'

I do not care to respond to this. If I speak now I'll only sound angry. As we approach London I decide it might be for the best not to see Natasha any more.

HANNAH CHARLES

I am walking through the wards during visiting hour, where happy families are cloistered around the beds of the gratefully alive. Patients are celebrating with their husbands or wives, children, brothers and sisters. The worse times are behind them. They are at the top of their tree as they feel their bodies being returned to them. The guys flirt with pretty nurses gliding past.

A sight for sore eyes, I am nevertheless drawn not to this euphoric picture, but to the patients who sit up in bed all alone, waiting for relatives who will never come; to the old woman being chastised by her daughter for breaking a leg. 'My father has just passed away and to have this happen,' she says. 'But you don't want to know about that. You've never been considerate of anyone but yourself.'

The Day Surgery, the Children's Ward, Fracture and Physiotherapy offer no comfort. Maternity is a sucking wound on my soul.

There is no respite back at the mess. Mavis sits in front of the phone in a flood of tears, her face red and puffy, chain smoking in the non-smoking hospital, risking disciplinary action. Her unrequited passion for the male nurse came to a head the other day, when she confronted him in the canteen before an audience of medics, accusing him of tormenting her, flaunting himself, parading his (several) women with the intention of hurting her. The nurse did not defend himself, so as not to humiliate her more. He left his lunch uneaten on his tray and walked out.

The amphetamines and antidepressants locked in the pharmacy cabinets read like librettos. Chloral hydrate, Dalmane, Flurazepam, quazepam. Even the antibiotics look good. I make £3.80 an hour and it's never going to get better. Maybe Natasha is right. Caring is a selfish act. I feel like I've lost my appetite for it.

Geena has telephoned every night, person to person. Her first few days in Cape Town have been bleak. Her spirit nosedives from a lack of progress. Each day she takes the 300-metre stroll from her guest house to Claremont Post-Adoption Centre only to get the same news: no show. She buys Chinese take-away and goes home to watch South African TV (shit) until she can fall asleep. No safari for her.

I cannot sleep. I eat like a bird. I can't read.

I call in sick at work, throwing three duvet-days in a row.

On the third day Geena calls to say she has found the foster parents.

The foster parents are overwhelmed to see her, who at thirty-two does not resemble in any way the infant they'd taken care of for a few months. They know nothing about her father, but give Geena the name of her birth mother.

Hannah Charles. Hannah Charles. Hannah Charles.

She takes the advice of the adoption centre and starts calling all the Charleses in the phone book; in Parkwood, Mitchell's Plain, Elsserivier, Belgravia, Kuilsrivier, Blue Downs, Wynberg, Belhar, Mannenberg, Mandalay – only to realise that most of these are townships. Hannah Charles is unlikely to be living in a township.

She fumes at the adoption people that she isn't getting anywhere phoning, so they try to trace Hannah Charles through the banks, through their credit applications. When that draws a blank they study the electoral rolls, but as HC is probably British (from London, according to the foster parents), unless she's acquired South African citizenship she'd have no voting rights. The libraries, universities, doctors' surgeries turn up nothing.

I am impressed by Geena's resolve, the way she is equipping herself out there. The girl who has refused to grow up is finally maturing, and with a fortitude that accompanies late flowering. In her voice I hear a thoughtfulness hitherto absent. So when she asks me to do something for her, I am more than happy to oblige. In fact I go about it with more energy than the mission requires.

In the public search room of the Family Records Centre a big heat is generated by people looking to authenticate themselves. The vast majority are old souls fighting against time, dragging leather-bound indexes off pine shelves and slamming them down on sloping pulpits. The birth indexes are red; marriages green; deaths black – irony colour coding. Everyone is self-absorbed, the place primed for tragic discoveries. Under a glass roof people sit exhausted by their failed hunt, or emotionally drained by what they did find. There are no children anywhere in the building. There is no sense of playfulness in the air. The refrains you keep overhearing contain one of two monosyllabic, sexless nouns: death and birth (marriages being off in another part of the building).

The exhausting waits, the patience, the fraying of patience . . . these are operative feelings.

I look through the indexes from 1945. Within a few hours I've picked a trio of Hannah Charleses: Hannah L. (b.1946); Hannah D. (b.1949); Hannah C.R.B. (b.1950). I order all three certificates at £22.50 each. Expensive day out. For a hospital porter.

The following morning I return to collect the certificates. Only Hannah D. Charles was born in London, in the district of Fulham. From the Register of Electors for 1949 I note the names of a dozen of her then neighbours and cross-check those names in a current Register. Three of them still live at the same address.

Fulham, a pre-war working-class neighbourhood, is now a poor Sloane Ranger's Chelsea. People who can't quite afford the Kings Road shuffle a few miles west to New Kings Road. And boy, is it New Money. You can get Laura Ashley poisoning from just inhaling the air. Every other shop is a fabric emporium or a cast-iron-fireplace showroom. In the streets behind New Kings Road cars are parked bumper to bumper. Alarms fire off brittle cacophonies. No one comes out to quieten the herd. One of these vehicles is a Land Cruiser just like the one driven by the bad father at Heathrow. As I walk on I start to fantasize about tracing him. This is just the kind of place he would live. When I find him I'll say either a) Sorry, my friend, I overreacted. You're a good dad, anyone can tell that. Your son is loved, protected, safe in your good hands. It's just your methods are different to mine. I made a bad call, sorry, sorry, sorry; or b) punch the fucker in the throat as hard as I can. And if that doesn't bring him down I'll clutch his balls in my hand, like Gene Hackman does to a redneck in *Mississippi Burning*.

Standing outside *the* house in Fulham, Hannah D. Charles's former home, I feel no emotional correspondence. I start knocking on neighbours' doors. An old lady, with a timid lopsided man behind her in the doorway, looks baleful as I ask the rehearsed questions: 'My mother was good friends with Hannah Charles, who used to live in number eight? In the fifties, sixties? Anyway, we found some photographs we think she would like and wondered if you knew where she is living now?'

But they can't respond to my lies. They don't know her. Fulham is a gypsy camp, family and kinship a long-gone turkey.

When I get home to Highgate there is a fax on the floor under the machine, hand-written from Geena.

On the thirteenth day over there she has found what she is looking for.

CAPE OF GOOD HOPE

Monday, 28 September

Mark, it was a such chance thing. I was feeling a little adventurous and took a 'sunshine cruise' around Table Bay. I got talking to the skipper and when I told him what I was doing in South Africa he said he knew some English yacht charterer called Joel *avec* a wife called Hannah. He also tells me where his house is. So now I go there and guess what? I see a beach house on the Atlantic Ocean. I knew it was The House straight off. I walk round the back and I'm trembling all over. Sitting on a deck-chair on the patio is this bloke in his late forties. I don't know him, he doesn't do anything 4 me, but this house is definitely the one, so I go, 'How long have you lived here?' He almost jumps out of his chair I gave him such a shock. He says, 'For ever.' So I say, 'Then I must be your daughter.' He laughs at me, gets up and walks inside the house! He doesn't invite me to follow him or nothing, but I do anyway. 'So what's all this bullshit?' he says. It was dark inside after being on the patio where it was terribly bright, like almost blinding, but now this room gets suddenly bright too. I turn around and there's a woman standing there, and she says, 'Your place has been laid at our table for the past twenty-eight years.'

You know my 'epilepsy' helped me to find Joel and Hannah, don't you? The hallucinations led me to their door. It makes me think the brain was acting independently somehow. I saw them in my head. I saw their house by the sea. What did Natasha say – the brain has the power to solve its own mystery.

I can't tell you how this wall of emotion that hit me felt when I met her 4 that first time. That was only yesterday and I'm having such highs and lows like never before. I didn't know I could feel such emotion. When I started to poke about down here I thought I'd just be normal in the way I did it. I'm not a drama queen, you know that. But hell, I've discovered my birth mother! And my birth father. His name is Joel Sugarman by the way (they are not married – too cheesy!). He says that he denied being my dad when we first met to protect my mother. I understand that now.

We spoke 4 an hour on our first meeting. The time went by as fast as a blink of an eye. We agreed I should come back today. I'm meeting them again in about an hour. Oh Mark, I'm shaking all over waiting for the time to pass. I feel nervous just writing this down. I am overflowing with curiosity and love. How are (your) mum and dad taking this? If they'd have told me B-4, maybe I wouldn't be so overwhelmed now. I feel a real distance from them, I must say. They feel unnatural to me.

Tuesday, 29 September
We went on a drive today 2 Kalk Bay. Kalk Bay is the next town to St James. Around the bay a bit is Simon's Town. There's a real British presence there. Buildings have

names like Prince Albert Mansions and Whytes. Hannah and Joel own a yacht-chartering company and have some boats moored in the harbour in Simon's Town that they have to bring back to Cape Town. Joel said he'll take me out sailing soon, but not yet.

In Simon's Town we saw whales calving in the bay and Hannah and I looked strangely at one another. I keep flooding over with feelings about how she gave birth to me. She is so beautiful. I was part of her once. None of it seems likely. I keep thinking I'm dreaming, or hallucinating still and that in a minute it will all end and I'll collapse on the floor in a seizure.

I have never been in love, but this must be it. This is why I've been holding off, for this moment. A lot of things are making sense to me now.

I never want 2 be apart from them. I just want to talk to them, B at their side, they are so light and fresh and interesting. We have yet to discuss why I ended up where I ended up. With the drugs and shit.

PS: When you see Natasha next, tell her that I got to square the circle.

Wednesday, 30 September

I can't stop myself from crying all the time. Last night I dreamed I was crying and this morning when I woke up I *was* fucking crying. It's not altogether wonderful, I can promise you. I feel weakened by it. I'm in a trance when I'm not with them. I wish I could just stop existing for the hours that I wait B-4 I can be with them again.

Today they are bringing a yacht around from Simon's Town to Cape Town, a twenty-hour sail. They didn't invite me 'case I got seasick. The Cape of Good Hope is very volatile with no place to put in, so if they hit bad weather I'd not be able to get off the boat. They said they'll take me sailing on a more relaxed, shorter trip, like to Robben Island.

Guess what? They took me to Robben Island when I was a two-year-old – on Christmas Day! Remember when we were going to Natasha's that first time and I heard that song 'White Christmas' in my head in the taxi? Well, Joel said he sang that same song to me when we went to Robben Island all those years ago. Oh my giddy aunt!

I don't think he was dreaming about snow though, do you? More like a racist joke. I'm dreaming of a White Christmas . . . on Robben Island when Mandela was banged up there. I hope I'm wrong about that. It would put a stain on things. But then again everyone I meet here is a racist, blacks and whites live such separate lives, you'd never think this was Africa.

Thursday, 1 October
The sun is shining, it's a perfect day in Cape Town, and I'm being torn apart by thunder. The love I have newly discovered I now live in fear of losing. I wish there was some formula, an equation 2 help me through this. Didn't Natasha say there were amicable, like friendly, numbers?

Problem is, I don't know how often I should see Joel and Hannah. I don't want to rush it and spoil all the good. Thing is, I went to see them on an unscheduled visit, at Misty Cliffs (that's the name of the place where they live). I thought it would make me feel better, just turning up, you know? After all, who needs to be constantly announced to your parents. I wish I hadn't gone, they were not 2 pleased 2 see me. They were distant and bad tempered, particularly Joel. He really shut me out. Granted, he was doing some business with some black guy (who'd arrived in a Mercedes), which kind of puts Joel in the clear as far as being racist is concerned, I guess. But it was a terrible moment nevertheless and I left there in tears. I could cry for England out here, I tell you.

Friday, 2 October
You know, Dad . . . your dad is old enough to be Joel and Hannah's father. Joel and Hannah are closer to our generation in age and spirit. We're into the same things, same music (hip-hop, hard-house, drum and bass), and when I look at them I think, hey man, I've got your genes. I got your hair colour, nose, ears. I even got your love of the sea.

There are some sources of irritation, but I don't want to think about those. I want my real mum and dad to B perfect. But the fear I have that they could B anything less than perfect puts the fear of God into me. I know this is unfair, no one is perfect, but it still hurts me deeply. I'm feeling some anger, or something that isn't as pure as what I felt just days ago. What is happening, Mark?

Thing is, Hannah is being quite secretive, Joel too. They whisper to one another in my company. I can hear them in the lounge when I'm in the kitchen. They invite me 2 the house but treat me as a guest. Like I'm not encouraged to explore the house or anything, wash up the dishes after dinner, like you'd expect 2 in your parents' house.

It's changed. I don't know why. I want to ask them, plead with them not to shut me out.

Saturday, 3 October
They took me sailing today. I adapted very quickly. I didn't feel at all seasick. No way Jose! I've got my sea legs. Things are brilliant again. We just needed to be doing something together, I guess, instead of dredging up the past.

Joel has lots of boats he charters, but he's got his own yacht for racing and stuff. It's thirty-eight feet long and very fast. Joel showed me how to change a spinnaker and use the winches, keep good your course. You should see me at the helm. Captain Geena. Out there in the bay you see whales, you see dolphins and great big seabirds with long necks and huge wingspans. We fly along under sail, Hannah making coffee below, we have a nip of rum in that as well, smoke a little dope. I'm flying out here. They B cool, I tell you true.

We had this black African with us, name of Ernie, same guy who was in the house two days ago. He seems to be a business associate of some kind, Joel never said. But he was nice to me, Ernie. And Joel seemed to like that he liked me – his china and his girl getting it on.

Sunday, 4 October
I was 2 go sailing again today but Joel phoned me at my guest house and cancelled it. He said the weather forecast was a little bit iffy. It's now the end of the day and the weather hasn't changed. It's fine and dandy. What's the fucking matter with him? I'm going to phone him now, ask him direct.

Hi, it's me again.

I've just phoned, spoke to Joel. Joel said he was pleased I'd found a good life for myself and that he didn't want to spoil things for me. How could he spoil things for me! What is that supposed to mean? When he or Hannah say things like that I fear they're losing their interest in me, that they are offering me up for adoption all over again. It's too dreadful 2 contemplate.

Something has changed. The feeling I get that I'm losing them grows stronger every hour. I am so desperate, I can sense a change coming over me. I haven't had a single

seizure or whatever it is I get since I've been out here, but
I feel one holy mother of one building. I'm going down
there right now.

Hi, me again, much later.

I've just been over to Misty Cliffs and confronted them,
told them how they make me feel like a guest. They treat
me as a visitor who will soon be leaving. So then Hannah
asks me if I feel let down. I didn't know what to say. How
can I answer such a question. I got angry and said, what
choice did I ever have over what happened to me, aged
three? She said she and Joel were out of it when the Social
put a care order on me. She obviously finds it difficult 2
talk about this part. I asked her what she meant by Out Of
It and she said, You know, just fucked up generally. They
were old hippies. Chemical heads. They emigrated to
South Africa at the end of the sixties.

Friday, 9 October
I'm sorry I haven't faxed you for a few days, but I've
moved in with Joel and Hannah and they don't have a fax
machine in the house. I've had to come into town to send
you this.

The thing is, Mark, I've decided 2 stay here in South
Africa. I've found my real family and I want 2 build back
the bridges. I think they do too. They've even said in
time I can be part of the family business. He's been promoting me like mad to Ernie. I think Ernie is actually a
gangster (he always travels with bodyguards) but a very
affable guy too. He speaks very good English. You know
what he said? 'Crime is just another form of redistribu-
tion in an adversary culture.' He also said this to me: 'If
you've never been hungry you can never know how ago-
nising can be a single slice of bread in the home. Either
you get it or your brother does. If you get it you know

114

you've stolen the food right out of your brother's mouth.'

Ernie's never had any schooling but respects education. He says the townships have to build their own middle class, which will take a generation or more. So in the meantime his men protect the township schools from vandalism. The 'Coca-Cola academies' he calls them. He protects the whole community in fact (Ernie is not modest, let it B said). If a man is burgled he can go straight to Ernie and within an hour he'll find the thief and give him a smack. If a victim of rape went to the police, the white police, they'd open a file, if you're lucky, and that would be that. But Ernie has men on the ground. He'd get that scumbag. His local intelligence is supreme. Ernie, he do rock and he do roll.

Please don't try to persuade me to come back there. I'm making a fresh start. My life begins now. I am going to become the person they can never reject, so help me God.

PART THREE

'The sea is as near as we come to another world.'

— ANNE STEVENSON

CORRUPT ARCHITECTURE

The taxi driver rakes the N2 at 100kph and explains how this highway was known as the Road to Hell during the interregnum. He can hardly contain his excitement as he tells me how in those days a white driver could run aground at a human road block, then see the carriageway behind him rolling up like a black carpet. Rocks would rain down on his car and if he couldn't find a way to ram through the crowds he'd get dragged out and stoned to death. Or necklaced. 'If we find corpse that has been burned, that's political. If we find corpse that has been shot, that's criminal,' he says. He offers me the joint that he's been smoking all the while, then adds, as a little side dish, an account of a businessman killed on the N2 only the other day, when someone dropped a paving slab from the bridge, coming through his windscreen and stoving in his skull . . . He cranes his torso around to smile at me and pulls the wheel, stampeding a herd of oxen idling along the hard shoulder. Cow herds flip into the bush to escape this hunk of German engineering spinning at them like a dart. I look at the seething squatter camps nosing up to the carriageway and recall how they wanted to host the Olympic Games here a couple of years ago. Fat chance. The tourist board has a real PR problem with this airport–city artery.

I do not travel well at the best of times. Being under-prepared only exacerbates my anxieties and for this trip I've arrived with a scream caught in my throat and nowhere to stay. As the driver fills the car with acrid dagga smoke I rifle through my Rough Guide for a guest house recommendation. The Kornhoop sounds a crib in a manger. It's in Observatory too, where my folks lived all those years ago.

I feed the info to the driver and feel a little more relaxed now that's settled, until I spot the 'Cautions to the Lone Traveller' section in the guide. That long list of the many ways of dying a violent death undoes me.

My father explained something to me before I left, that there are eleven tribes in this land and at least eight of them want to kill the white man. On to every cow herd we zip past I project a homicidal instinct. Even my driver's not exempt. I anticipate him pulling off the highway, burning my white flesh with a blow torch and then eating me.

Does this make me racist?

He who is free from sin cast the first stone.

I happen to concur with Baudelaire's disgust with reality. Too much reality is bad for you, it can make you go mad. Bravo to the New South Africa, but I'd just as rather be in England.

My taxi turns off the N2, arriving in Observatory a minute later, and my wish seems to come true. This little suburb is full of imported British post-industrial Gothic revival architecture, ornamental pillars and balconies. When my parents lived here it was the home of candlemakers, timber-yard and railway workers. Now it's overrun by students from the University of Cape Town. Groote Schuur hospital, where Dad worked, is tucked in under the mountain nearby.

The Kornhoop is run by an Englishman from Hull and I admit to being grateful for that – a northern caricature offering sanctuary in the southern hemisphere. Welcome, greetings and salutations. How is the smog over London?

It's just as well he has a vacancy. Having cleared three layers of security to get inside the compound – razor wire, electrified fence, vicious dogs – I'd refuse point blank to leave.

The landlord is kind enough to arrange car hire for me, then ruins it all by adding his own list of cautions. Don't go near the townships in the car. Don't wear jewellery in the car. Don't carry a camera. If held at gunpoint do not resist . . .

For an hour or so I lay on my bed waiting for the hire car to arrive, with the landlord's ten commandments crashing the gears inside my head. I drift in and out of sleep. Voices of children playing in the garden sound like bathers on a distant beach. I think about my father and mother being woken at night by security police knocking on doors, hunting blacks without passes; and then a prescient remark Geena made about my father when she was a young girl slips through: 'Daddy's lost because he didn't birth us.'

I am woken conclusively by the sound of electronic security gates rolling open, and the voice of an English woman remonstrating with her children for venturing outside the compound: the landlord's wife, who is to remain invisible, hidden from all the dangers of this land.

A car drives into the compound. My time has come. I sit bolt upright and drain a bottle of mineral water infused with kiwi. The landlord raps on my door and introduces a burley Afrikaner holding a clipboard. I sign the paperwork as he stands over me, his short-sleeved shirt reeking of sweat. As he copies down the number of my English driving licence he too imparts safety warnings: Keep the petrol tank filled up. Lock the doors when driving. At red traffic lights don't get stuck between traffic. Keep the handbrake off and the car in gear and check the wing mirrors constantly (tilted down to show hijackers sneaking up on their hands and knees).

I feel tempted to lie down again on the bed and wait for whatever is going to befall me.

The Afrikaner takes me through the instrument panel as I sit in the driver's seat of the rental car. Then he regales me some more. 'In this car you must use certain tactic. For instance, you get into the car, first you know, you shut your door, lock your door, put the central locking on, check the mirrors just to see if there's nobody right next to you. If you go to the shop, before you get out do the same. In the shop, is there anybody in the shop that is a potential robber? Is the people walking around carrying weapons? Because you don't know what's going to happen next in this country. We free as democracy and we free of speech and all that, but we, you can't live free here.'

'Do you want to come with me?' I ask in all seriousness. But he just laughs. With a borrowed map of the Western Cape I set off.

I drive through the gates of the Kornhoop and the sky falls on top of my head. Black cloud rolls over the ubiquitous mountain, menacing and bloated. My hands shake on the wheel. The map on the passenger seat communicates nothing. I keep checking my doors are locked. The windows are frigidly sealed. I am frigidly sealed. They will drink my blood here. I shall be buried in this land.

Ten minutes later I'm in downtown Cape Town. All the pavements are being worked by black vendors, all the cars driven by whites. At traffic lights Africans try to sell me racks of plastic coat hangers. I avoid their eyes, keep the car in first, hand on the handbrake, release button thumbed in.

Cape Town is not a big city and soon I am out the other side, cruising past the ocean, brown-skimmed with burnt salt and lipping at the row of white hotels. The municipal corruption is visible in the architecture, the laundered gold and diamond hauls in the façades of these Bavarian palaces with their white fretwork balconies, flying German city-flags. Along the promenade gnarly old Boers in shorts and knee-high socks walk with the aid of staffs.

I change down and plug deeper south, carving through the corridor between mountain and sea. No sooner do I begin to relax a little as the land becomes depopulated when anxieties of a different kind fill my head like a flock of crows worrying a carcass. Geena is not expecting me, has no idea that I am on my way. Natasha suggested her flight was in part a bid for freedom from me and I have come to tell her that our relationship from this moment on can be entirely on her terms. I have some doubt whether her terms can be defined without me, but if she wants to stay on here, so be it, I will not try to talk her into coming back to England. If I sense she is happy. But how can she be happy among strangers in a land trembling with tectonic irruptions? Hannah and Joel are newly mindful of her (even though they haven't paid their dues!) and helping her to broaden her horizons, introducing her to a variety of activities and people. What exactly can parents in name only offer her? Do they know how to read her mind? Can they help her formulate her unspoken thoughts? I have been in this country less than four hours and feel less than sanguine about its future. (A vast image out of *Spiritus Mundi* troubles my sight.) I can't get it out of my mind how a single truth has landed Geena here. Truth can be so pernicious. Natasha's dictum that when the truth is ugly only lies are beautiful has some substance to it. Yet we cannot undo what is done. Geena may require a passage of time to come to terms with this truth of her origins, a passage of mourning for what could have been. Grief will be her friend, but I hope not a friend for life. I am her friend for life. My arrival should signal my commitment. This is what I want. I want our amputation to be reversed.

The mountain wraps around the Cape like a Wall of China. There is a sheer 1,000-metre drop to the ocean that sparkles in the sun. No barrier either. A country built for thrills. The adrenalin courses through my veins like an uninvited guest. A single sneeze, yawn on my part and my mission could be over before it begins.

The road eventually curves back inland where solitary vendors flogging firewood, carved giraffes, strange fruits at road-side stations slip harmlessly by. The ocean comes back online as I slow at a four-way junction. A small child materialises at my window proffering a single orange in the palm of his hand. He must regard my hysterical gestures of the arm as offensive and runs off to hide in the bush. I lurch on up the empty road. My windows are still sealed and the car is baking.

I drive high above a beach where the blue sea pumps onto the white sand. It is deserted like the end of the world. I relax into chronic weariness. But not for long. I see the sign, Misty Cliffs, and stop the car for the first time since leaving the Kornhoop. These are the coordinates. This is where Geena has gone to ground.

Like the beach the road is empty, scraped clean of vehicles. I turn off the engine and open the door. My mouth yaws open and the ocean, so blue and wild, tastes like raw meat.

A solitary clapboard, clinker-built house with a corrugated-iron roof sits below the road. It is unnumbered, unnamed, but it is the one. I look for signs of life, and see none, although the air seems rigid, expectant.

I leave my vehicle and walk, turning my head every step. How long would it take to run back and lock myself in? What is the point of no return? I project myself onto the safety of a yacht I see out on the ocean. Then I think of solo yachtsmen falling overboard, seeing their boats sail off without them, five thousand miles from land.

I take one last look at my car and venture down the gravel drive. Bright ocean light glances off the tin roof and hurts my eyes. Foliage of pepper and rubber trees climbs the wall to a domed half-landing window bracketed by green shutters. A set of wooden steps with ivy and lemon grass wrapped around the handrail descends to a front door. Behind me the mountain races up a kilometre.

I stand by the door composing myself. I decide against ringing the bell and wander around to the side through a garden of proteas, jasmine, bougainvillea, hibiscus. A large pool of black water is bordered by white stones, while the ocean just there builds waves the size of three-storey buildings. Still water and volatile water have the same properties but are as different as man and woman.

The rear of the house is the main show, so close to the ocean it seems to be floating on the water. Shutters are closed over French windows on the ground and first floors. I step onto the stone patio below the veranda. The roar of surf is constant and oppressive. The light is filled with millions of water particles, like a sky of mirrors. Sand flung up by the wind stings my face. Wind chimes tinkle in the empty space.

I look all around the house, through gaps in the shutters. Inside I can see iron candelabra hanging from the ceilings. On a kitchen table three plates and three glasses have been discarded. The surf rambles on like city traffic. I cannot see, hear or smell Geena. All vestiges of her have been salt-blasted and cleaned away by the sea breeze.

NOUS SOMMES DU SOLEIL

The sea in Table Bay shimmers like a dish of mercury as I drive along the docks road. The early evening sun perforates wind-screens and fires up the cars parked around the entrance to the Cape Sailing Club – the other place mentioned by Geena in dispatches. I reverse the Nissan into a small gap and walk back along the road to the sailing club.

A black doorman in a white tuxedo bars me from making a clean entrance. 'I'm looking for Joel`. . .' I struggle to remember his last name. 'Sugarman.'

'He here, sir. Please sign the visitors' book.'

I stroll into a crowded bar. I can't see Geena anywhere. I don't know what Hannah or Joel looks like. I stare into faces seeking familial resemblances. Everyone looks cock-a-hoop. And bloated. Their skin is pock-marked as though the well at the oasis is poisoned. After covering the floor I wander outside onto the marina, heaving with a few billion rand's worth of yachts. I can't see her among the cocktail drinkers either, so I decide to ask.

I tap a man on the shoulder. He turns around smiling. The smile on his face falls to his feet. When I ask him if he knows Joel Sugarman he regains his smile and points down to a man in Hawaiian shirt and faded Levis standing on the deck of a yacht. 'You better be fast,' he says. 'He's about to go out racing.'

From the marina I walk down onto the pontoon, which moves beneath my feet, to get a better mark on my man. His long grey hair is tied in a ponytail. Both his ears are distended with Maltese crosses hooked to silver rings. His skin is wrecked by the sun.

As I am absorbing these first impressions he catches me staring up at him. 'You look as though you've lost something,' he says.

I count down a few seconds. 'I have. I'm looking for Geena.'

'Who are you, then, china?'

'Her adopted brother.' This is the first time I've ever had to use that scarlet adjective.

He gives a half-smile. 'She didn't tell me you were coming.'

'I didn't tell her I was coming.'

'Well she's not here, china.'

'Have you any idea where she might be?' I always knew where Geena was at any time of night or day.

'I could hazard a few guesses.' He stroked his unshaven chin. 'Can you sail?'

'No, I don't think so.'

'You don't *think* so?'

'I've never been on a yacht before.'

'You can wait till I get back, or come with us and we can talk out on the water.'

'I'll come with you.'

Some men have no blush, no capacity for humiliation. Within seconds of meeting this man I am following his orders, untying the bow rope from the pontoon bollard, casting off, riding in the back of his yacht.

There are three others onboard. As we make way I am introduced to James Willmot, a portly guy in his early fifties,

127

wearing a pair of half-framed spectacles and a silly moustache that looks as if he's misplaced a postage stamp under his nose. James introduces his son Kenno, who is my age with a powerful build underneath his surf T-shirt. Not once does Kenno look me in the eye. The other sailor is black, and is not introduced.

There is something about this handsome African that suggests he is not some capacity-building exercise for these white men. He is no Billy Budd, no man of sorrows. Well dressed and confident, he sits in the helm with his hands resting on the coaching behind his back, like the real man in charge of the enterprise – the foreman, the general. His eyes are focused as if he knows that this is now his country and he is just humouring the white men with their toys. He has the most gravitas.

Joel takes the yacht out of the harbour under motor power as Kenno and James pull sails out of their bags. In the fairway dozens of yachts are waiting, running sails up the masts. When a klaxon honks the yachts break free of the pack and span out across the water. The wind is slight, but gusting. The blue mountains grow sultry behind us as the sun streaks the ocean red.

Joel, James and Kenno work in concert, expressing themselves in a nautical language. They talk of stays and halyards, sheets and tell-tales. Their easy familiarity contrasts with my embarrassment for being here and the strong isolation of the black sailor.

The way Joel obsesses, trimming the sails, shouting orders to Kenno and his father on the winches, reveals him as a competitor, a guy who wants to win, even a game like this.

After an hour he still has not told me what I want to know.

'How long is this race going to last?' I ask.

He does not answer me directly and instead shares his prosaic ideas. 'The southern seas are unpredictable, dangerous, beautiful, don't you think? The only order is the order you impose. Through navigation. There's no truth out here, baby.

Only the one who wins is true. The sea's my analogue for South Africa.'

'Where do you think Geena is in this unpredictable, dangerous, beautiful place then?'

'Perhaps she's at home with her feet up.'

'I've been there. No one was around.'

'You've been there, have you?' I get no more from him as the race beckons again.

Afloat with the man who'd made her, abandoned her, and found her again, I concentrate upon the memory of Geena's face until I begin to feel seasick, like reading in a moving car. I stare at the horizon to recover. Love cannot withstand seasickness, as Byron once said.

In the last leg of the race the wind falls and all yachts are becalmed. The voices over the shortwave radio consider whether or not to abandon the race. But since only the commodore on the bridge can make that executive decision, we wallow under limp sails for another thirty minutes, listening to the exchange of flat jokes crackling on air. Joel remains in a winning state of mind the whole time, concentrated and remote. But why is this? Why is an old hippy working himself up over an amateur competition?

We limp in (third) eventually, a result that placates him. In the marina, Joel, James and Kenno strip the yacht and then, minus the African, we make for the clubhouse bar.

There is the game out at sea and then there is the game in the clubhouse. Yachties are the tourists of the ocean, filling the void with legerdemains. We sit at a table overlooking the harbour and I wait in silence. I wait for Geena to make an appearance, hoping she will say, Let's leave this place and go home. Or some such thing. But all I hear are mock-heroic stories of races won and lost and the wind whistling in the rigging. The beer goes straight to my head.

Our party meanwhile is getting bigger. There are now ten at

the table, with Kenno and Joel at opposite ends. This is how the social life of the club works, I figure; a quorum built from knowing one or two persons who introduce you around. They all sound English to my ears. I also detect a strain in their voices, like an imposed censorship on mentioning the obvious realities, the bitter social truths beyond the harbour walls. These things have to be constantly blanked out of their conversations, like expletives on TV, in order that they may enjoy the life they've created for themselves. For similar reasons, I have no doubt, no one asks questions of me – who I am, where I've wafted in from. In such a country it is expedient to mull along without prizing open pasts. We are all uninvited guests.

I glimpse the African who came sailing with us, fending off drunken yachties trying to give him their drink orders. I turn my gaze on to the docks, where men seem to be toiling out of sight, as if not to embarrass the opulence of the yacht club in their midst. In any other maritime port there would be dilapidated bars in place of this yacht club, sparsely populated with seamen counting down their shore leave in glasses of whisky. When I look back again the African has gone.

Kenno starts telling anyone who will listen about his last sail around the Cape, when the wind had been 'on the nose' all the way. Knowing his ETA was going to be delayed, he made a ship-to-shore call home. The African maid answered the telephone. Here Kenno imitates her African voice. '"The master he not at home." "This *is* the master," I say.'

Everyone gets off on that, but not so much as Kenno, who releases a gaited bellow of a laugh. It is like nothing I've ever heard before either, like shrapnel bursting. He gets to his feet and bends over to touch his toes, as though his hysteria has to be nipped in the bud, cut off at the diaphragm before it engulfs him completely.

I upend my bottle of Windhoek. When I lay the empty bottle down again my party is wandering away from the table.

'Where's everyone going?' I ask.

'To see James Willmot's *Flying Dutchman!*'

In a dry dock we converge around an eighteen foot sailing dinghy, as James Willmot says, 'I didn't argue over the price. Soon as I saw it I got my cheque book out.'

'My Golf GTi . . . same thing,' says his son. 'Saw this car, man, just got my cheque book out.'

I need something to fix upon, and stare at the neatly coiled ropes under gunwales, the polished brass tackle, the wooden mast lying on its side. I meditate on the order of things because I can't engage in this discussion, I don't understand what it's for. I don't know where I am or who I am with. My ears ring and my head swims with booze.

There are more people at our table when we get back. A black waiter delivers the orders and I see Joel making a quick calculation. The waiter is an Amstel short. As Joel speaks sharply to him, a woman I haven't seen before lays her hand on Joel's arm, seizing the opportunity to change her order to pink gin. The waiter is grim faced as he struggles with her English, the speed it's delivered. I hear Joel say to her: 'You think these people will know what bitters are?'

She rises from her seat. 'I'll go in with him.'

Joel laughs at her receding back, revealing his top gums, his small crooked teeth blackening. Then he becomes rather serious suddenly, pointing at the sun sinking into the ocean. *'Nous sommes du soleil!'* he cries.

I draw conclusions. I think I've got this guy's number: an old hippy clinging onto his youth, a man in pursuit of the sun, the rays, the good times. I do not feel threatened. I reckon I can take him.

I also allow that this might be a very big mistake on my behalf.

Minutes later the woman returns, laughing, holding up her glass of pink gin like a trophy. As she passes me I catch a whiff of rose-musk issuing from her cotton skirt.

131

'That's my wife!' Joel boasts proudly.

I open my mouth and the wind literally takes my breath away. Hannah Charles, Geena's mother, the fixed foot of Joel's compass.

I try to catch her eye under the heavy fringe hanging like a curtain. But she does not know who I am. Joel has not even bothered to tell her.

Thirty minutes later everybody gets to their feet. This time they are going for good. 'I'll drive,' James Willmot says.

'You've had too much to drink,' a woman who appears to be his wife says.

'If you can walk you can fucking drive.'

'There are road blocks all over the Cape tonight, James, don't be stupid.' Mrs Willmot's voice is very north London. Her face too seems familiar. I even toy with the possibility that I've wheeled her around my hospital.

'If they smell drink they blood-test you on the spot. If it's positive they throw you straight in jail. No quarter given, not even to the ladies.'

'I'm not walking home, Jennifer, and that's a fact. I don't much like walking out there to my car.'

'Fuck it,' says Kenno. 'We'll drive in convoy. Hit a road block . . . we ram it.'

As we are walking towards the door of the club bar, Joel stalls and turns to me. 'Are you okay for a lift?'

'Yes, I've got a car.'

'Great. See you then. When I catch up with Geena, you want me to give her a message?'

A message! I think about it for a moment. 'No, it's fine.'

'Where are you staying?'

'The Kornhoop.'

'In Observatory.'

'Yes.'

CHRISTMAS IN CAPE TOWN

I rake my bed until dawn. Sleep is not going to come, so I go to my window. The light spreading over the Cape like a crystal dome ordains me. I go back to bed and when I wake again it is noon, by which time the light is ominous and heavy, evoking Hemingway: In Africa a thing is true at first light and a lie by noon.

I am beginning to fear there is something sinister about Geena's absence. I need Joel in my sights if ever I'm going to find her, that much I decide. But first I need to eat. I get dressed ready to go into Observatory to find a restaurant.

I end up driving around in circles, past the same women pushing prams, black road sweepers and hawkers, students sitting in cappuccino bars, with nothing but the day stretching out in front of them waiting to be filled. The skyline is clogged with electric tram wires. Clouds drift lugubriously off the mountain. I pass the entrance to my dad's old hospital and then further along the Main Road, in Rondebosch, I turn off for my dad's old ivy-clad, English-style university campus that my ancestors helped build after they were through digging the harbour.

At a barrier I stop the car and get out. I think of my father standing here before I was born, staring down at the salt flats spreading endlessly into the haze, and for a moment I feel connected to the land of my parents, and where Geena, a grain of sand in this same landscape, is now groping for an identity of her own.

My anxieties have taken the edge off my hunger. I set back for the guest house, arriving to find Joel and Hannah sitting in a Range Rover Discovery outside the gates. There are two passengers in the rear seat. I search for Geena's face among them but don't find it.

Joel pokes his head out of the tinted window and invites me for a picnic lunch.

'Is this pure coincidence?' I ask.

'Nah,' says James Willmot through a crack in the back window. 'We are all very friendly in this country. We came to find you, man.'

'Mark, this is James,' Joel says.

'We met last night,' I say.

'James is my stockbroker,' Joel adds, as if that explains anything.

'You hungry?' Joel asks.

'I could eat something,' I say, already climbing into the back seat next to Jennifer Willmot.

'Hello again,' she says.

Joel's hair resembles a beaver's tail draped over the back of his seat and irritates me, as does Hannah smiling inanely when Joel enquires whether I've found Geena.

'No,' I say. I look across the seats at Hannah's bare brown legs. She flaps the edge of her skirt to get a little breeze up inside her thighs. Her rose-musk is quite vivid despite the window being wide open. I notice the doors are not locked. 'Have you seen her?'

'Geena is not returned to us yet.'

'You're not worried?'

'No, no, I'm not worried.'

'But this is a violent society.' My observation makes James smile.

'Like the man says, violence *is* society.'

'What *man*, James?' Jennifer objects.

'If you live in a dangerous place you keep your eyes and ears open and it becomes less dangerous than a place where your guard is down,' James continues. 'Living on amber alert keeps your brain charged up. Someone tells me something, a name, a telephone number, I remember it. Only need telling once. And that's good for business.'

'Geena doesn't know her way around,' I say.

'You can always find your way around here using that mountain as a transit,' Joel explains.

'That's not my point. Anyway she doesn't drive.'

An hour later we enter the nature reserve at the most southerly point on the peninsula, and stop at the Cape of Good Hope. The sea is so cobalt-blue it seems like a dye job and makes me recall one of Natasha's prejudices, about men with blue eyes being dishonest. I'm feeling very prejudiced myself.

Hannah lays a tablecloth on a grass shelf above the beach and opens a hamper of cheese, bread, cold meats, fruit. Jennifer Willmot starts to rub sunblock into her face and neck, then offers the tube to me. When I decline she touches my cheek. 'Don't be so macho!' I stare at her thick wrists as her hands go to work on her neck and face, and ankles that are scarred with mosquito bites.

Joel produces a bottle of chilled champagne and glass flutes. Nearby a large African family is frying fatty lamb over a wood fire. Joel does a good job blotting them out, by meditating on the ocean and bragging about his business acumen. 'We do game fishing . . . tuna, broadbill, swordfish. We do executive cruises, sunset parties, champagne breakfasts, crayfish lunches, overnight adventures. We take them out, put them down on Seal Island and bring them back in, all for three hundred rand a pop.' He tells me that he and Hannah came out here for a sunshine holiday thirty-five years ago, liked it so much they decided to stay. He got into the yacht chartering business by just going down to the water and getting started. 'Now that's something you could never do back home.'

'Next Christmas we're going to sail to Robben Island and eat dinner there,' Hannah stammers with excitement. 'Family Christmas.'

'A family Christmas . . . You mean with Geena?' I ask anxiously. Next Christmas is a long way off.

But Hannah doesn't answer me. I begin to realise she is not quite with the programme. I look across at Joel who seems underwhelmed by the idea. Perhaps it's the idea of a *family* Christmas he doesn't savour. Joel is crowding fifty-five and not happy about it, if the talismans of the sixties he still carries on him have any significance: rings on every finger, semi-precious stones on leather thongs around his neck, and that long hair mocking his ageing face.

After we've eaten the cold meats and drunk the champagne Hannah gets up from the grass to stroll like a barefoot squaw down to the sea. Jennifer ups and follows. Joel winks at me and opens another bottle. Let the girls do their thing, we do ours.

I see my opening. 'Do you know why I've come here, to South Africa?'

'China, it never occurs to me to ask anyone why they come to South Africa. You're just here as far as I'm concerned.'

I'm verging on trying one more time, but James takes the initiative away from me. 'So what do you do, in England?'

I pause for a second. 'I'm a student,' I say.

'You'll get on with my wife, then. She teaches in a university.' He breaks off to laugh. 'A kaffir college.'

'Is it true what they say about England now?' Joel asks.

'What do they say about England now?'

'That it's had its day. It's all shagged out.'

'I'm not quite sure what you mean.'

'The south of England's tipping into the sea is what I've heard. The whole country's tilting. Sea's receding in Scotland and rising in the south, with all the thermal warming and stuff. They reckon in fifty years, hundred years, places like Canterbury will be underwater, like Atlantis.'

I drop my head to cover the grin breaking on my face. While down there I stare at his big silver rings in lurid fascination.

'I'll tell you why I've come here.' I pick up my head. 'To try to persuade Geena she's better off back in England. If I ever find her.'

'Cool,' Joel says and turns to watch Hannah gliding along the fringe of the water with her arm around Jennifer.

'Is that it? That's all you have to say?'

'That's it. Period. She's a grown woman.'

I grow cold in the sun, drinking this man's champagne as though we have something to celebrate. I prime myself for another salvo, but Joel's inscrutability makes this harder than it should be.

'So where is she, Joel? If you don't know, why not?'

This time Joel doesn't bother to reply. He makes a rude gesture towards the Africans, who've just turned on a car stereo, then starts packing away the picnic. He tosses a full flute of champagne onto the grass and throws everything into the hamper. He shouts to Hannah, waving his hand for her to return.

Travelling back to Cape Town I do not talk at all. Instead I listen to them and gain an impression of how tight Hannah and Joel are. They've come a long way over the years. A lot of water under the bridge allows them to share an easy, uncomplicated affection. They talk a great deal and give plenty of airtime to the other for expressing half-lost thoughts. Their humour is dull to me but hilarious to themselves. When Joel isn't changing gear they are holding hands the whole time.

They are still holding hands as we climb up Lion's Head above the city. We'd dropped the Willmots off at their house in Constantia and now Hannah and Joel lead the way along the narrow path, the imprint of Hannah's knickers showing through her white jeans. In the Range Rover earlier she told me she was 'into' Tai Chi, Alexander Technique and I can see it in her comportment.

Darkness is falling fast. We have to scale a sheer rock face at one point, aided by chains bolted into the rock. Hannah goes up easily, but I have to suffer the indignity of Joel pushing on my ass from below.

When I was six and Geena was ten she fell off a swing in the park and I carried her all the way home.

The city lights pour weak candle-power into the crevices and reveal the big drop, should I lose my footing. We reach the top of Lion's Head as the sun is shaking hands with the moon below the horizon. At the summit a big gathering of people is waiting to watch the moon rise; as dispiriting a sight as the time I climbed Snowdon to discover a restaurant up there.

Resting on a rock I inhale marijuana fumes. I look to see who's skinned up and Joel hands me the joint. With his other hand he points to a yacht out at sea, lit up like a beacon. 'That's *Elinor II*,' he says. 'One of a dozen I've got flying out there tonight.'

Hannah smiles at me through the dark, in an almost seductive way. She says: 'You look like Geena . . . I mean, you look like her like I look like Joel. You know, people who spend a lot of time together start to look alike.'

'I guess so,' I say.

'My little girl's all grown up. But she looks happy, like the sun is shining through her. Only people who have been loved shine that way. Your parents loved her, I can tell, as if she was their very own. Like I would have loved her . . .' Her voice caves in, trails off, trembling at the edges.

Joel jumps to his feet, suggesting we go down the mountain some. He claims the crowd has distracted him from his meditations. Bad karma, so many people in one place. I wonder if it is Hannah's reminiscences that unsettled him.

It is brighter now the moon has risen, which makes going down easier than coming up and I don't really need Joel's help, even though he hooks his hand under my arm. I wonder if he is as solicitous of Geena as he is of me, her adopted brother.

At an unpopulated spot on the path we stop to look at the view of Cape Town, a huge sprawling light show. It is almost totally silent, apart from a solitary dog barking, delivering a clear note on the thin air. How can that be, the only sound in such a big city to reach our ears? Cities need to live in the imagination, through literature, before they can live at all. But I don't have a book guiding me around Cape Town, just Hannah and Joel, and the only sense of their city I get is of a love-sick dog barking at the moon.

THE TAVERN QUEEN

During the night I dream about wheelchairing the woman with her dead child on her lap through the hospital. At the end of the corridor where the mortuary should be I find myself in open country. The hospital bursts into flames behind my back. There are no shoes on my feet. The mother's cries rumble in my chest. She pleads with me but I can't hear her for all the drumming of blood in my ears. The help I so desperately want does not materialise.

I hear my burnt lungs sucking oxygen from the room as I come awake. The child in the wheelchair was Geena. Sitting up in bed I recall something Joel said: Geena is a grown woman. Not strictly true. Geena is child *and* adult. And in some cultures it is as dangerous to be a grown woman as it is to be a child.

I am almost forlorn with grief. My head spins and my heart shakes like an untuned engine. She has disappeared into the vortex as my parents had predicted. This country has devoured her. Every hour that passes I feel her becoming less than what she once was. I long to see her before me, to lock onto her eyes. This absence of substance, of flesh and bone is unbearable. My attempts to go back to sleep are thwarted by involuntary visions of her lying in a garret with her head smashed and bloody.

A knock on my door saves me from spiralling further into unmanageable fear. I turn on the bedside lamp and look at my watch. It is past midnight. At the second knock I open the door and find the landlord standing there in his dressing gown and looking miffed. 'You've got a visitor.' Behind him is Kenno. The landlord stays just long enough to satisfy himself that Kenno is welcome before leaving us to it.

Kenno comes into my room, picks up my copy of Melville's Short Works from the bed. 'You reading a book, china?' he asks.

'That's the general idea.'

These are my first communal words spoken in many hours and they tow the heavy freight of sorrow and fear through my body, scorching my organs on the way. But it heals me. I feel patched up.

Kenno has to take some credit for that, I'm damned to say. He smiles at whatever expression I hold on my face. 'Want to come out with me to find Geena?' he says.

I throw on my jeans and grab my leather jacket and wallet. 'Let's go . . . china.'

In Kenno's Golf GTi we take the Main Road south – the white man's ley-line that runs from Cape Town through all the glittering suburban satellites to the true paradise of False Bay. Although at that hour the only people out in this promised land seem to be black prostitutes.

In Constantia Kenno makes a brief pit stop. He parks outside a white suburban house surrounded by high walls that I recognise as his parents'. He opens the security gates with a remote control and runs in.

Kenno reappears at a pace. He zaps the gates shut and dives into the car. 'We're getting outta here. Now!'

'What's the matter?'

'My cousin's visiting from London. He wants to come with us.'

'What's wrong with that?'

'What's wrong with that? He just say in there: "Can I come too, I'm looking forward to having a glass of wine." Jesus Christ! You say: I'm gonna get shitfaced tonight. Or: I'm gasping for a few beers. Or: Get me inna fucking bar. I could murder a bloody drink. Something like that. Not: I'm looking forward to a glass of fucking wine. Jesus Christ. How the hell we came from the same family, I don't know.'

'I know how you feel,' I say.

I see signs for Mowbray, Rosebank, Diep Rivier flash by. We are journeying around the posterior of Geena's right temporal lobe.

'How long has your family been in South Africa?'

'Three, four decades back. But I was born here.'

'Do you have any black friends?'

'What do you mean?'

'It's just that I don't see white guys hanging out with black guys.'

Kenno belts out one of his explosive laughs. 'I got black friends.' He kicks the laugh into touch. 'Watch this.'

He takes a sudden right turn, ramming up into third, and in no time we are cruising along an unasphalted road. Everything has changed, from white to black, from First to Third World in an instant. On each side of the road are rows of grimy hostels barricaded behind corrugated iron. Men hang around drinking and conspiring, watching us. From pane-free windows women shout down to the men in loud unleaven raps. Dust coils into the air. The wheels of the car dip into small craters and collide with overflowing refuse bins.

Kenno pulls over, hits the lights and keeps the engine running. A man drifts across the road to Kenno's window. He says something, in patois, eliciting an annotated remark from

Kenno. 'You kid me, man! Do we look like police? You just lost yourself a deal.'

He drives on a hundred metres and stops. Another shadow appears at the window wearing a woollen hat with a Nike symbol stitched on the front. He wants to see the money. Kenno gives him five rand, promising another five when he comes back. The man vapourises into the night.

'Keep an eye out,' Kenno says. 'If he isn't back in five we're splitting.'

I do as he tells me. No one approaches the car except for dogs, curious as to who is sitting inside like lanterns.

Kenno keeps up a nervous, shifting monologue. 'Why do dogs sniff the bitch they wanna fuck? Ever wonder? Never look at her face. Just fight and fuck, like the South African Army. How'd you score in London, Mark? Routines are different every places. Where's this *wus* with my drugs?'

'These your black friends then, Kenno?'

'Don't get sentimental about the kaffirs after just a couple of days out here.'

'Is that what they are to you, kaffirs?'

'We're still discriminating in favour of them, aren't we? And we're the minority here.'

'Oh, surely you don't need an English tourist to explain that to you.'

Kenno punches me in the arm. 'You think it's all our fault, don't you?'

'What, what's all your fault?'

'Listen, china, when the colonists first penetrated the African interior they discovered the people hadn't invented the wheel. They couldn't read their own language. They didn't know how to tell the fucking time. No vineyards, orchards. Farmers didn't understand contour ploughing, nothing like irrigation. They couldn't build higher than one storey. There was tribes on the seaboard didn't know how to build boats, let alone navigate. They couldn't make glass, couldn't grind lenses for telescopes. We gave 'em all that. And since the colonists checked out . . . war, famine, genocide, fucking mayhem . . . Hang ten, here comes Johnny.'

The car pitches beneath us as the dealer leans on the door and palms the dagga through the window, rolled in a strip of yellowing newspaper. Kenno gives him the other five rand. 'Take a good look at us, *poes*. Remember our faces. Remember it was us who gave you a tiger today, okay? Number one.'

Kenno turns on the lights and we are travelling again, the fastest moving object in Parkwood.

'Oh yes!' Kenno bangs the steering column with his fist. 'Look in the glove compartment. You'll find some Rizlas.'

I put my hand into the glove compartment and feel cold precision steel. I withdraw fast. Kenno laughs as he leans across, stuffing his fist into the glove compartment.

He tosses the Rizlas into my lap. 'Jack one up, china.' He smiles, giving me some rare eye contact. 'Don't worry, Mark, we all pack pistols here. Mine's a Luger nine mil that you just feeled up, with one in the chamber.'

'You pack a pistol but still live with mummy.'

He winces, rumbles a laugh through his thick lips, and rides fast over my remark. I do what I can to roll a joint in the moving car.

Kenno recovers composure with a new narrative. 'I was driving around last week up on Modderdam. Apache country. I get stuck between a van and truck at the lights. Two kaffirs get out of their van and start ambling back to my car. So I point my Luger out and put three rounds into their van. The kaffirs run off and I drive straight to the police station. I'm waiting to report the incident while this cop is having an argument with some old fruit over the desk. He takes him into a back room and leaves me all alone with a MAG 58 and full clip on the desk. Gun to go. Only in South Africa, man! When he comes back I tell

him what happened and he goes, "Why didn't yah just plug
'em, man." Ha . . . ha . . . ha.'

Ha fucking ha. We are in Diep Rivier.

Kenno pulls over outside a busy pub and I pass him the
joint. 'Is this where Geena is?'

'Maybe.' He lights up, takes a slug. 'Jesush chrish!' He passes
it to me. 'Take a toke offa diss one, china.'

I follow him out of the car, tossing the joint into a bush. He
storms the pub with his broad shoulders hunched. Inside, leer-
ing Voortrekkers jam their torsos into my face. Heat blows out
of their swollen lips. Oak-trunk thighs strain cotton chinos.
They try to scare me, but only the women actually succeed. In
frocks and heavy eye shadow, heavier perfume, they are like
men in drag.

The music is Neanderthal and a lot of noise for just two gui-
tarists playing over a recording of drums and bass. They wear
their hair like Led Zeppelin. Kenno reappears clutching the
necks of three bottles of Amstel.

'Who's the third bottle for?'

'I thought I saw Geena as we came in,' he says. 'Looks like
she's gone again.'

'You fucking with me, Kenno?'

'It's your sister I'm fucking.' He laughs into my face. 'Only
kidding, china.'

'She's not my sister anyway.'

'Then you don't mind if I do?'

A bullneck slaps him on the back and he turns his head
away. This performance is repeated every few seconds. He
seems to know everyone and everyone knows him. This is
Kenno's town, all right, all two square miles of it.

Kenno begins moving in on the women. Two heavy-set girls
look to be quite enthralled by his spiralling, shaking laughter,
until he latches onto the tall blonde, who covers her breasts in
a defensive way with her arm. As he shouts in her ear she

stares straight ahead as though through a lens, sipping her beer diffusely. The band finishes on a number and I hear her reply to him: 'Sorry, I'm on a different wavelength completely.'

On the rebound he puts his arm around me. 'I was lining them up for us, china, but they're married to some sailors from Simon's Town.'

It is almost 2 a.m. 'I think I'm ready to hair-out.'

'You need to chill,' Kenno replies. 'Night's young.'

'I'm going to find a cab. You don't need to take me back if you want to stay.'

Kenno shoots off a salvo of laughter. 'You'll die before you find a cab out there.'

I turn and walk out, the liberation from the smoke and unreason an instant gratification. It doesn't last too long, however, the euphoria of escape. Prostitutes are packed into shop fronts, their pimps all giving me slight nods of their heads. I'll die before I find a cab . . . could be true enough. Something prevents me from going further out. I think it's not the presence of danger that holds me to the spot but a memory of a red line painted on the pavement outside the Dark Side of the Moon.

Kenno comes outside. 'Let's ride. I've got some more ideas *vis-à-vis* your sister.'

He revs the GTi, spins the wheels, drives over the pavement and we are gone. Kenno cranks up the volume on the stereo. A mobile phone plugged into the cigarette lighter goes off, whereupon he turns down the volume to take the call. Call over, he cranks up the volume again.

'Was that Geena?'

'No, man, it ain't that easy.'

'If she calls let me speak to her, okay?'

'Listen, sport, I don't think you fully appreciate what your sister, that ain't your sister, is doing these days. She's down on the fucking farm. She's gone, man.'

'Just find her for me.'

'Sure, china, anything you say.'

The night increases in tones of black. As we enter the town-ships I start to feel a great pull in my gut. I have no idea where we are in the world. A sign says Guguletu, but a name is noth-ing, a name is just someone else's idea. As we go, a big population clogs the concrete roads. I imagine they can regis-ter our white flesh behind glass. Heads turn and eyes open wide; some coruscate.

Kenno pulls in at a petrol station, just like the one where two German tourists were shot dead a few days ago, which I'd read about in the local paper, its front page like an obituary column. A pair of brown Cat boots appears outside my window and Kenno cranes himself out of the door.

A tall thin African pushes the back of Kenno's seat forward and climbs into the back of the car. I look at him once, quickly. There are no introductions.

A mile on we stop to let the African out, who disappears into a leaning shanty. Kenno turns off the engine and turns up the stereo. I turn it off. 'Are we still trying to find Geena, or has the plan changed?'

'We are, china. We are.'

'Who's that bloke?'

'A real bad guy in a real bad place.'

'I mean his name.'

'Sipho. But don't tell him I told you. Sipho's our scout.' Kenno turns on the stereo again, until the phone rings. Call over, up goes the volume.

'Who was that?'

'Someone for our scout.'

This little pantomime repeats itself for the half an hour we wait in the cul-de-sac. Men and women drift by like shadows on the stage flats of a pantomime. Eventually Sipho returns with a woman. As she squeezes into the back seat the car fills with a smell of wet nail varnish.

147

Kenno announces we are running short of fuel and we go back to the same petrol station. Sipho pumps gas into the tank, but makes no cash transaction, I notice. He just waves to the woman sitting behind wire-reinforced glass. As he climbs in I hear some stray remark issued from the forecourt. So apparently does Sipho, who motions for Kenno to stop. I am pushed against the windscreen as Sipho forces my seat forward to get outside.

The first clue I get of something going wrong is in the stiffening of Kenno's shoulders. He's observed something in his rearview mirror and reverses the car at speed. Through the windscreen I catch sight of Sipho kicking some guy lying on the ground. His kid-leather boots split open the man's lips. Blood blossoms on black skin. Framing his head are patches of petrol spilled on the forecourt refracting the spectrum, like a peacock's feathers.

Watching the violence through the windscreen is like watching TV with the sound off and I feel immune from its effects for an existential moment. Then Kenno opens his door and the sound rushes in like wind. Cries and whimpers. I gulp the warm air. The woman in the back seat yells. Kenno dives out and pulls Sipho off his victim and into the car. Both of their bodies are racked with laboured breathing.

'Would somebody please tell me what the fuck is going on?' I shout as we are driving off the forecourt.

Sipho speaks to me for the first time. Ice has been broken. 'That man insult me, so I have to show authority. That is auntie inside. He hang round here otherwise, maybe rob auntie.' He takes off his boots for some reason, and the woman massages his shoulders. 'This is my wife, Nadira.'

Nadira smiles at me, her freshly lacquered fingernails sinking into the flesh of Sipho's neck.

We beat on until Khayelitsha and emerge from the car into a crowd of flyboys wearing chunky gold crucifixes on neck chains the thickness of a ship's hawsers, all listening to a car stereo. Hip-hop meets the scriptures.

Sipho settles things with the gang, who allow us to advance towards a tavern.

A woman studies us through a steel grille in the door before releasing the bolt. She stands in the doorframe, hand on hip, smoking a cigar. When I hesitate in the entrance she hauls me in by my lapels, sliding home the bolt behind my back.

It is slamming inside. My neck rocks up solid as Sipho pushes me through the crowd to the bar. He abandons me there. Women dance to Hi-Life belting out of speakers, their shoulders leaning, black dresses hanging straight down their backs. I allow myself a second of appreciation as they dance around men hunched over wooden tables and working on litre bottles of Castle. A handsome woman in a headscarf counsels me in English. 'Why do you come here?' She sounds angry, her eyes bulging. Someone else brushes into me and hisses in my ear, but I can't understand what he says, can't talk back to him. I might as well be on the bottom of the sea. These people are screens onto which I project my prejudices. I see savages, victims, revolutionary heroes. My white skin is a liability and burns like a furnace.

Sipho comes to retrieve me. This is not the right place.

'What is the right place?' I ask.

'Where Ernie is, is the right place.'

'Who's Ernie?'

He doesn't answer me but hooks my hand in his and guides me towards the door. I have a distinct feeling he is enjoying himself, protecting his gleaming white trophy, his own home-boy.

Riding again and Kenno starts cursing. 'I can't drive without a drink. Got any money, Mark?'

I say I do.

He stops the car and I give him 150 rand.

'Tell me one thing in return,' I say.

'What's that?'

'Does Joel know we're out here tonight?'

'Joel? Sure. He's the skipper.'

'Doesn't he know where Geena is?'

'Who knows what Joel knows, man.'

He vanishes through an unmarked door. Sipho and I follow, leaving Nadira behind. Inside a shack we negotiate a labyrinth of stacked beer crates, a single bare lightbulb illuminating the corrugated-iron walls, to where three men work diligently behind an iron grille. Lying on a mattress behind the grille is a Cape Coloured with a shaved head and stumps for legs. His hands are buried in a metal tray full of coins and notes. A folded wheelchair is propped against the wall and a chrome-plated pistol sits on top of the money. Kenno orders thirty-six cans of Castle, a dozen Amstels, a bottle of Cape Verde brandy and a carton of full fat milk, spending every penny of my 150 rand.

It is now 3.30 a.m. The mobile keeps ringing and Kenno keeps driving, stopping occasionally to check out some she-been or tavern, but we never stay more than a few minutes, never find what we are looking for. I wonder all the time if we really are looking for the same thing. Geena seems more like a fiction than a reality.

For the second time that night I fight off an image of Geena as no longer among the living. Her face again appears covered in blood, surrounded by a halo of refracted light in a petrol slick. I shake my head furiously, flinging off the image and suck on my beer can. In the back seat Nadira cuts her brandy with milk, drinking from a small green-tinted glass that she procured from her bag.

Then I get plain bored; how easily the body relaxes its guard. As Kenno stops at a red traffic light Sipho punches the back of his headrest. 'Go! Go!' he shouts. 'Hijack location!' Kenno releases his manic laugh for the first time in an hour and guns through on red.

It starts to rain heavily. The car aquaplanes, carrying its heavy load lightly. Dust turns to mud in the streets that have no names, ordinance, which appear empty but are actually teeming with millions of people waiting to drink my blood, should the car fail or skid into a tree. A respite from my ugly thinking comes when the collapsed geometry of the townships is replaced by open fields. Farmlands detonate with rock falls and crumbling escarpments. Torrential rain pushes up barley seeds from the soil. Trees crumble from termite engineering and sag in the wind. Flies hover over newly formed pools. Lizards sit on rocks flicking their tongues at easy prey. In the thorn trees birds wait strategically for the lizards to have their fill before shaking out their wings and dropping down on them.

This land that favours the predatory is sibling to the spaces in my head. It is the land that has swallowed my sister.

Kenno has the mobile phone open permanently now, speaking in English-Afrikaans patois, his voice full of anger and stress. The rain switches off and we stop the car to piss. My moist clothes cling to my skin. There is dust in my ears, nose, congealed in my honey-coloured hair as I stand with my flies open. A crowd emerges from the darkness, drifting silently by. A loud crackle of multiple gunfire ripples through the air from some way off. I feel tense again, feel *white* again. A car cruises by our stationary vehicle, and some black faces stare at me. As they slow Sipho pulls a revolver from his belt and points it at the car. The car speeds on, leaving us its exhaust fumes.

'You have to pull the gun before him otherwise there a possibility he will shoot you first,' Sipho begins my basic training. 'You must produce your gun and point at the driver, the one who drives the car, or hit him on the forehead with the butt of

151

the gun so he can not see clearly, you see. I fire my gun every month. Every week. Maybe in a month I use sixty bullets. After I shoot people I run away. I do not know if they are dead, but to shoot a person in the head, I'm not sure is going to be alive. There are people who do not belong to here. And they must die, you see.'

Kenno, who had wandered off into the bush with his cell phone, comes running back, zipping up his flies and snapping his phone closed. 'Okay, we're gone.'

'Another shebeen?' I say.

'We've found your sister, *poes*.'

A white Mercedes is parked under a mural on the exterior wall of the tavern. The mural depicts three bodiless heads floating like balloons on the thermals of a desert landscape, the Hottentot mountains smoking moodily in the distance. Each of the heads is named: Hammer, Milky, Benny, and captioned: 'fallen but not forgotten'. In the foreground there stands one building, this tavern itself, an idealised centre of the universe.

Just inside the door, Kenno fights a verbal battle with two men in T-shirts and jeans. 'We've got business with the *baas*,' he says, but it takes Sipho to get us through the courtyard of beer crates and into the inner sanctum.

The tavern looks recently vacated. Bottles and glasses and overflowing ashtrays have yet to be cleared from the tables. The kinetic of a dancing, drinking crowd is still palatable on the small dancefloor, which is illuminated by fairylights around the perimeter. The air feels like it has been greased. The breeze-block walls are painted black and the corrugated-iron ceiling curls at the edges.

One man is seated in a booth down the far end, with four others leaning against the wall beside him. He is African, about fifty years old, lean and handsome, in Lacoste shirt and jeans, white trainers. As we move closer I struggle to recall where I've seen his face before.

The four men standing, letting me notice their shotgun, rifle and two handguns, distract me. My sense of self goes, washed clean by pure chemical fear.

I remember where I've seen him – on Joel's yacht.

Just as commanding but no longer silent, he volunteers his hand to me, only to me. 'I am Ernie Sisulu.' He slides down the bench seat. 'Please . . . join me, please.' I sit down beside him. Kenno and Sipho sit on his other side.

Sisulu snaps his fingers and a young Indian girl materialises. Walking in behind her is Geena.

I stand up in the booth. Geena, there's Geena . . . the refrain keeps playing in my head as if I'm trying to convince myself. I've made the positive ID, but the context – the gunmen, the setting, *Africa* – is so alien I cannot quite believe myself. I can't fire up obvious connections. André Breton once wrote that a shoe is a shoe, but put it in an oven and it becomes something else. Right now, Geena is something else.

But she keeps on coming. Eventually she is close enough to be able to stretch her arms across the table to hug me. 'I can't believe it,' she echoes my sentiment.

A reply is well beyond my reach and I stare at her open mouthed. On some occasions nothing you say or can't say can ever relay your emotion.

She has changed her appearance. She has gone halfway across to the other side. Her hair is loose under a rolled white scarf. She wears a wrap printed with yellow and red flowers and a Victorian lace blouse – the kind her mother would wear.

She watches me angling, paying out line. The stress I am under triggers stress in her, like a faultline opening up beneath our feet. We have always felt what the other feels. My predicament is her predicament, is one predicament.

Geena is diverted by the Indian girl, who holds a plastic litre

153

bottle of Coke and some glasses on a tin tray. Everyone's attention, including the armed guards', becomes focused on Geena as she shows the girl how to serve Coke without it erupting over the edge of the glass. I look from the girl's huge sad brown eyes, concentrating on the glasses, back to Geena, gently guiding the girl's hand. Like some carer, I think. It's not just her appearance that's changed.

The moment lasts maybe fifteen seconds at most and yet I am left cracked at the completion of the mime.

Sisulu places a proprietary arm on Geena's shoulder. 'Let us talk, Geena. Then you come back.'

I am incensed by the way he gives her an order, and by her compliance. The guys with the weapons are an inhibiting device against me actually saying something.

Geena withdraws from the room. Then Kenno and Sipho drift off, leaving me alone with Sisulu. I feel exposed and frightened by the milieu, lessened somewhat when Sisulu begins to speak. My survival is guaranteed, at least until the end of the story.

The story starts with the Indian girl. Two years ago, at fourteen years of age, she was kidnapped from a Durban orphanage and sold to a brothel in Cape Town. She was discovered by a social worker and sent to a reformatory. From there she escaped and found her way to one of his taverns. (He has five taverns on the Cape Flats.) He gave her shelter, until she ran off with his money, returned, did the same again. Yet he feels great sympathy for this young girl, Kubasni, as he himself grew up in an orphanage. He wants to help her make something of her life, if she would only stop running away with his money.

Then he meets Geena while at his friend Joel Sugarman's house. He instantly takes to Geena and decides she would be a good mentor to the Indian girl. So he introduces them and watches with satisfaction the way Geena handles the girl. She understands how young people think without even knowing the language. Geena tries to persuade him to give Kubasni responsibilities. Let her serve drinks in the clubs, man the cash tills. At first he resists but then makes these concessions. The girl has not run away since. So impressed is he by Geena he promotes her to his tavern queen. He is very proud. All taverns are managed by women, but Geena is the only white tavern queen in the Cape Flats. She has become a symbol for unification in South Africa.

He calls her, 'A silk of a lady.'

Sisulu moves the subject on from Geena and Kubasni to politics. He tells me how he voted for the ANC in the first elections, voted for changes, but is still waiting for those changes to be implemented and in the meantime has to suffer political interference in his business, which is intolerable. Politicians fast forget where they come from when they move out of the townships to go live in some white suburb, like Newlands.

He pauses to moisten his parched throat with a drink of Coke. His abstinence, like his comportment and soft voice go against the grain. Only now do I notice the clutch of barmaids, prostitutes – or both – sitting behind a pillar in the shadows, composed in silent relief at the end of a working night. The women drink Coke, like Sisulu, but unlike him they smoke.

This political interference, he continues, has recently taken a turn for the worse. Muslim Fundamentalists are summarily executing what he calls the 'rightful leaders of the community'. These fundamentalists justify their murders on the grounds that *they* are protecting the community. But the Mohammedans don't smoke dagga. They have no use for hookers . . .

He notices a minute shift in my expression and adds: 'What else for us is there to trade? The whites have cornered all legitimate markets.' The fundamentalists are just religious fanatics who know how to make bombs and are versed in the ways of

155

guerilla warfare. It will be a hundred-year war, he predicts. 'Like your War of the Roses.'

That is why he has to keep moving around, because there is a price on his head. He points to his armed bodyguards. Not even his men know where he is sometimes. He never sleeps in the same bed two nights in a row. One night police raided one of his taverns in Old Crossroads, and were surprised to find him asleep in the bar.

The smile etched on his face suddenly falls. His expression is sawn-off as he ends the story. The story is over and so is my time. He has been here for one hour already, too long, and has to get going. The Indian child goes where he goes, and Geena also.

He stands, leaving me scratching around for the surface. *Geena goes also.* The armed guards flutter like flags in a breeze.

'I'd like to talk to Geena.'

'I can give you no more than five minutes.'

The journey into the courtyard is lost time. I find Geena in there, sitting on a stack of beer crates, swinging her legs like a child in a playground.

'I've just been told I've got no more than five minutes with you alone. How did this come to pass?'

'I'm busy. I've got a job to do.'

'You call this a job?'

'Don't impose yourself on me!' She holds out her hand, fingers splayed as if I am about to strike her. 'In London I couldn't afford the downpayment on a glass of beer. Here I feel like I've found a real purpose in my life. That's not so bad, is it? Better than watching TV until I die.'

'You might die quicker than you think out here.' She lifts the collar of her white shirt to her ears as though a cold wind had blown through the stifling courtyard. 'I thought you liked your life in London?'

'It was fun being a nobody. But not as much fun as being somebody else.'

'Joel, Ernie . . . these are not your people.'

'So who are my people, Mark? Tell me that. At least this is my country. I was born here.' Her confidence startles me as she crows of her contentment. 'Joel and Ernie have given me something I've never had before.'

'You go where that man goes, do what he tells you to. What kind of life is that? You're virtually a prisoner.'

'I'm not a prisoner! Ernie has a chauffeur who takes me anywhere I want to go. I can visit Joel and Hannah any time I want. I take days off on the beach.'

'Ernie's a gangster.'

'I've seen this man you call a gangster hold a rally in a football stadium, Mark; I've been there. Thousands of people turned up to hear him talk. He has huge respect; I've seen that with my own eyes. He could be a politician if he wanted to but doesn't want to because politics is about power, not people.'

'So he told me.'

'What have you ever done in your life that is so original? A hospital porter, just like your dad.'

I inhale to clear my head. 'What's that smell? You wearing perfume? Since when have you started wearing perfume?'

'Don't give me any more grief, china.'

'China!' I recognise the scent – the same rose-musk Hannah sprinkles on her skirts. 'You're even talking like they talk.'

'My mate . . . plate, china plate. Cockney slang.'

'So who do you think these people are . . . The Kray Twins? Are you really that confused?'

Ernie Sisulu appears in the courtyard. He does not look at me, but says something to one of his guards. The guard puts a squeeze on my arm and escorts me out of the tavern, back to the car, where Kenno waits and Sipho and Nadira have fallen asleep in the back. I am placed in the front seat and the door firmly closed.

Geena appears outside the car. I roll down the window. 'Is it me you've run away from?'

'This is not about you, Mark, it's about me. Look at the light. Look at the land. Tell me it's not beautiful.'

I try to see what she can see, but there is desert all around me.

PART FOUR

'I knew that I had to purge the black fear from my white heart.'

— RIAN MALAN

FLYING MONEY

> From: Kornhoop@iafrica.com
> To: Natasha.r@goldstein.wolff.co.uk
> Subject: From Mark McLuhan

How appropriate to be telling you what has happened to Geena in an e-mail. E-mails do not belong anywhere, or to anyone, are free of controls. They are like mercury – slippery, with a life of their own. Like Geena herself.

If you could see her now, running township bars and nightclubs, instead of squandering so much of her time in them, you may well think she's not only integrated into South African life but integrated into black South African life. That is some achievement, no? Is this not a profound experience, breaking through the membrane between the races? In so short a time. So why can't I just encourage her, celebrate her emancipation?

I cannot because I do not believe she is being true to herself. By trying to replace her missed history with contemporary experience, she has spun a web of illusion around herself. She hasn't paid her dues to be integrated.

Mum and Dad paid their dues. They understood the dangers to body and soul out here, and then they quit.

You once asked me, walking along the Thames, what was I frightened of, about Geena coming here? I couldn't answer you then, but now what I'm frightened of is the company she keeps, that walks the earth with armed guards. Her parents exploit her love. She is a woman remade by virtue of her contact with these people. I can recognise revisions in her dress and voice; even her scent is borrowed. She is all at sea, shipping on water.

You said brothers and sisters are meant to drift apart. But she isn't my sister. Now that past has been rewritten we are free to be anything we want to be to one another. Friends, lovers . . . might that be what I am frightened of? Or is it my true motive for being out here? Wouldn't you want to consummate a relationship with your best friend?
    Mark

> From Natasha.r@goldstein.wolff.co.uk
> To: Kornhoop@iafrica.com
> Subject: For Mark McLuhan

I would certainly not want to consummate a relationship with my best friend! Part of the character of great friendships is the abstinence of sex. Do you really want to go down that path? Does she even know what is in your mind? Your behaviour might look benign but your thoughts are bloody. But if you do go down that path you should consider the consequences first. You will no longer be arbiter of what she needs. Lovers cannot control one another. They must have a democratic relationship that siblings rarely have. Siblings are more like dictators of neighbouring counties. You want your cake and eat it too. Moreover you could drift apart, like a majority of lovers eventually do. Then you'll lose the very thing you hold so dear.

I still maintain you need to let her go. She's already been forcibly removed from that country once in her life, don't make her go through it again. Consider how much she has overcome to regain something of her past. That shows great integrity and willpower. Respect that. I think it proves that she has an instinct for survival that you do not credit her with. Geena's soul is intact. Can you say the same for your own?

Natasha

> From Kornhoop@iafrica.com
> To: Natasha.r@goldstein.wolff.co.uk
> Subject: brotherly love

Leave saving my soul to me, just give me some practical advice instead. How do I find out about Joel Sugarman's business activities? What kind of business would a yacht charterer need with township gangsters who can't sail? Ernie Sisulu is one such ominous character to whom Geena seems to have pinned her future. And then there is the broker, James Willmot. He and Joel live in each other's pockets, sail together. Their office is the open sea where no one can record what financial schemes they hatch.

Mark

From the guest house I telephone my father. The phone is metered and ticks away like a taxi.

–Geena's gone native and I don't know what to do.

– Your mother and I went native, long time ago.

– I'd like to think she was emulating you, but this is not ANC she's mixing with. She's working for a township gangster.

163

– Are you sure he's a gangster? Crime doesn't mean the same over there as it does here.

– I saw the guns, Dad.

– Is she still having those hallucinations?

– The light out of nowhere . . . I don't know.

– Do you think she's gone, you know . . . (He can't bring himself to say the word 'mad'.) Is she still with us?

– She's still with us.

– Her parents, how are they?

– Her father's a piece of work. He got her the job.

– Mother?

– Not quite with the programme.

– I think I'd better come out there. I know the place better than you.

– You haven't been here in almost thirty years.

– I'll book a flight and let you know my itinerary.

LIGHT OUT OF NOWHERE

My father is due to arrive this evening on the flight from London. To kill time I go for a drive to False Bay.

I park at a railway station and walk alongside the tramlines on the edge of the breakwater. Rail, road and houses squeeze into this narrow corridor between mountain and sea. The tide lifts the kelp and rakes footprints off the sand as I sing the first lines of pop songs to myself: You're Not The Only One; Baby, When I Think About You I Think About Love; Yesterday All My Troubles Seemed So Far Away.

Blue trains with yellow stripes roll by in both directions, borne silently on the electric current. Flying steel crashes through my head like a virtual cortège. I glimpse first-class passengers reading newspapers sedately, the journey itself a meaningless aberration, while in third class Africans hang out of open doors, raising the hue and cry, leaving for the day their overcrowded shanties, coming down to False Bay to wash the sins off their hands.

Whales are breaching and flapping their tails 100 metres out. Like Geena, whales were once something else too; hairy land mammals who began to spend more time in the ocean than on land, feeding away from the competition, their bodies gradually elongating, losing hair, the skull streamlining for faster movement through water, nostrils shaping into blow-holes, front legs into fins, hind legs growing shorter and folding into the fuselage. That was a million years ago. Geena has been in-country three weeks.

Surfers are bobbing around over a reef, chasing waves. It is small surf and they are young boys. Schoolboys of the ocean. I look at the surfers again and wonder how much longer they will stay out there; how much longer Geena will stay out here.

I nurse a beer on the street outside a café, while the lowering sun bleeds both the ocean and all the beautiful people leaning against high-performance cars. What kind of person chooses to drive a Porsche or a Ferrari in a country where just a couple of miles away a million people are having to walk an hour to get water from a standpipe? The sky turns a dirty orange, the colour of industrial sewage.

An African carrying a six-foot wooden crucifix over his shoulder walks into Arrivals seconds before my father appears. Dad looks rakish in his trilby stained from decades of wear. Wisps of grey hair fall over his ears. In one hand he carries a blue plastic holdall and in the other a British newspaper. He wears a tie and the collar of his shirt sticks up over the lapel of his Harris tweed jacket. I do not let him see me straight away, do not want him to see my tears. I watch him become anxious before I duck under the barrier and cross the concourse. He smiles so happily, for a moment I think he's going to laugh.

We shake hands like men. 'How was the flight?' is the first thing I say.

'I got a sandwich about an hour ago. It was all right.'

As we walk to my car I tell him where we are staying.

'The Kornhoop,' he repeats. 'Don't know it.'

'It's run by a bloke from Hull.'

'Is he a Hull supporter? Good rugby league team, was Hull.'

166

My father holds an affection for the northern game of rugby league because it is more honourable than soccer, a sport corrupted by money and commercialism. I am indifferent to both, but comment nonetheless. 'Hull had a fierce pack of forwards.'

'When Lee Crooks used to play with them. Lee Crooks and Knocker Norton.'

It is at times like this that I realise men do not talk like women talk. We create a correspondence between ourselves and a third party: a landscape, a sportsman. When we talk about a footballer like Lee Crooks it's as though we are praying together. And that's all right because anything is better than talking about what we really have to start talking about soon enough.

Dad does not want to go to the guest house straight away. He asks me to drive him into Cape Town, for a peek at the docks before night sets in. I am still nervous about driving in this country; of paving slabs sailing down from footbridges, of losing the way and ploughing into some township. But I keep it to myself. I pass the turn-off for Observatory and head for Cape Town.

Groote Schuur hospital appears on the right. 'My,' says Dad. 'That's got bigger since I worked there.'

'You want to visit?'

'No I don't. It's not there where I made an impact. It was just a job. Someone else will be doing it now. No one will remember me.'

On De Waal Drive I hear his intake of breath. He taps his knuckles against the dashboard and asks me to pull off at the next turning. In a couple of kilometres I am able to grant his wish, then double back along a concrete road through the former sprawling black and coloured slum of District Six, now levelled to the ground.

I stop the car and he steps out. He puts his trilby on the bonnet of the car and stands there for a very long time without comment. It is unclear to me what exactly he is fixing upon in this barren wasteland. I see in my father's face none of the joy or lust that I experience in the presence of city ruins. Which makes me think that his nature is better than mine. He is a good man with no side at all.

Eventually he gestures towards the lunar landscape. 'Your mother and I danced here to penny whistles, walking guitar, *kwela*. To Elvis, Duke Ellington, the fast music that came off the ships.' As he inhales his whole body trembles. 'We got married at a Zionist church that was just over there.' He laughs briefly. 'And got mugged coming out of the church by this kid cracking pine kernels in his teeth.'

Table Mountain fades into the darkness as I drive back onto the highway, and Cape Town unscrolls in a pageant of light. The city's candlepower, the inflammation of the docks, the blazing cathedrals setting keel for open sea are preternaturally visible through the windows of the car. This utopia of artificial light and the applied mechanics of an automobile are merciful on us. We need all the comforts we can get.

'Can we go to the Kornhoop now and check you in?'

'I want to get going on this, Mark. Drive us to Langa first.'

'Langa, where's that?'

'It's a township.'

'We'll be killed before we get out of the car.'

'That's a silly prejudice, son. Have some courage. Drive back down the N2. I'll tell you where to turn off.'

WALKABOUT

The road is littered with bricks, timber, corrugated iron, burned-out cars. We are *walking* through it and I am out of my mind with fear. The car lays somewhere behind us, stalled in a ditch like a broken bird, its engine refusing to turn. As we walk I can hear the rasp of my own breathing. Things are falling around my head in the dark. Gravity is harder in some places than in others. In Langa gravity is original sin. Dozens of girls and boys emerge from shacks, like the dens Geena and I used to make, and follow in our wake. Small pebbles, sticks are thrown at us, like the patter of rain before the storm. There is no place to hide. I feel as naked as Adam.

'This is insane.' My words are detached as though from another's mouth.

'It's all right, son,' Dad tries to placate me. 'Ten years ago – maybe not.'

Everyday life is being conducted in the road: trading, ablutions, cooking. Cooking is a feminine activity and we gravitate towards the women, whose faces are painted with camomile, seeking a place of safety. Laid out on trestle tables are coconuts. Closer up, in the light of the fires, I see they are in fact sheep heads, their eyes fixed like glass. Women are searing the heads to sterilise the meat. We nudge aside the hot air and move on. A lorry container decorated with tobacco billboards and paraffin signs has been dumped in a road that is no longer capable of taking traffic. Two elderly men sit on deck-chairs inside, selling uncooked chicken and dagga. The chicken looks more deadly than the dagga. I hear singing, like a siren song. The two elderly men watch us pass and I sense their bewilderment.

We find the source of music: a dozen women singing a capella in the road and dancing to their own songs. It is very good too, both the dancing and the singing and for a moment I forget our predicament and lose myself in it. A dry red dust swirls around their ankles as they shuffle and stamp. Then one of the women notices us. She stops moving and laughs, to see such a sight as this. She intuits our tribe. 'Are you police?' she asks in English. The colour of our skin, the enemy uniform.

'No,' Dad says. 'We're looking for Erasmus.'

'Many men called Erasmus.'

'He is my friend, from a long time ago.'

'Erasmus Mlangeni who lives in New Flats, maybe.'

'That's him,' Dad sounds excited. 'Which way are the New Flats?'

'I shall fetch him for you,' says the woman. 'It is not good for you to be walking around on your own in township.'

She escorts us to a shebeen and tells us to wait there for her return. We enter sheepishly the simplest of constructions.

An old woman with her arm in a sling is stuffed into a plastic upholstered chair. Four men sit on a sofa, drinking, listening to jazz on a radio. An antique Pye TV in a walnut cabinet has the sound turned down, the reception like a snow storm. The film too is antique; Shirley MacLaine when she was eighteen.

We have created quite a ruction by walking in. I stand on the threshold with my mouth closed and a stupid grin flaming up my cheeks. Dad is not so stricken. He understands the protocol. Noticing the three beer bottles on the smoked-glass coffee table are empty he offers to buy a round. The old woman calls into another room and a boy of eight or nine appears with three litres of Castle. As Dad hands 15 rand over to the woman, the radio is turned right down and one of the men stands. He welcomes us to the township, to Shirley's shebeen, and thanks us for the beer. He sits down again and the music goes back up.

The four men move up to make room for Dad. Shirley, the shebeen queen, indicates to the empty armchair beside her. I sink down in the chair that has lost its springs.

The men start arguing playfully. 'Who is the best, Dinah Washington, Billie Holiday or Ella Fitzgerald?'

'Ella,' my father is first in. 'Ella's voice is pure like a child's.' I look sideways at him. We have been in this country together less than three hours and he's already become quite foreign to me, one of the others.

'You see her now, she's a big fat old woman.'

'But the voice remains young, you see.'

'Because God's gifts never age.'

Shirley adds, '*Ja*. Like me. I'm old and fat but I still make more money than a twenty-year-old man.'

The four men crack up.

'God bless you, Shirley.'

'God bless the brewery,' she says and splits her sides. 'Ah, I cannot laugh. It hurts my arm.'

Three of the men start to dance when Ella Fitzgerald herself comes on the air, dancing in the twelve-inch space between the coffee table and the TV set. The one who remains seated talks to Dad. 'We like to drink on Friday night because it was the only freedom they allowed us. You must excuse me, but I don't drink now.'

Shirley leans her healthy arm into my shoulder. 'Welcome,' she says belatedly. 'I have been to your country. Disney World. On first night in Florida I go to bistro. A waiter come and I drop my face. I will be thrown out for sure. But he give me a glass of water. Complimentary, this staggered me. When he bring me a menu I begin to weep. Why am I not treated this way in my own country?'

Shirley takes a rapid reading of the room, gauges the mood. She smiles with contentment that two strangers from far off can harmonise with the locals. Life is good. Life is short but good. 'We are safe here,' she says.

'Safe,' I repeat. 'That's good to know.'

'Yes, in the taverns you can easily be killed. Gangs shoot weapons to kill their rivals for drugs. Nigerians who bring in the cocaine. Mandrax from the coloured communities.'

The man sitting beside Dad picks up the thread. 'Asief-Ali was shot dead only two days ago in Park City Take Aways. Ishmail was shot dead in his butchery. These are innocent muslims, not fundamentalists. Anyone who wears a fez is targeted. They want Muslim businessmen in compensation for Staggie. I have heard it is thirteen they want dead . . . the Dixies, the Mongrels who reign in Grassy Park, the Hard Livings. Only yesterday a drugs dealer was shot two doors down by Muslims. They even shoot his dog, because the dagga was buried under its kennel . . .'

I do not understand what they are telling me, I feel swept away again in uneasy thoughts. But my father is quick to pick up on the front line issue. 'This war you talk of, it has replaced the political fighting?'

'In many ways it is more serious. Once we were on the same side. One enemy outside township. Now is all confused. And the police they stay away, after all those many years they come here.'

The talking stops upon another man's entrance. Of my father's years he wears a dark grey suit, holding the jacket closed. His eyes bear down on us under a cloth cap.

My father rises slowly to his feet and the man's eyes and

arms both open wide. There are no buttons on the jacket and it falls open to expose a large tear across his white shirt. His sharp pointed shoes have no laces.

'Clement!'

To hear my father's name on this man's lips is dislocating. Then to see him and Dad embrace is even stranger. I am seeing history as foreground.

The man laughs for several seconds, exposing quite a few gaps between his teeth. 'Upon my soul,' he says finally. 'You may have perished before finding me.'

'Our car broke down,' Dad explains and laughs. He can't help himself. 'Electrical failure.' He laughs again. 'We had to walk here.'

'It is not very practicable, the grid.' The man laughs with him.

Then Dad introduces me to Erasmus.

'Greetings and salutations,' Erasmus says and squeezes my hand.

What started as an ordinary weekday night in her shebeen has turned into something quite exceptional and so now Shirley is up for a party. She hollers in Xhosa to the same boy trying to catch forty winks in the bedroom. The boy staggers in with a crate of Castles.

'Tonight we drink for free,' she says. 'Welcome, welcome. Tell everyone in America that life is good at Shirley's.'

Erasmus doesn't hesitate, he snatches a free beer by the neck and sits down next to my father, displacing the other men. His big arm rests on Dad's shoulders. They look into each other's eyes, inspect one another's grey hairs. They grin without blush. 'I am very happy to see this man again,' Erasmus says to me. 'Your father saves my life once.'

I have nothing I can possibly add, but it's fun coasting along. If bad times engendered this friendship then they are far more bonding than good times.

'Erasmus, how is Miriam? How is she?'

'Miriam, alas, is dead.'

'I am sorry to hear that, Erasmus. She was a fine woman.'

'And your wife?'

'Very well,' Dad says. I assume it's the same woman that I know.

'Your father is a very brave man. Clement has been even arrested by the police, lose his job on account of me.'

'At the hospital?' I say.

'You saved mine too,' Dad returns Erasmus's compliments. 'You had four broken ribs, fractured collarbone, a broken ankle from the farm. I came to visit you here and got beaten up outside your house.' Dad turns to me. 'Erasmus limped out of his bed on crutches to plead for my life. I would not be here today if he hadn't.'

'We are brothers for always.'

Shirley offers Erasmus another bottle of Castle, but he declines. He senses that since we've come all this way to find him, at some risk to ourselves, that we must want to talk to him in private, about more pressing matters than the past. He takes a few minutes to say his farewells.

We walk through the night and I am scared again. Shirley's sanctuary is a lot more manageable than the outside environment. Men stagger out of dark places smoking Mandrax and fall over in the road. The red light in the shebeen window recedes.

As we are crossing a shambolic courtyard between a cluster of two-storey hostels, Erasmus says, 'We call these the New Flats. Which is manifestly absurd of course. One time build for male migratory workers, now house entire families. It is corrupt here, but not so corrupt. We live too close. Everyone spits, even the women, which I personally deplore. I don't think it is done in good circles.'

I am so curious about his biography, where he learned to speak such archaic English, that I ask him directly.

'While in Robben Island I read all Agatha Christie novels,' he replies.

His remark kindles shock in my father's face. 'That I didn't know.'

'Yes, indeed, Clement. Twenty years and thirty-eight days.'

My father too has lived in gaol, it always seemed to me, and for the same amount of time. But his suffering is slight compared to what twenty years of imprisonment has done to this fine friend. A very poignant moment follows as they stare at each other, across all the intervening years. The time span shrinks in a matter of seconds.

'But now we are in Langa,' Erasmus changes the subject. 'So welcome. Welcome to Langa, which takes its name from a man who was also a prisoner of Robben Island. This man was a chief of the Hlubi tribe.'

We follow him up the wooden stairs running along the side of the hostel building, its whitewashed walls deeply ingrained with mud and dirt. A strong wind starts to blow from off the top of the mountain. Erasmus inhales on the wind before his door. 'Can you imagine Cecil Rhodes having a slum like this named after him?' Erasmus says. 'The man who plundered our gold and diamonds has a beautiful granite memorial on Table Mountain.'

We enter by a door on the second floor, straight into a communal kitchen. The room is bare except for a wooden table where three women shave white cabbage into a plastic colander. Their mouths drop open on seeing two white men and their hands freeze in the air. In a small pantry two large pots of water simmer over Primus stoves. There is a strong odour of paraffin.

I follow Erasmus leading Dad by the hand into a small room. It is furnished with bunk beds made from recycled timber and bound with rope. The mattresses are lined with old newspaper, as are the shelves on the wall. Clothes hang from nails. I count three men sleeping in there.

175

'Your brothers?'

'You are perfectly correct, Clement. We have to take shifts to sleep.'

We sit on the edge of an occupied bunk bed. Dry newspaper rustles beneath us like autumn leaves. Erasmus takes off his cap and looks directly at Dad.

'My friend,' he says. 'I feel there is much troubles that has brought you all the way here.'

'Troubles?' Dad plays the word in his head for a few seconds. 'I've been gone a long time, Erasmus. The despair I've felt you can't measure. It's put a strain on my marriage. I've been far away from troubles, but also from those sweet days we spent together, a community I once held as dear as my own family. We went away not like Slovo, like Mbeki for heroic reasons. We went away for Geena, my adopted child. And what does she make of herself in a free world where there is so little suffering? I love her as I love my son. But she makes me so . . .' As he gathers his next statement, those words of his, never uttered in my presence before, become wild things turned loose in my mind.

'I don't know what I'm saying, Erasmus. They're just the ramblings of an old man. Excuse me, please. You remember Geena, don't you?'

Erasmus strokes his chin. 'I remember an infant in a pushchair only.'

'Well she is here now, among us, but not with us. Come to trace her roots.'

'What roots, if she left here in a pushchair?'

'Her parents are here. Joel Sugarman.'

'I do not know the name of this man.'

'What about Ernie Sisulu?' I ask.

'Yes, of course. He is township's showbiz tycoon.'

'What kind of man is he?'

'Let me quote a greater mind than my own, Mark. Hercule

176

Poirot has said, "Evil walks the earth and can be recognised as such." But I think the body is a cage. Through the bars, the wild animal looks out.'

'You are perfectly correct,' I add, like Countess Andrenyi on the Orient Express.

'I don't know why I thought you may be able to help, Erasmus.'

He picks up on my father's despair and wants to say something to alleviate it. We sit in silence for a few moments. The man sleeping behind us grunts a few times.

'You mention Geena and this man Ernie Sisulu close together. You believe her to be in some peril.'

'Geena is working for Sisulu, in his taverns,' I say. 'I've seen it with my own eyes.'

'Then that is not so good. Allow me to tell you something. For many year in Robben Island, political prisoners were mixed in with criminals. It was very bad for us. You see, for a petty thief to graduate into a gang he must prove himself while in prison, by killing a man while there. Only this counts. Thieves are known as 26s; assassins, 27s. They arrive as 26s and leave as 27s, having slain the political men.'

'What are you trying to tell me?'

Erasmus places a hand on Dad's shoulder. 'What I am trying to tell you, Clement, is Sisulu is a 27. He is a killer of men. I am very sorry to have to tell you this.'

'Geena claims he protects her,' I add.

'A gangster always demands a crime from his friends before they can enjoy his protection. But who will protect him now from the fundamentalists? His people are loyal but his people cannot protect him forever. I have heard that he has politicians and policemen on his payroll. He has newspaper editors on his payroll. But none of these people can save him from the fundamentalists. They will kill him, Clement. It is only a matter of time. If your daughter is there you must go and get her.'

'She's thirty-two years of age. That's easier said than done.'

The two old friends fall silent and stare deeply into one another's eyes.

Dad sighs heavily. 'I suppose we should check in to our guest house, Mark.'

Erasmus objects: 'Please. You must be my guests tonight.'

I close my eyes, praying the offer is declined.

'Of course,' says Dad.

Erasmus walks us to where we abandoned the car to retrieve Dad's bag. But the car isn't there. It has been hauled away, along with Dad's holdall. 'Dad . . .'

'Yes, yes, I know.'

'What did you have in it?'

'Only my clothes.' He drags out his passport and wallet from his breast pocket. 'These are all that matter.'

'We'll have to buy you some more clothes tomorrow.'

'I hadn't banked on staying that long.'

Erasmus turfs out one of his brothers from his bunk. Dad and I top and tail on a mattress filled with straw. Erasmus sleeps on the floor alongside his displaced brother.

During the night I hear mice scurrying across the bed. They wake me constantly, nibbling at my fingers, cleaning my nails with their teeth. Long into the early hours I hear car horns blaring, children crying in their sleep, dogs fighting, the hullabaloo from a shebeen that never shuts, and the movements of people who have learned to cover great distances without light. There is a rhythm to all this coming and going, which picks up in tempo around dawn in the throats of cockerels and in the sound of women beating laundry against a rock by the standpipe. A breeze lifts the bright red muslin hanging over the door. Women drift past just to look in at us, the ghosts in the machine.

There is an African custom that requires a man to show hospitality to travellers and strangers. No matter how poor they are they're obligated by this custom to feed us. So in the morning, with Erasmus and his non-English speaking brothers, we sit in our T-shirts and underwear eating maize porridge from the same enamel bowl. We eat with our fingers, and for the first time in my life I witness my father enjoying a meal.

Erasmus and Dad catch up on life. Erasmus works now as a tour guide in the former maximum security prison on Robben Island. When Dad asks how he could bear to see that prison ever again, Erasmus replies simply: 'It's a job. And jobs are scarce.' He works a two-weeks on, one-week off rota. On his week off he lives here with his three younger brothers. Their rent is 7.50 rand a month, a pound a month, which he pays, the only one in the family with a job. What I paid for my Ted Baker shirt draped over the back of a chair could have settled their rent bill for five years. 'Going back to the island isn't so bad. Not as bad as I felt coming home after twenty years. I was a virtual stranger.' He couldn't understand where so many cars had come from, why so many people were drunk. People he loved were old and the young wouldn't talk to him because he was still considered dangerous by the authorities. For twenty years he had slept on a concrete floor, only to be offered another floor by his mother. He had two teenage brothers he'd never met. It felt depressing to be free. At least now on Robben Island he has a small house of his own.

After breakfast Erasmus walks us to the train station. On the way he browses around the ubiquitous trestle tables laden with empty bottles, second-hand radios, old clothes. We have no one but Erasmus to talk to, while he talks to the traders and the men sitting on the ground stretching drum skins over Calor-gas stoves. He introduces us to them all. We shake hands around a hundred times and our journey of about a kilometre takes over two hours to complete. When Dad explains that in London people do their shopping for a week in one hour at the supermarket, Erasmus claims that is the saddest story he's ever heard.

He leaves us at the station with a closing remark. 'You are a good man, Clement McLuhan. That is a proven fact. But things have become very confused since you were last here. You cannot fight men like Sisulu with goodness. If you need me to help you fight you know where to find me. I may be old but I still have some arrows in my quiver.'

FOREIGN BODIES

There's so much torque applied to my heart I can hardly breathe. I am drenched in sweat, and somewhere along the way I've misplaced my shirt. A dirty white T-shirt is all I have to cover my dirty white flesh. We are sitting in third class, the wrong class carriage of the Cape Town-bound train, and everyone seemed affronted by us, operating a kind of reverse apartheid. What's our game, trying to save a couple of bucks? No one says anything, but it is all in the eyes to read. I hang my head low like an abandoned marionette. There is no oxygen down at my waist, it's like sucking air from an oven. The doors and windows flung open don't do it, either. The train is stationary in Langa, as dead outside as it is inside.

When at last I hear electricity pumping through the length of the train and the hydraulic doors begin to hiss I raise my head and the first thing I see sitting opposite me next to my father is a ragged Boer, his arms resting on two aluminium crutches, staring cock-eyed at me. Of all the places he could sit he chooses the white ghetto on a black train. As the doors seal he places his hand on mine. I am too startled to resist. Quite gently he takes my hand, places it to his chin and rotates his jaw. Through my fingers it feels like he has a mouthful of rocks.

He lets go of my hand. 'My jaw's pinned together with wire. I've got a metal plate in my skull. I got metal rods from thigh to ankle in both legs.' He sounds quite proud of it.

My father introduces the wry note. 'Stay clear of magnets, friend.'

'*Ja*!' he laughs. 'And lightning. In thunder I dive straight under the table.'

As the train clatters forward he moves deeper into his declaration of endurance. We sit there hostage to his story. He tells us how he served with the Defence Force in Angola and stepped on a landmine; that did for his legs. Disabled out of the Defence Force he drove a truck for a while on his metal pins, until he was hijacked and his head smashed with a crowbar. The hijackers were white men, he adds, still unable to conceive of such a thing.

He is going to Maitland for his weekly treatment, at the Alexandra Care and Rehabilitation centre. The hospital, he says, is full of kaffirs who just lay in bed with nothing seriously wrong with them, snapping their fingers at the nurses, making them dance like their slaves. It's all fucked up now, this country, now the kaffirs are calling the shots. They get free medical aid, welfare support, jobs, while he has to pay his own hospital bills.

The Boer is as colour blind as he is crippled, living as he does in the townships. I guess they let him live because he's already one of the walking dead.

As the train decelerates for Maitland he asks us for money. Dad digs into his trousers and palms the man 5 rand. As the train stops in the station he eases himself out of the seat on his crutches and paddles to the door.

'You know . . . it's not the kaffirs that fucked you up,' Dad says to him. 'Your own race conscripted you into the army and two white guys hijacked your truck.' As the man alights from the train, Dad adds, 'That was worth five rand.'

*

The landlord of the Kornhoop greets my father with the same brief on the dangers facing the white traveller. A bit too late, I think. Dad lets the warnings roll off his back. When he is through the landlord tells me I've got e-mail. I wonder if he's read it or not.

'We've had my car stolen,' I explain.

'From where?'

'Langa.'

'Langa! Jesus Christ!' He looks contemptuously at me. 'Don't tell the car hire company that or they won't let you have another one. Do you want another car?'

'Yes.'

'I'll give them a call. My laptop's in the kitchen.'

He shows my father his room as I fire up the laptop.

> From: Natasha.r@goldstein.wolff.co.uk
> To: Kornhoop@iafrica.com
> Subject: For attention of Mark McLuhan

I've taken the liberty of finding out some things re: your adversaries, from Compliance. The broker you mentioned, James Willmot, works for a small house of thirty-five employees. In the past eighteen months he's made over twenty requests to purchase interests in several banking funds on Joel Sugarman's behalf. What's suspicious is the way he sold each of those interests after just a few weeks. The transactions made J.S. a loss, from the charges incurred, but he seems prepared to sacrifice yield and performance for the purpose of obtaining the cloak of legitimacy for his money. It looks like he's layering cash, instructing his broker to integrate plain vanilla into derivatives instruments.

The corporate culture Willmot belongs to is so ego-driven he may have gone wilfully blind to his company's money-laundering avoidance rules. Even if suspicions about J.S. were raised there's now a powerful set of reasons to do nothing about it. The broker's in a struggling business and can't afford to turn any clients away.

Compliance are regarding this as serious enough to merit passing on their findings to the Financial Services Board in Cape Town. The South African financial market is not a palm-fringed jurisdiction and the FSB can act on suspicion only in the pursuit of flying money. They may demand Willmot give access to his client's accounts. If they do, then J.S. will have to show legal receipts for his cash profits. If he can't they may go to the Attorney General to prosecute them both. But that could take years, which I don't think you've got.

Natasha

> This communication is for informational purposes only.
> It is not intended as an offer or solicitation for the pur-
> pose or sale of any financial instrument or as an official
> confirmation of any transaction, unless specifically
> agreed otherwise. All market prices, data and other
> information are not warranted as to completeness or
> accuracy and are subject to change without notice. Any
> comments or statements made herein do not neces-
> sarily reflect those of Goldstein Wolff incorporated, its
> subsidiaries and affiliates.

The same Afrikaner who rented me the first car comes to the Kornhoop with a Nissan Micra. He confiscates quite a lot of money from my credit card before getting me to sign the paperwork. Meanwhile my father has showered and dressed back in the only clothes he possesses. I worry a little because tonight we have been invited to dinner at the Willmots'. Joel and Hannah are bringing Geena. I don't want him to look like a pauper. I don't want them to gain an unfair advantage over him. I don't even tell him the content of Natasha's e-mail.

The Willmots' house is situated just off the Main Road artery at Constantia, surrounded by a high wall crowned with razor wire, arc lights on the corner posts, 'Armed Response' shields bolted onto the electronic gates, burglar bars on all the windows. We drive inside the compound and park on gravel under the over-hanging branches of an acacia tree. As the gates roll shut on oiled castors we get out and walk, following the moist emerald lawn to the swimming pool marbled with midnight-blue Turkish tiles. The whole garden smells fragrant. A trellis canopy over the pool is entwined with bougainvillea and jasmin. Jennifer and James Willmot are sitting by the pool on garden furniture. They both rise to their feet as I introduce my father.

James decides there is a nip in the air and invites us inside the house. Three rooms interconnect through open double doorways. Each room is large, with high wooden ceilings. The walls in one room are painted lime; lemon and pink in the other two. There are stuffed sofas scattered everywhere, apart from in the dining room, where the oak table has been laid for supper, with Sicilian plates, silver candleholders and tall cut-glass wine goblets. I wonder where their son, Kenno, is, and whether he is joining us tonight.

We are the first to arrive at the Willmots'. James leaves his wife to entertain us in the lime room while he goes to open some wine in the kitchen. Jennifer starts telling Dad that she and James are from Muswell Hill in north London, as I browse through their large collection of CDs, vinyl and tapes. I read the names – Ladysmith Black Mombasa, Johnny Clegg, The Dark City Sisters – off the sleeve notes as Jennifer adds to her back-ground story: 'This house would be well beyond our means in London.'

James reappears with a bottle of chilled Stellenbosch

chardonnay and clutching four iced glasses at their stems, like a bouquet of petrified lilies. He serves my father first, who stands stiffly with the wine glass in his hand.

He asks my father what work he does.

'I'm retired now, but I used to be a hospital porter.'

'Me too,' I add for ballast. 'Still am.'

'I teach at a university for blacks and coloureds,' Jennifer says, as if there could be some connection.

James smiles wryly at me. 'You told me you were a student.'

'And you told me your wife taught in a kaffir college.'

Jennifer sees the evening getting pulled out of shape and tries to rescue the situation. 'I teach European literature.'

'To black South Africans?'

She fences back, 'Yes. Unashamedly. European literature is simply better than black South African writing. Black literature falls somewhere between agit-prop and social realism. If they choose to reject the books on the syllabus that's fine by me. But it's a stronger student who rejects Eurocentric literature than accepts an impoverished form.'

'How do you call into question the colonial order with literature that uses its terms and procedures?' I ask. 'I would have thought metafiction . . .'

'Like Coetzee, you mean?'

'Possibly.'

'Where does a hospital porter learn about Coetzee and metafiction?'

My father adds: 'When I lived here black Africans were forced to learn Afrikaans. Colour in pictures of Voortrekkers. Assimilate stuff like South Africa began when Diaz rounded the Cape. What's changed?'

Jennifer rattles her sabre again. 'I don't think you know how the education system in this country works, Mr McLuhan . . .'

'Call me Clement.'

'My students come from the townships. They have very low

levels of education and even lower self-esteem. English is not their first language. But I do not patronise them with simple works of literature. I give them the greats.'

Jennifer excuses herself on the pretext of tending to dinner in the kitchen, followed by James.

'Better take it easy, Dad,' I whisper. 'We've got a whole night to get through.'

'I don't know how the education system works!' he mimics Jennifer.

From outside the house I hear the electronic gates roll open and tyres crunching gravel. I know who this is but my father seems oblivious. Moments later Hannah walks into the room where we stand, followed by Joel. Behind Joel is Geena, in green combat trousers and a low-cut vest.

My father clocks her, but dampens any urge he may have to embrace her, leaving the first moves to her. The last time they saw one another they'd hardly been on speaking terms.

The real object of his fascination is Hannah and Joel. Why do the ones who abandon us intrigue us more than those who stay?

Geena does make the first move and advances across the Kilm to embrace Dad tentatively. There is an exchange of pleas- antries, platitudes until she asks, 'Why have you come? You've come to see me, but why have you come?'

'I think you've answered your own question,' Joel laughs from behind her.

'This is my dad,' Geena says and for a moment Joel and Dad look at one another, not sure who has earned the title.

Geena raises her eyebrows at me: this is going to be some night.

Joel steps forward and shakes my father's hand.

'This is my wife, Hannah.'

Hannah asserts, 'It's a pleasure to be able to thank you from the bottom of my heart.'

'For what?' Dad replies.

'Don't be so dumb,' Geena says. Hannah puts her arm around Geena and I see Dad wince.

James and Jennifer reappear in the room. Joel kisses Jennifer, and embraces James. Hannah kisses both the Willmots. My father looks marooned, the drink in his hand untouched.

This is the first time I've seen Geena with her parents, who crowd around her, their fulfilment in the bag. I stand firmly at my father's side. The floor opens up between us, our emotion smoking up the room.

'How's your epilepsy?' Dad asks.

'I don't have any anxieties; I don't have those. So no absences, pre-seizures, hallucinations.'

Hannah speaks to Dad from across the divide. 'We've worked on that problem, haven't we, Geena? We sit together in a darkened room with our eyes closed and concentrate our thoughts on a little spittle in the mouth. Then we swallow the spit, taking the malfunctions of the brain into the healing heart.'

Dad looks wretchedly at her. 'I always thought when you swallow, the spittle goes to the stomach.'

'What's the ETA on dinner?' Joel asks.

'A few minutes,' Jennifer says. 'I hope you're all hungry.'

'Starving,' Joel replies.

James seats us at the table, placing Geena between Dad and Joel, with Hannah next to me on the other side. I notice a little card above my plate with my name on it. Same for Hannah, for everyone. James pours wine and then takes his seat at the head of the table. From the kitchen Jennifer carries an ostrich casserole in a large earthenware pot.

Hannah begins tossing the salad in a glass bowl. 'Nice salad spoons, Jennifer. Are they from Zulu/Natal?'

'KwaZulu/Natal,' Joel corrects her.

'I love them, they're carved.' Each lettuce leaf that flies out

188

of the bowl she picks up in her fingers and stuffs into her mouth.

They make my father the centre of attention. He twists in his chair as they ask about his South African heritage. He does not touch his food, his cutlery exactly where it was placed, and tells them that his mother was housekeeper to an Afrikaner family, in charge of their black domestic servants, about twelve in all.

He shines the light back on them. 'Your maid and gardener . . . how much do you pay them?'

'The going rate,' says James.

'Thirty pounds a month?'

'Two hundred rand, about thirty pounds, yes.'

'Each?'

'No, they're a married couple.'

'Quite a bargain.' The Willmots' rip and tear at the ostrich casserole like a murder of crows.

'In my mother's day the servants slept in a bunk house in the backyard and ate outside off enamel plates – same as the dogs.' My father watches them squirm with obvious relish. 'The family only used to talk to them when they wanted the swimming pool skimmed or the toilets cleaned, their babies nursed when they were sick.' He shouts in Afrikaans: '*Waas die boy!* . . . Even the children ordered them about like that. Kids eight or nine speaking with a voice like a jackhammer, obese because they'd never get out of a chair if a servant was around to fetch something they wanted. The family never saw where their servants went on their weekends off, knew nothing of their lives in the townships.'

Geena lays down her fork. She takes what my father has said as her cue. 'I know how they live. Belhar, Crossroads, Khayelitsha; I've been to all those places.'

'Which village in Khayelitsha?' Dad asks briskly.

'Village four. Ernie has a club on Christmas Tinto.'

'Christmas Tinto?' James says. 'Is that a street?'

'Tell us about Ernie?' Dad asks.

'He likes me because I'm the only one who can tame his orphan girl. An orphan like me.'

'You're not an orphan!' Hannah smiles.

'I just have the identity of one.'

'We all assume several identities before we find the one we really want,' says Joel.

'If you have an identity crisis this is the country to be,' James laughs. 'Everyone has an identity crisis here. Several identity crises.'

'What's the girl's name?' Dad asks.

'Kubasni.'

'This Ernie Sisulu, he trades in prostitution?'

Geena's face repeals the hostility she last showed him in London. 'He's given me a job. Which is more than I had in England.'

'So what's the pension scheme like?' I ask. Geena stares at me with prejudice.

Dad twists round to face Joel over the top of Geena's head. 'You got her this job with the gangster, is that right?'

'To call Ernie a gangster is a prejudice, Clement. You've been away too long. In townships the black economy is the economy.'

'But you got her the job?'

'These things follow their own course,' Joel replies. 'Geena makes her own plans. I just facilitate them.'

'Lay off, Dad!' Geena says.

'This is confusing,' Dad smiles. 'Two fathers at the same table.'

Joel cups his chin in his hands. 'Have you heard of that Chinese proverb, Clement? "If you love your children, send them on their travels".'

Dad makes sure he has good eye contact with Joel. 'Is that

190

what you were thinking when you put Geena up for adoption?'

'We didn't put her up for adoption.' Hannah's voice shakes with emotion.

'Ever think about coming back, Clement, to the new South Africa?' James Willmot's postage-stamp moustache glistens with ostrich stock. 'Workers are allowed to go on strike now. And what do they do? They dance. Illegal immigrants are leaving because the crime rate's too high.' He laughs a version of his son's manic roar, seeking approbation from his friends.

'I thought you'd respect that I work in a township,' Geena says, 'rather than serve drinks in the yacht club.'

'We aren't political,' Jennifer throws in. 'One way or another.'

'Who wants more wine?' James asks.

As he serves wine, I get up from the table to use the bathroom. I don't need a piss, I need R&R and float around the house, exploring what looks to be Kenno's bedroom. On the walls are posters of Springbok rugby stars, the British band Prodigy and black rappers NWA. I make a loop back to Geena's childhood; her room in London twins with this one. They are both children trapped in adult bodies.

I walk back into the dining room in time to hear Geena say to Dad, 'We're sailing to Robben Island on Friday. Me, Joel and Kenno.'

'Where is Kenno tonight?' I ask.

Joel replies, 'He had to work, skippering one of my charter boats around Table Bay.'

'He works for you too?' I ask.

'Kenno has always worked for me. He's my *poes*.'

'We can't land on Robben Island though,' Geena resumes. 'It's a national museum, or something.'

'When we first came to South Africa,' Hannah adds. 'When we first came here we could. We used to sail in a flotilla from the yacht club for a champagne picnic on Ladies Rock.'

'Did you visit Mandela while you were there?' Dad asks.

191

Joel's lips stretch tight. 'Let me tell you something, Clement. When Genghis Khan wanted to invade Japan he had four thousand ships built. Japan hadn't a hope in hell. Then a hurricane blew up out of nowhere and sunk the entire fleet.' He pauses to take another toke on his wine, then bangs the empty glass down on the table. 'Life is what life is, is what I mean. You have to make the best of it.'

Dad leans back and knits his hands behind his head. 'You know, Joel, I've seen a lot of Englishmen like you making it big here, because there was never any competition from the nine other tribes who also live here. They were barred from entering business, the skilled trades. But there's a price you're going to have to pay for that. In order to stay on here you're going to have to start over again, with nothing. Otherwise you're all going to be killed, picked off one by one until you are all gone.'

'It's worse than I thought.' Dad is sombre as we are driving back to the guest house. 'Those people are too cute to be believed. Geena's been completely seduced by them, their glamorous evil.'

'I don't think they're evil. Glamorous, maybe.'

'Maybe you don't know enough yet to make judgements, Mark.'

'So what am I missing?'

He tells me that the great deception among white South Africans is they think they've achieved redemption by removing apartheid. He says they're fooling only themselves. It has been removed only in the pejorative sense. But his worst contempt is reserved for people like the Willmots, Joel and Hannah who emigrated here during the troubles. 'They're opportunists. They got well heeled only because the dice were loaded in their favour. It's a rigged market. There is absolutely no credibility in their achievements. I couldn't swallow a mouthful of their dinner. There's a cancer on the vines from where they bled their wine. Let's go get a hamburger somewhere. I'm starving.'

'Hamburger, at this hour?'

'They dump their child onto the adoption services. She returns and they act like she's been off to boarding school for the past thirty years. These people look out for themselves only. You know Geena's problem? Her desire for identity has overpowered her moral principles.'

I finally tell him about Natasha's e-mail message, how, in her bank's opinion, James Willmot is probably laundering cash for Joel on the stock market.

'I think we should try to find out what kind of partnership Joel has with this Ernie Sisulu, don't you?'

'How do we do that?'

'Through Erasmus. If he can't find out no one can.'

THE ENCHANTED ISLE

My father is eager to hitch a ride on Joel's yacht to Robben Island. He is prepared to humble himself before the man he calls white trash in order to keep Geena in his sights. He can work on her moral principles a bit more if he can be near her. I can't tell if he's driven by logic or by the emotion of a mourning parent, but since what drives my motives is less than clear, I do not try to dissuade him.

While he goes off to find Erasmus I prepare myself in the same way I always do before embarking on a trip: I read up on the place. In downtown Cape Town I find a second-hand volume on the history of Robben Island in Clarke's Bookstore (pay top dollar too) and sit with it in a café on Loop Street.

Reading the histories brings to mind *The Encantadas* that I was reading back in London. Like Melville's Isles, Robben Island is pervaded by a primordial evil affecting all who land there. The first sailors to arrive in the sixteenth century rowed ashore on a tender, scooping up penguins in their arms. Being their first encounter with Man these 'feathered fish' let themselves be herded from tender to ship like Noah's animals onto the Ark. They trusted and were eaten. Seals too were slaughtered, clubbed to death where they lay on the beach. One Dutch mariner noted in his log: 'Great numbers of sea-bears are found here which bleat like sheep but are very unlike them in taste, and for my part I could not eat them, nor the penguins, because they too much tasted of fish-oil, although most of our crew found them good and preferred them to bacon.'

From these first days of settlement Robben Island was used as a place of incarceration. Tribesmen captured during the frontier wars, leaders of resistance to the Dutch East India Company, Indian princes and Muslim holy men, British and Dutch convicts were all imprisoned there. A sanitorium was built for lepers, lunatics and women with 'vener' disease. They were brought to the island to convalesce in the fresh air, but found no cure. The original malady just got worse. The sick and the fragile complained of the damp, the glare and isolation. While out on their forced constitutionals they found themselves having to buckle down under howling south-easters and the great north-westerly gales lashing the island in curtains of rain. Perched on rocks in the harbour they would gaze at Cape Town nestling under Table Mountain at the foot of the Dark Continent, like a Dantesque terrestrial paradise viewed from purgatory.

From these sources it would seem that every governor employed to take charge of the inmates, the livestock, failed miserably as human beings. They allowed whole flocks of sheep to perish, let fire beacons go out causing ships to founder on the rocks and treated the sick and the criminal alike. They stood by as convicts raped the lunatics and the lunatics raped the lepers. Victorian Calvinists attempted reforms – clothing the naked inmates, introducing cricket, painting classes, fishing. Chaplains gave lessons on morality. Nurses were brought in to the leper colony. As an experiment in Rousseauian ethics, convicts were given parole and lunatics allowed to roam freely on the island. The lunatics drowned while having epileptic fits and the convicts combined forces with the lepers and killed the nurses. Together they commandeered the asylum and petitioned the Queen of England, demanding from her table napkins, beer to go with dinner, cruets and extra sugar for their tea and coffee. When they were eventually captured they were taken out in long boats, weights tied to their bodies and thrown into the deep.

This is how things stood up until and including the present day.

CAR WRECKERS

The charterers are a family of six just returned from Namibia. Four blond suntanned children run around on the pontoon, letting off steam after being cooped up for weeks. Kenno is hosing down the deck. Joel sits in the cockpit completing the paperwork with his customers, checking the logs. He shouts at Kenno to keep the hose pointed down, before going below. From inside the cabin he starts throwing soft bags into the cockpit. From the cockpit the charterer passes them to his wife on the pontoon, who loads the bags onto a trolley. They round up their children and set off for their car parked in the Waterfront, waving goodbye over their shoulders.

This is the moment my father chooses to make his move. With Erasmus trailing he steps onto the pontoon. On seeing them, Joel's smile falls off his face like a clam from a rock.

Dad makes his appeal to Joel. 'Need any more crew?'

'Not on this trip, china. Another day.'

'Where is Geena?'

'Geena's not here, Clement.'

'I thought she was sailing with you.'

'Sometimes plans change, you know?'

'So where is she?'

'Your guess is as good as mine.'

'I doubt it.' Dad's voice tumbles to the ground. 'See you when you get back.'

'I'm sure you will.'

The Waterfront is teeming with tourists as we watch from the quayside Joel's yacht skim silently out towards Table Bay, with the main sail halfway out. Seeing Kenno and Joel sip beers on deck I think I realise the attraction that sailing holds. Out at sea you can lose your mind and all its programmes. No emotion in the ocean. The sea is a clean slate. No one can come after you out there.

Dad says: 'Can we rent a boat somewhere to take us out?'

'Why, what for?' I ask. 'There's no Geena out there.'

'My instincts tell me to follow them.'

'Why do they not take us?' Erasmus asks. 'There was plenty of room. Is it because I am an African?'

'It's me they don't want on board,' Dad says.

'I have good idea,' Erasmus says. 'Follow me.'

He leads the way to the Robben Island ferry terminal. A hydrofoil stuffed with tourists is about to leave. Erasmus gets us onboard without a ticket on account of being an employee of the museum. From the deck we watch a family of Cape seals sleeping on a small landing beside the ferry. One of them wakes, belches and vomits a few dozen oyster shells before going back to sleep against his mate's stomach. Black and benign, they are cursed with a slowness of movement, making them easy prey for killer whales and sharks. Which is why they are here no doubt, in the safety of the Waterfront, an added attraction for the tourists.

We sit in the wheelhouse with the skipper, Kenneth, a friend of Erasmus's. Kenneth is a Transvaal Boer, with a handlebar moustache as stiff as a coat hanger. What strikes me most is how tight they seem to be. I ask Erasmus how they met and he tells me Kenneth had been a warder on Robben Island when he was a political prisoner. Now they both work for the National Museum that runs the island. I decide it would not be politic to probe any further.

Less than an hour later the island comes up on the prow like a raft floating on the sea, just as it did for Bartolomeu Diaz, Vasco de Gama. The tourists with their cameras and video recorders must be thinking the same thoughts as those early explorers and Dutch settlers who gazed through their telescopes and wondered: Is it possible to have pleasure on this island?

At the harbour the tourists are disgorged onto the island. As we step on land behind them I fancy that I can sense the enchantment. The sunlight dazes my senses and a droning sound emits from just above the threshold. We stroll past the gift and souvenir shop, which Erasmus informs me is run by Mandela's former warder.

'If you wish you can purchase pictures of Mandela's cell from there. Prison maps, biographies of heroes of the struggle.'

I wonder how Erasmus feels coming back. Is it possible for him to have pleasure on this island?

We board the coach, which does not go immediately to the prison but takes the tourists once around the island. Outside the leper cemetery (segregated even in death) they each take a few frames. In the quarry the guide tells us the glare on the lime wrecked the eyesight of the ANC's high command. At the beach, she points through the window at white crosses marking the sites of unsuccessful escapes by men so desperate they plunged into the icy sea to take their chances with the sharks.

The tour guide knows how to exploit all these histories. She knows that the deeper the misery, the greater the show. Tourism in a dystopia shows up the rust spots on the human soul.

Where the coach turns round for the prison tour, the three

of us get out. Erasmus makes the lighthouse, enveloped by shrub bushes, our destination.

Just a walk for Dad and me to the lighthouse; it is something quite monumental and profound for Erasmus. He keeps stopping every four metres. He takes a second to reprogramme an old habit of turning through 180 degrees as though he's reached the wall of his cell, before moving on, only to stop and repeat the whole thing. It's a staccato performance and a hushed one, as he takes the air, listening to the barely audible cacophony of insects underfoot and the sight of birds alighting the stumpy bushes.

Botanically, the island is pared down to a scattering of salt-blasted shrubs and stagnant ponds floating on limestone. It is not beautiful at all. 'How does it feel coming back to this wilderness, Erasmus?' I ask.

'It is better to face your demons than not, I think. This wilderness failed to conquer my faith, so it feels good to show tourists around my prison cell. Other men who were incarcerated here try to bury the memory. But I think it is wiser to recall painful memory. One should only bury the dead.'

The lighthouse keeper evolves out of an open garage; a black man of the shadows. He and Erasmus shoot the breeze for a moment before he opens the lighthouse for us. We climb the narrow winding staircase to the glass lens at the top from where we view the whole island through curved glass: its quarries, its jail – that grey hell by the harbour, where the coach has now arrived. I see springboks, ostriches, cormorants down on the ground, but no seals, no penguins.

Tied up at a disused jetty we spot Joel's yacht. Joel and Kenno are small, insignificant figures way down there on the surface of the Earth, carrying large bundles wrapped in green oilcloth on to the jetty. We watch as they walk into the scrub with their cargo over their shoulders.

'What are they doing?' I ask.

'Good question,' Dad replies. 'Shall we go and see?'

'Let us wait a little longer,' Erasmus cautions.

In the next half-hour Joel and Kenno make several journeys into the scrub carrying these bundles, returning empty handed each time. Eventually they cast off and set keel for the main-land. As the main sail and jib are raised we hear the engine cut. The light over the water, so blue when we arrived, begins receding from the earth by degrees.

It takes another twenty minutes to descend the lighthouse stairs and walk to Fire Hill and the old wooden jetty where Joel had moored. From there we retrace his and Kenno's path into the scrub. We discover nothing there but a car wreck just inside the bushes. Its engine has been removed and the tyres have rotted away, but otherwise the car is relatively undam-aged. On the windscreen someone has painted the score of the 1995 World Cup Rugby final: New Zealand 18 South Africa 19.

By now it is getting too dark to see and I suggest we get back to the mainland.

'I have a better suggestion,' Erasmus says. 'Tonight we stay on the island, have a good time. In the morning we come back here and make more extensive search in good light.'

'Stay here?' I repeat. 'Tonight?'

'Erasmus survived twenty years,' Dad says. 'One night won't kill you.'

'Besides,' Erasmus adds. 'We have missed the last ferry.'

When all the tourists are gone, when the island regains its com-posure, everyone with business on the island goes to the bar, a one-time abattoir. My father and Erasmus stick to the beer. I order double rums and Coke and in an hour I am drunk. But not so drunk that I hallucinate this: a dozen ex-political pris-oners in a merry tryst with their former warders; old enemies in one another's arms, dancing the *toi*, a township war dance.

As shocking is seeing my father right in amongst them, being all the things that he is not: loud, talkative, drunk, happy. What a change in form profound friendships can bring.

I hold my own on a stool at the bar. Ex-prisoners and ex-warders talk to me, occasionally all at the same time. 'This bar as you now see is only a short walk from the prison,' Erasmus says. 'But it took twenty years for me to get here.' He chuckles, his lively old eyes smiling, shoulders bouncing up and down inside his jacket. Another ex-prisoner from Venda (who can speak all eleven South African languages) says, 'My release date was 2003,' and he just chuckles too. 'The boundaries between prisoner and warder were very blurred,' Kenneth, the hydrofoil skipper adds. He reads the scepticism off my face. 'I know how that sounds to you. But we are like family now.' Erasmus puts an arm around Kenneth to confirm his remark. 'You must have forgiveness in this country, or the Devil will have His day again.' In His day, Erasmus continues, a university atmosphere prevailed among the prisoners, which accounts for their lack of bitterness. Before books, newspapers, radios were allowed on the island, the inmates held oral seminars in the lime quarry, teaching the younger men to understand the objective movement in history and their place in it. They saw the big picture, while many warders, who couldn't even read, shrivelled into nothing. I think of how this kind of education policy echoes my father's belief, that knowledge should not be shackled to commerce, that it should be more like the tenets of faith. It must stay pure to mean something, as a defence against tyranny and brutality. Erasmus adds: 'One day in the quarry we heard a child's cry. It was a little girl and it went through us like lightning. We stood there dead in our shoes. It was first time in ten years any of us had heard a child's voice.' But whoever she was the warders rushed her off before the prisoners could see her.

Around one in the morning women stroll into the bar to

claim their men. They dance together, the men and the women. Even my father gets waltzed around the floor. My drunken spirit continues to soar, seeing Mandela's vision of a racist-free, fully integrated society coming close to being achieved on the very ground where the National Party sinned its worst.

My father belongs to this dignified past. I feel proud of him, and frightened for Geena because her father belongs to the warped past. She is never so far from my thoughts that I can forget what I'm here for. My father has similar thoughts. He gathers a few old comrades around the bar to discuss the topography of the island, and where contraband could be hidden safely.

In these days of liberty Kenneth, Erasmus and the others see themselves as keepers of the island's true legacy. It must never become a freak show. The struggle is now a quixotic one, pitched against Harvard students' requests to hold raves in the courtyard of B section, and property developers who want to build a five-star hotel, an airport, gambling casino and golf course on the island. This consortium of white men insists the botanic value of the island is minimal, that the marine reserves are less rich than expected, thus clearing the path for their business plans. McDonald's yellow arches may soon be appearing outside the leper cemetery.

To defend the island against these men the tour guides have done their own survey of the island's flora and fauna, etc. And so they know the area around Fire Hill where we watched Joel unload his cargo. They know all about the car wreck.

'That was Frikkie Joubert's official car, remember him? He governor here in the seventies and eighties. The man who put Sobukwe in solitary on separate compound. This king among men! Once when we taken by bus to the lime quarry we saw him led from his cell. Sobukwe, he took handful of earth and let it slip through his fingers. So we would remember our motto, "Sons of the soil".'

'I was his warder,' Kenneth says. 'On the six to one p.m. shift. Sobukwe would share his food with *me*, man!'

'This Frikkie Joubert, what a bastard. He cut back our visiting rights to one every six months, stood over us as we talked through the screen. For thirty minutes our families would help us remember our lost identity. If anything political was mentioned, old Frikkie would cut the visit short.'

'If that is his car,' Erasmus says, 'we must look at it again. In my heart I know that car will reveal something to us. That car is devilish sacrament, you understand.'

The party ends around 3 a.m. Erasmus escorts us to the guest house where we have been given a room for the night. His ability to navigate through pitch darkness impresses me, as my father sings slurringly at his side. As we make distance I ask Erasmus what he was imprisoned for, twenty years ago.

'I was *accused* of going to Cuba, the Soviet Union, Egypt and Nigeria for military training.'

'And did you?' I ask.

'Oh yes!' he says. 'I was recruited into the military wing by Chris Hani and Joe Slovo, you see.'

We pour into the guest room, laughing. An Afrikaner girl in pajamas appears on the threshold. She and her family are staying in the adjoining room, visiting the island for the fishing apparently, and we have woken her. Curiosity fights with anger in her expression at such a drunken mixed race reverie.

She steps further into the room. 'Why are you back so late?' she says.

'Excuse us for misbehaving, miss.' Erasmus stays as polite as he can. 'But whose island is this?'

I can't remember what time I drifted off to sleep but when I come too for a moment I think I'm in the hospital, surrounded by Mavis, Ginger and BJ in the porters' mess. It is a blissful sensation, as the bright morning spreads across the walls. But soon I discover I am laid out on a bathroom floor, with a towel under my head. When I try to move, my head stays on the towel, poisoned and protesting. I remember things. I remember twin beds in a room. My father snoring. The floorboards creaking under my feet as I escaped to the bathroom to be sick.

When my father appears in the bathroom he says nothing at all to me, as if such sights as this were normal. He leans against the wall to pee into the toilet bowl. I have never seen my father with a hangover and I do not care to see him with one again. He has crawled out of bed in the same clothes he came off the plane wearing. His tie is still knotted around his collar. Fumes rise off his skin and his buff trousers are spotted with blood from where he'd cut himself sometime during the night.

Erasmus arrives to take us to the mess for breakfast and we walk there in an ill silence. The glare of the sun hurts my eyes. The mess is packed with tour guides, ex-warders, cooks and cleaners watching a Mickey Mouse cartoon on the TV with the sound turned off. We are given large enamel bowls of porridge and mugs of weak tea. It is as much as we can do to drink the tea before staggering back into the light from the gloaming. It is on everyone's mind what we have to do.

As Dad and Erasmus look inside the car wreck, I open the boot. There are oilcloth bundles on the floor. I am still quite drunk as I untie two leather belts fastened around one of the oilcloths, and jump back quickly when I see snakes spilling out of the oilcloth. I peer again into the boot. They aren't snakes at all but metal barrels, all greased up.

I shout to my father and Erasmus. They run around the car to the boot and Erasmus throws up his hands. 'Lo and behold!' Then he astounds us both. Pulling back the oilcloths he chants: '9mm Super Stars. Walther P38s. Berettas. M92 Lugers. R4s. R5s. 9mm Uzis. Two Sterling L2A3 submachine guns . . .' He covers them over again with the oilcloth, as one would a corpse. 'All Defence Force issue.'

205

'And they are Joel's . . .' My father makes the connection.

'I have heard charter boats going to Southern Namibia, someone there boards the vessel when the sailors are at luncheon and hides weapons or drugs on the vessel. The sailors return without knowing they carry this cargo.'

'You'd make a convincing Inspector Poirot,' I say.

Erasmus smiles vainly. 'You are too generous.'

'Do we go to the police?' I ask.

Erasmus laughs. 'No, my friend. Many in the police belong to a third force. If Joel is selling arms in the townships, as I suspect, they would encourage him.'

'Why would he do that, sell arms?' I ask.

'He is an adventurer, no?'

'So this was the prison governor's car,' Dad says.

'Ah yes.'

We stand around the car in a state of painful frigidity. The deadlock is broken when Erasmus bends down and picks up a large rock. He raises the rock above his head and hurls it at the windscreen. The laminated glass folds around the rock. He picks up another and dumps it onto the bonnet. Then my father joins in. He and Erasmus laugh as Dad smashes the headlights with a stone.

Then the laughing stops. It dries up on their faces, which become contorted with rage. In concert they pull rocks out of the ground and begin to smash every piece of glass there is on the prison governor's car, the rear window, the side windows, the rear lights. I would be embarrassed by the sight of these old men pelting the vehicle with whatever will come out of the ground, but it is too serious for that.

After they have dented the bodywork and broken all the glass, Erasmus, heaving for breath, gets in behind the wheel. Still in his state of frenzy, Dad rolls up his sleeves and starts to push the car on its wheelrims. The blood pumps through his limbs and raises his tattoos like blisters on his forearms. The car begins to roll down the slope. As it gains momentum, Erasmus jumps out and helps Dad push. They get a good speed up as the car rolls out of the scrub and onto the jetty. They let go just before the car plunges into the water. In silence they stand shoulder to shoulder watching the car, with its weapons, slowly sinking into the ocean until there is nothing left of it to see.

THE GREAT SWEET
MOTHER

At the beach house Hannah is all alone, pacing barefoot across the polished wood floors. Her white lace skirt hovers on a breeze blowing through the open French doors. In her hand she has a well-bitten drink. A quart of vodka perched on the rattan bamboo coffee table is half empty. It is eleven in the morning.

'You want a drink?' she asks both of us.

Dad shakes his head. 'No thanks, but you go ahead.'

She freshens her drink and tops it up with tonic water. Her eyes magnify through the bottom of her upended glass.

'Where is Geena, Hannah?' Dad asks gently.

'Geena? I don't know.'

'What about Joel?'

'Don't know.' She drifts away from us, borne back into the past. 'When we first came here we lived in this Bedford van. Now look at us.' She laughs briefly and drains of colour. Her eyes turn down. 'Are you sure you don't want a drink?'

'This was in the sixties, right?' Dad settles into a faded pink sofa.

'*Ja*, end of the sixties.' She stares at her reflection in the mirror above the mantel, searching for all the intervening years, then turns to meditate on the empty ocean. 'When we first came, in those days you could drive thirty clicks out of Cape Town and not see another car. It was full of animals, flowers like you never see in England. Those fynbos, you know?' She pauses to catch something moving out at sea. There is nothing there that I can see. 'I don't know where Geena is,' she repeats, her words slurred.

'You like the sea, don't you?' Dad says.

'Very much. Each wave, you know? Each one's a happening.'

'Swinburne called the sea a great sweet mother,' I tell her. 'Like you . . . a sweet mother.' And she falls for it.

'Joel didn't want children. He just wanted to be out there all the time.' She points towards the ocean. 'When Geena was a baby he went away a lot, hitching rides on yachts as crew. Sometimes I wouldn't see him for months when he was delivering . . . Durban, Mozambique, places like that. It was just Geena and me, in this house.' There is a shake in her voice, as though she still fears absence.

Then she brightens, far too fast. 'After Joel bought his first yacht we've never wanted for anything. He bought one boat, then two, then three. Now he has a fleet.'

'How did he raise the initial capital?'

'I don't really know,' she says and I believe her. She is as blind to how Joel raises money as she is to most other things of this world. How Joel makes money, makes *them* money, she doesn't see. Not because she chooses not to see, but because she has no way of judging character.

'Hannah,' Dad cuts in. 'You are Geena's mother. But you lost her. How did that happen?'

She looks at him through bleary eyes. 'I'm not sure I should tell you.'

Dad leaps out of his seat, pours her another drink.

'I mean, it's none of your business, really, is it?'

'Of course it is.' His raised voice inhibits her. Hannah picks up her replenished glass then puts it down again immediately.

'Drugs was definitely our scene then. Like alcohol was to my parents . . .' She stalls. The mention of her parents springs a trap.

'But now you drink,' Dad pushes her, 'like your parents.'

'Oh, you know . . .' she laughs, a dry flat howl. 'It means a lot to me to see her again.'

She moves suddenly towards my father in an attempt to embrace him. Dad holds her off at arm's length. Hannah drifts off to stand inside a circle of wax that has dripped from the candle chandelier onto the wood floor.

'Are you hurting, you and your wife?'

'Yes, yes of course we are.'

'I suppose,' she sighs, 'you have a right to know what happened.' She becomes coherent now, her voice clearing. 'Joel and me, we were out of it on acid. There. I've said it.'

'Said what? Go on.'

'We were all sitting at the kitchen table when Geena started making small noises in her throat and fell off her chair. We couldn't raise her. We took her to the hospital, the doctors pumped her little tummy. At the Groote Schuur. They kept her overnight to run blood tests and when we went back the next day there were police and social workers waiting for us. LSD had showed up in her blood tests. I think she'd eaten one of our micro-dots lying around the kitchen.' The tears come now, welling in her eyes. 'They let me carry her to the social worker's car. On a glorious summer's day in January I held her in my arms. I smelled her hair.'

She stops to gather breath. Outside the Atlantic waves make the sound of canvas ripping. The sky is a hard dish shuddering pink and yellow from the dalliances of the sun, its hypocritical pure light pouring onto the water. The outline of the mountains in the east seem fluid, muffled by stacks of cloud.

'Just one little mistake, one silly mistake and they took her away from me.' Hannah walks to the fireplace and takes a hard steady look at herself crying in the mirror. 'Geena was taken from me like a sack of potatoes. I put my hands together, you know, like I'm praying? And she copied me, sitting in the back of the social worker's car. She put her hands together.'

I watch Hannah weeping silently, feeling as indifferent to her as to the ocean outside. My earliest memory of Geena as a young girl was the way she used to place her hands together in bed, at the table. No one knew why. Now I know why she stopped. She stopped praying when she lost faith.

I feel a strong urge to be alone, away from all parents, and remove myself onto the patio. The sequence of events roll over in my head. Geena aged three, sees a micro-dot on a table and eats it – and the seeds of her personality are indelibly forged. But mine also, *before I am even born*.

The wooden house seems to float under me. I seek out something concrete in the past to anchor myself to, when Geena and I were children – the time she set fire to some ferns on the disused railway line. When the fire got out of control she ran home and then a policeman came to our flat. I heard my mother talking to him at the door and Geena's name used. I went into the kitchen, cut a piece of fruit cake and wrapped it in greaseproof paper. I put the cake in Geena's hands and told her to run, run away from home. I helped her out of the bedroom window, using a sheet to lower her to the ground.

My instincts now have reversed. I am trying to rope her back in, play the escape backwards.

I walk across the beach to where they are surfing out at the kray fishery. To get a closer look I climb over the rocks that are pungent with rotting kelp. Beetles scatter out of the kelp and into fissures. The sea licks at my feet. I look up and the surf is like a storm in the sky. Foaming escarpments fifteen feet in height explode, sending up shrapnel of atomised water particles. Galileo once described nature as an encyclopedia that can be read as a text. I see no text in the sea.

I retreat to a slip road where several cars are parked in the dunes. Men in various stages of undress strip the UV covers off their surfboards, remove leather caps from the sharp fibre-glass tips. One man massages his board, as though it were a living organism. They are mature men, unlike the schoolboys who surf the more protected breaks of False Bay. They are reserved and unsmiling as they make mental preparations, contemplating the man-eating waves marching silently lee-ward. There are no signs of celebration, no cries of joy. But having come this far, at some point they have to enter the water and face their fears.

They do not take their eyes off the ocean.

There is only one girl around, in a blue sweatshirt and grey pin-striped skirt over bare suntanned legs. In the dunes she picks wild flowers to put in her long hair, bleached white by the sun. I catch this Afrikaaner beauty's eye and she smiles back at me. I see no fear in her face. I think of how Geena and I used to pick wild flowers and how such innocence can never be retrieved. It is a once in a lifetime thing. The unconscionable ocean pounding the white toneless sand frightens me. I can hear my own name called in the wild.

I catch a glimpse of a surfer as a wave is breaking over him. Seconds later his flimsy board is sent spinning in the wind, the leash that connects board to surfer taut, the surfer himself trapped inside the internal combustion of the wave. I wait for a long time for him to show. I begin to fear for him. The girl con-tinues to pick flowers. When next I see him he is paddling up a sheer glass wall, flailing his arms, his tail fins popping out of the water as he goes over the top.

I follow his progress to the reef beyond the kray fishery, the pilgrimage objective. He is identifiable from other surfers by the bright pink panels in his wetsuit. The rip is so strong he is having to constantly paddle across the bay to stay in position. He keeps trying for waves, backing out at the last moment, losing faith. Finally he catches a wave. He accelerates down the blue face before disappearing behind a curtain of tumbling white water marbled with sapphire. He reappears like a high soprano, bulleting up the face that is stretched like skin, and throws himself off the top. I can sense his relief from the beach as he falls like Icarus into the trough behind the wave.

From above the beach I watch the waves for a very long time, hurling frosty clouds into the sky, through which seagulls hover on the wing. What I see comforts me. The bigger sets always seem to travel in groups of three. A prime number. A *trinity*. There *is* order to nature. Someone's hand is at work.

I brim over with a desire to share this discovery. I say to the Afrikaaner with flowers in her hair: 'Galileo was right,' and she beams me a beatific smile.

My dad is ready to leave when I return. Hannah has given him some vague coordinates where we might find Geena. We get going to pick up Erasmus so he may lead us into the unknown.

> From: Natasha.r@goldstein.wolff.co.uk
> To: Kornhoop@iafrica.com
> Subject: For attention of Mark McLuhan

I've seen my two children for the first time in four years. We played in the living room at their father's house, while he went out for a walk. We had two hours together. They are so thrilled to be with me it's painful. I don't deserve such love. I cried when I left them. Their father is willing for me to take them to my flat for the next visit. If that goes all right I might have them to stay over. I hope they like cats. If not, then sorry, cats, you're going to have to go.

It's not your children who hold you back. It is your love of your children that holds you back. Some parents do not want to be held back by their kids and desert the flock. I believed myself to be one of these people, that I was making a rational decision to be free. I thought family was a kind of holy prison, and mathematics became my escape from its painful sadness, from being slave to ever shifting desires.

214

My children have helped me revise my position. I do not want to give up on those who love me. I do not want to break free of those bonds. Which makes me understand you more now, Mark, why you are so possessive over your loved one. But I want to tell you before your platonic love gets metamorphosed into sexual love, that you have to feel desire first. Do you feel desire? And, if so, do you feel ashamed of the desire?

Natasha

SURFACE TENSION

Physical desire cannot withstand physical fear. It is easily displaced by danger and goes beyond reach so long as the danger lasts.

Erasmus drives us to Belhar, stopping outside a rickety tavern in the heart of the township. A line of expensive four-wheel drives and Mercedes is parked outside in the dark. Erasmus takes a moment to share some lightweight information. 'These are the safest vehicles in South Africa. No one dare steal these cars because they belong to the gangsters sitting inside.'

'How do you know this?' Dad asks.

'My intelligence is still good.'

The first thing I see as I enter the tavern is the young Indian girl, Kubasni, lighting men's cigars and cigarettes with a trembling hand. They are all sitting around a table. The second thing I see is Geena serving them Coca-Cola, a Cinderella figure among these big men with shorn heads and dressed in designer sports gear. Joel Sugarman is also here, his face shining like a lantern.

We cause immediate consternation in a dozen trigger fin-

gers by simply walking in unannounced. I feel curiously
detached. I have never seen a gun fired in my life, and what
these bodyguards hold in their hands seem more like toys. I do
not believe them.

This is the theory. In reality if it wasn't for Erasmus our
future might have been bleak.

Ernie Sisulu gestures with his arm and the bodyguards back
off. The six crime entrepreneurs at the table all appear to know
Erasmus, and are respectful. They know him as a political, an
untouchable with special status. One such privilege afforded
him is, you don't tell lies to him. So when he asks a straight
question of Ernie he receives a straight answer.

He asks why Geena is needed in this meeting and Sisulu
points at Joel and replies in Xhosa. Erasmus translates for us:
'He says Geena is his guarantee against this white man betray-
ing them.'

Joel shrinks hearing this information. What he might have
hitherto thought secure is not confirmed.

Erasmus asks Sisulu again to release Geena into our cus-
tody. Sisulu laughs and says, this time in English: 'You walk
into our meeting uninvited and try to trade with me? What
with do you come here demanding things of me?' He sees the
determination in Erasmus and adds, 'When the deal is complete, maybe then you can have her.'

'What deal is this?' Erasmus asks.

Since he cannot tell lies to Erasmus he explains the problem
like it is. 'The Islamic brothers. Oh boy, what a headache
they've become for Dixies, Hard Livings, Mongrels, the
Respectable Jesters. The deal, the deal that is going to solve
our mutual problem, is guns. But stronger weapons than the
pistols and shotguns we possess.'

He reveals how he and the other gang leaders (enemies for
so long, now historically convening) have foot soldiers
amounting to several hundred men who they want armed with

military weapons. This is where Joel enters the picture. Joel has offered to be their armourer.

'For us to trust a white man, he has to offer a security,' he adds, pointing at Geena. 'This you will understand, Erasmus.'

Geena stares at Sisulu, at Joel. If she believed she had a job running Sisulu's taverns, acting as mentor to the Indian girl, she now knows she's been used as bait. In the background I hear my father's gently coaxing voice, trying to reason with her. It is calm and fearless. 'I want to bring you back into the safety of those who love you, Geena, if it's the last thing I do in my life.'

She does not move. She is rooted to the ground. I see her begin to tremble as Dad snatches at her arm, trying to shake her to her senses. She breaks into a sweat, her hands flicker by her side, eyes roll up into her skull. For the next few moments she is lost to everyone in the room. She occupies a space all her own.

The gangsters appear quite frightened by her seizure, as though she is possessed. Men who give and take life as casually as cigarettes are highly superstitious and look at Geena as though their luck is about to change for the worse.

Geena revives and returns, almost. She tells everyone that she's just seen two naked people making love; making love and surrounded by fire. Joel hears this and laughs. 'Hey, how did you do that? You were only a small kid when you used to watch us fuck in front of the fire.'

Sisulu has had enough of this family altercation. He relieves one of his bodyguards of his handgun and points it at my dad, standing in his cloth cap, his tie loose at his throat. 'There is no way I will shoot you, Erasmus,' Sisulu says, 'I cannot do that. But I'll shoot this mother if you don't all leave. I promise on my children's lives. He's a dead man unless you fade away.'

Geena flings herself between Dad and Sisulu. In different circumstances I might have celebrated this gesture of protection.

I notice that Joel does not move from his seat.

'I'll kill her as well, no problem,' Sisulu adds. 'I've done it before and I don't feel a thing.'

We have no choice but to back out of the tavern, without Geena. At the door Erasmus faces off with Sisulu standing there with his gun. 'In the past you and I fought a long war with a common enemy. What has happened to you Ernie? Now you are less than a man. You are nothing.'

'It hurts me to hear you say this to me. You are a hero, a prince among men. But this is the new politics, Erasmus. Religious war is the new war we have to fight.'

We back right up to where our car is parked. Erasmus takes the wheel and drives us around in circles, with tears in his eyes, crying hard for his country.

DEAD RECKONING

The afternoon starts off simply enough. The objective is clear in our minds. I'm sitting in the back seat of Kenno's car, skewering into the township of Guguletu. His casual jocularity belies the fact that we are carrying a few dozen hi-tech weapons in the boot. He acts like he's immune from judgement. This is a criminal activity but who is going to bring him to book? No police out here. The gangsters are more powerful than police and it is with them we are doing the trade. As far as Kenno is concerned it's all part of the adventure of living on the new frontier. Guns in the boot makes this boy feel like a man.

Sipho is riding up front with his cell phone open, speaking in Xhosa, breaking off the call every few seconds to tell Kenno to make a right, or a left. The streets have no names, just numbers. NY85, NY56 . . .

We are tracking down Sisulu by mobile phone. But as Sisulu is moving around, for security reasons, it proves quite difficult. It occurs to me that this method of herding by cellular phone is also the preferred mode among Geena and her friends in London. But their desire was always to come together into the same pasture, while Sisulu's desire is to remain elusive. His instinct is a nomadic one.

More of Erasmus's top dollar intelligence secured my ride with this crew. His mole in Sisulu's camp (a bodyguard; you cannot lie to Erasmus, remember) passed on information about a delivery of weapons being made today. The delivery boy was to be Kenno. Erasmus, Dad and I paid him a visit to persuade him to let us shadow him in our own car. Since we knew where he was going and what he was doing, Kenno had little option but to agree to it, but insisted I ride with him and Sipho. I couldn't very well grass him up if I was sitting in the back of the car. And so we progress through Guguletu, with Dad and Erasmus following us in the hired vehicle.

We pull over for Sipho to take an instruction on the cell phone and a crowd surrounds the car. They rattle the locked doors, bang on the roof with bare fists. I stare at their faces and beyond to the other car stopped just behind us, which has been left alone by the crowd. The power of that man Erasmus.

After a few moments of siege Sipho tells Kenno to get going and to take a left on NY72. In order to get past the crowd Kenno drives over a puny garden, someone's attempt at optimism, and chugs into an empty street – a vacuum compared to the one we just left – and we seem to fly as though in a small air-craft.

Where the road terminates in a mountain of rubble a white Mercedes waits, its snout pointing outward. Inside the Mercedes is Ernie Sisulu, a phone to his ear. Sitting next to him is a bodyguard. In the back seat is Geena.

Kenno cuts the engine fifty yards short of the Mercedes. I push the back of Kenno's seat, eager to get out. But Kenno won't budge. He tells me to stay cool. Sisulu's bodyguard has a pair of binoculars trained on us. We have to wait until we clear security or Sisulu will fly.

We sit in the road for five, maybe ten minutes as Sisulu's bodyguard attempts to ID the passengers in our car and in the car behind. With each minute that passes I grow closer to hysteria that they will drive away. Around us Guguletu is unnaturally quiet; an outer-space silence, like a foreshadowing.

We hear it break at the same time. An ululation keeps on growing and growing. A moment later a cloud of dust rumbles towards the cars and a dense and formal Islamic crowd appears behind us.

'Fucking hell!' Kenno cries. 'Fuck, fuck, fuck!'

'Get out the car!' Sipho shouts. 'Get out the car.'

We bale out so fast Kenno neglects to remove his keys from the ignition. He tries to double back to retrieve them, but is seconds too late. The vehicle is now surrounded by the marchers. I estimate a few thousand in the crowd, chanting in Arabic, dividing me not just from Geena but from Erasmus and my father. I feel afraid without them.

If it is unfortunate that we have driven into the predestined route of this march, it is much more unfortunate for Ernie Sisulu. For him to be in this place at this time is almost providential. Certainly that is what the leaders of the march sense. With shawls around their faces, carrying Kalishnikovs above their shoulders they start to run towards Sisulu's Mercedes. Geena is trapped in the back seat and there is nothing I can do. There is nothing my father can do either. I keep seeing split-second flashes of his drawn white face framing his startled eyes. Red dust colours his grey hair. I hear Kenno repeating over and over, 'This is going off! This is going off!' and his manic laughter.

Sisulu is taking stock of the situation, looking for an exit. He wears shades, but his terror is audible in the way he revs the engine. He has nowhere to go. Behind his bodyguard Geena's head bobs from side to side.

I cannot move in the crowd, buffeting me around as the gunmen reach the Mercedes. I see the bodyguard fleeing the car, then Sisulu throw the Mercedes into reverse. He tries vainly to batter a way through the pile of bricks and mortar.

I hear my father cry out as the masked men fire their Kalishnikovs into the windscreen of the Mercedes. The crowd stampedes at the sound of gunfire and I'm flipped over a picket fence, with several bodies on top of me. A lonely desolation prevails. I hear four more gunshots and the sound of splintering glass. Sipho's Cat boots appear briefly between the feet of the crowd. I also glimpse Kenno, dropping onto his knees. Sipho's boots start running. He is fast distancing himself, bolting into the heart of the crowd where he can be camouflaged. My stomach contracts violently as though from chronic hunger. My mouth salivates.

I fight with all I've got to get back on to my feet. Through a gap in the crowd I see Sisulu being pulled out of his broken windscreen over the bonnet of his car, his blood streaked across the white paintwork. Then the marchers flip the Mercedes onto its roof. Children begin to dance on the exposed undercarriage.

I hear myself moaning, because I want to be right there beside the Mercedes. Briefly my mother's face flashes before me. I hear my father shouting my name, but can't see him. I can't see Erasmus. Sisulu is laid out on the road just twenty yards away. His body is kicked and stoned with bricks, lumps of wood as the crowd empties their lungs: 'Allah-hu-Akbar . . . ALLAH-HU-AKBAR!' I see young faces looking full. Then Sisulu is shot again. His head jerks as each round enters, and explodes like a watermelon. Petrol is poured over his body and it is set alight.

The marchers cleave apart, escaping the reach of the flames. I feel the heat on my face as I run through the gap towards the Mercedes. Young boys celebrating around this *auto-da-fé* look at me as I push through, moving with a strength I'll never experience again.

An imprint of Sisulu's body has been left behind in the dust before he was dragged away and burned. I kneel down and put my hand through the broken rear window of the car. The car rocks on its roof as the children dance on the undercarriage. I smell my sister. I smell the rose-musk that she sprinkles on her skirt, like her mother. Connected only by this olfactory thread I stretch in further and feel a hot sweaty hand, like the hand of a child. I pull Geena through the rear window.

Geena is unconscious as I lay her on her back. Her face is bloody. I lower my ear to her mouth, feel her carotid pulse. She is not breathing and her heart has stopped. I make sure her airway is clear then put in four breaths, pinching her nose with her head back. I test the carotid again, peel back her eyelids and check her eyes. One of her pupils is dilated. Just the one. I give five massages to the heart to one breath. Every three cycles I check the pulse, eyes, breathing.

A blow is delivered to the back of my head, but it does not stop me. The pain spreads around my face, spiralling down my neck and back. I make no effort to see who my assailant is, and keep working. I may still be conscious but there has been some interference to the function of the brain. Messages transmitted to and from my nervous system for the protection of my body are short circuited and it cannot make its usual decisions in such a crisis as this. I feel nothing, not even numb. Numb is something.

I check her mouth, ears, nose, eyes. The one eye is still dilated. I check for cerebro-spinal fluid discharging from her ear. I continue resuscitation and then she comes around. Only then and only for a second do I look up. I'm expecting to be struck on the head again. Instead what I see is Erasmus standing over me, keeping the rowdy boys away, saving me like he once saved my father from a fatal beating thirty years ago. I manage to give him a brief smile before returning to work.

Her pulse is weak, her breathing paradoxical. As she inhales, a section of the chest wall caves in. At least one rib is broken in two places. Her eyelids flutter and she looks at me, confused and distant. Now her heart is beating again her facial wounds start leaking. She has contusions to her forehead, lacerations on her cheek from flying glass. I feel down her neck, arms, legs for fractures. Her skin is clammy and cold, her face is ashen and her lips are blue.

Under normal circumstances I would not move her and just wait for an ambulance. But there are no medics in this fallen world. I pick her up and carry her over my shoulder and stagger away from the Mercedes. A breeze lifts her yellow cotton dress over my face. I run blind, straight into my father.

As he is pulling me towards our hired car it bursts into flames and clears my mind. It is so fabulously clear that I remember that Kenno left his keys in the ignition of his VW.

We work together, Dad and I, laying Geena on the back seat. Her mouth froths like foam on the sea. I rest her head on my lap as Dad gets in the driver's seat. I don't know where Erasmus has gone. I seek out my father's eyes. He looks out of the side window briefly, returns my stare and shakes his head. 'Erasmus will be okay,' he says.

The moment he starts to rev the engine I feel sanguine. What else can possibly befall us now? The car feels as impregnable as a castle of steel. Multiple petrol explosions under the bonnet are going to rocket us to safety. Cars can get you into trouble, but they can get you out of it too. We all of us have cars. Cars are common to all men, cars and TV sets.

My optimism is not sustained. Cars are not common to *all* men. My father keeps losing control of the vehicle. He can't even change gear. How did this come to pass, that I am in the back and he is at the wheel? Our one big mistake.

We start to skid and the car sluices sideways. Suddenly I am looking out the offside window, then the nearside window, then the offside window again at the bleak salt flats, the drifting cloud, the cruel shadows. We scatter township pedestrians through pale grass, with looks of fury on their faces. If they could stop us they would cut us out of the car like fruit from a can.

He navigates out of the township by the dead reckoning of his memory. On Baden Powell Drive I see his shoulders relax, and immediately he loses control. He throws the steering wheel too far to the left on a bend and the front wheels carve into sand. The car comes to a stop and the engine stalls. I sit there for a few sliding seconds, not quite believing the sight of our bonnet buried in a sand dune.

In the silence I hear Geena's laboured breathing. Her fingers start to worry the hem of her skirt.

My father swaps with me and sits in the back with Geena. Now her head is on his lap. I pull the car out of the sand dune and drive back onto Baden Powell Drive.

We discuss briefly which hospital we should aim for. Groote Schuur is the obvious choice. It is the only one we know.

Then Geena starts to talk, quite clearly. All she wants to do is go home. My father and I both bite back the tears.

'I want you to go home too,' he says. 'But we're having a bit of difficulty agreeing where that is.'

'I have a terrible headache and my chest hurts like hell. But otherwise I feel okay.'

My father strokes her brow. 'You need medical attention.'

'I've got the two best porters in the business, what more do I need.'

'You need a doctor, Geena.'

'I've heard that before somewhere.'

We drive her to the Groote Schuur hospital in Observatory. From the car park I carry Geena in my arms and follow Dad into the building. He seems to know exactly where he is going. The A&E resembles a field hospital, with black casualties sitting on the floor, in chairs, nursing wounds seeping through dirty bandages. It is all lacklustre and blue emotion. Dad goes off and comes back with a porter wheeling an empty chair. I lower Geena into the chair and follow the porter to find an assessment nurse. The nurse tells us there is an eight-hour wait to see one of the doctors. I tell her Geena has a suspected head fracture and demand an immediate CT scan. I explain that she has a broken rib that might have punctured her lung. She is a front-line, blue-light casualty.

She lets us jump the long queue of Africans to the doctor's door. When your family is on the line, when your adopted family is on the line, politics, ethics go to hell.

'You've had a knock to the head too,' the doctor informs me, playing his fingers along the back of my skull. 'There's a lot of congealed blood around here.'

Only now does my head begin to hurt. 'It's all right,' I say. 'It's nothing.'

Geena enters the great machine. For the next hour she belongs to the CT and X-Ray attendants. Dad and I stroll up and down the long white thoroughfares of Groote Schuur, clouded with nurses and doctors, patients. There seems to be at least four tribes represented here. My father tells me that thirty years ago the patients had all been white, the doctors and nurses were all white, the hospital porters all black . . . with one exception.

We are called into a treatment room where the Afrikaner consultant explains that the CT scan revealed a fractured skull, but no internal bleeding. In the X-ray we see a rib broken in two places, but no punctured lung. There is no treatment required, being self-healing injuries.

I feel a sudden rush, like an infusion of joy. Hospitals are beautiful. Science and mathematics are beautiful. Perhaps Natasha had prayed for us and was heard.

The doctor insists Geena stays in hospital under observation for an absolute minimum of forty-eight hours. But she has other plans. 'The last time I was in this hospital, I went in with one set of parents and came out with an entirely different set. I have no intention of it happening again.'

She tells the doctor she is discharging herself. We persuade her to compromise. So for forty-eight hours read twenty-four.

BOYES DRIVE

At the highest point on Boyes Drive, Joel pulls over, switches off the ignition and kills the lights. In the distance the ocean drones on eternally. He produces from his breast pocket a ready-rolled joint, torches the end and passes it into the back seat to me. I don't hesitate, even with my father in the front. I suck greedily at the skunk and quickly feel the effects.

'This is my favourite spot in all Cape Town,' Joel muses. He points to the vast lunar expanses of the Cape Flats far below us, where a million squatter campfires wink in the night. A new melon-slice moon hangs in the sky. 'Hannah calls those lights down there stars that have fallen from the sky.'

'For every one of those lights,' Dad says, 'is a person trying to survive.'

'*Ja*, the unlucky sperm club.' Joel finds this amusing. 'Have you ever read the Icelandic Sagas, Clement?' He flicks the joint out of the window. A few dozen cicadas stop rubbing their legs together. 'It's like the Sagas down there. In a township if a man kills your brother you're obliged to kill him. To show honour to your brother. A brother who's not avenged is a man whose memory and reputation means nothing. It says to everybody, you do not love him. And you'll be branded a coward and your reputation will mean shit also.'

'The Sagas are medieval,' I add. 'No one had guns. If there were no guns . . .'

'They'd kill each other with a bone.' Joel laughs.

The sound of bells ringing in a Dutch Reform church rises on the thermals, like a bird of prey.

'Why do you want to help them kill themselves, Joel? What do you get out of it? Is it just for the money?'

'Not my hand on the trigger, china. The sins of this country pre-date me. Anyway it's not murder, it's suicide. Suicide with company. Life is cheap down there, like you say, Clement. Death's a welcome release. Give them a firearm and you save them the wait.'

'That's big of you, Joel.'

'Oh come on, Clement. Fucking hell. I'm not selling to politicals, white extremists or anything. There's a war going on out there with one side more tooled up than the other. I'm redressing the balance. I sell guns to people who can't get them legitimately. Because if you haven't got a piece in the townships you are less than a man who has. It's as simple as that. I've lived here over thirty years, and I'm telling you, there's no justice out there, no law courts. It's dog eat dog.'

Joel lights up another joint. This time he doesn't share it with me.

'A third of all Africans are HIV positive anyway, d'you know that? Guys with the disease are raping young girls because they think virgins can cure them. For us maybe sex produces new life, but in the townships it's the source of death.' He pauses. 'If they don't kill each other with guns they'll do it with their dicks.'

'This isn't getting us very far, is it?' Dad says.

'I'm just telling you like it is.' Joel's eyes are completely chimped out with the dagga. 'Guns are the new gold in South Africa.'

'And you're Rhodes's heir-apparent?'

'In Rhodes's time there was a future for whites in this country. I don't think our future's going to hold out much longer. I intend to make as much as I can, then split. Me and Hannah, to London. See you there, maybe. Have a curry one evening down Brick Lane.'

I feel my father flinch. 'Give me a good reason why I shouldn't tell the police about you.'

'Quite frankly, Clement, I doubt they'll be interested.'

I remember the story of Kenno's about when he went into a police station, how he was left alone in a room with a semi-automatic rifle and a full clip of bullets on the desk – and find myself deferring to Joel's wisdom.

'I could take the police to have a look at the arms you've stashed on Robben Island and in the back of Kenno's car.'

'Clement! I'm impressed.'

Joel waits a moment and then puts his hand into a compartment in the door. Ceremoniously he hands Geena's British passport to Dad. 'You give me back what's in the boot of Kenno's car and I promise, cross my heart and hope to die, never to see or contact Geena again. That's what you want, isn't it?'

My father inspects the passport in his hand. 'Okay, that's a deal.'

'You see, Clement? Now you're in the arms business, just like me.'

TRINITY

With Geena clutching her bottle of pain killers in the back seat, I set a course for Langa. Driving along the N2 in Kenno's Golf I check my rearview mirror constantly, each time seeing Ernie Sisulu tailgating me in a burning white Mercedes. His killing plays back in my head on a loop, his mutilated face like a portrait, watching over me and speaking in a language that is the language of the living, but uprooted and turned over in the soil to become something else; a plant with pale flowers. But the recall has no emotional impact at all. Certain events are so horrific a certain rationality kicks in and converts the unbearable into cartoon. Only when I recall Geena lying unconscious on the ground do I feel nauseous.

Someone has said of Macbeth that when he kills Duncan he crosses a line and can never go back to being what he was. Killing is like losing virginity. Both are irrevocable experiences, and very intimate. Some of the gunmen who killed Sisulu were teenagers. I saw their faces when their shawls fell and their eyes changed instantly, turning passionate.

My father carries Geena in his big arms up the steps of Erasmus's hostel. Her stiffness, the furrowing of her brow, the alarm in the eyes, all the somatic expressions of anxiety absent

232

for so long, place her once again in the rational world.

Erasmus emerges from his room in boxer shorts. He looks mortified to receive us improperly dressed. He returns briefly to his room, re-emerging in my Ted Baker shirt.

He apologises for wearing my shirt.

'Keep it,' I say.

Erasmus prepares a meal of salted *snoek*, okra, hot peppers, sweet potato on a bed of rice. We all sit down on the floor and eat from four corners of the same bowl, as Erasmus breaks the fish and vegetables with his fingers, delivering morsels to each of us as we need them, like a croupier. Geena eats little, complains of head and chest pains and asks to lie down.

We put Geena into one of the rooms, turfing out the family that occupies it. As I lay her on the soft mattress her small hands cup the back of her head. Her pale blue cardigan is twisted beneath her.

That night I sleep in the same bed to watch over her; like we used to, like children again. The air is hot and viscous. When I sense her sleeping, I too fall asleep.

Some time later the feel of her naked flesh pressing against me wakes me. She has taken off all her clothes. Her eyes are wide open, seeking me out. 'It's all right,' she says softly and strokes my hair. 'What will be will be.'

I stare back unable to move a single limb or muscle. Her hair is tangled around her eyes and nose, stuck to her face with sweat. A humid smell rises from her armpits and neck. Outside a storm rumbles and in the distance the sky cleaves with yellow sheet lightning. The curtain over the doorway keeps rising and falling with the draught and I glimpse the family of four we have displaced, lying on the floor of the kitchen, looking very small against the wall and sleeping through the storm. I maintain the same rigid position through the rest of the night. I stay on watch. Her refrain keeps replaying through me. *It's all right. What will be will be.*

Just before dawn breaks I submit to sleep. I am jolted awake by a mouse nibbling the food beneath my fingernails. The room is bathed in bright, sharp light, full of puns. I don't know where I am for certain. Then I hear someone moaning from another room, which helps locate me. I sit up on my elbows and see Geena's ruffled hair evolving out of the pillow. And it brings me down. I remember. The sheet that has covered us has fallen on the floor and I see for the first time since we were little and pre-pubescent her long, slim body, naked except for her white socks. Her pubic hair curls in great whorls, like a wind has spun it, fanning off down the inside of her thighs. Light, but lengthy. Her ankles are downy and her armpits unshaven. Her pelvic bone protrudes. On her stomach below her navel is a little scar that I didn't know about. Her breasts are small with one nipple ingrown. I keep thinking how foreign a body she looks.

My desire, for so long confused, cannot be sustained. This is my last revelation in a journey of revelations. If I'd hoped to stay pure by refusing all others' love but hers, avoid the corruption of a stranger's naked flesh against my own, I am now inclined to think that the only way I can ever love anyone else is to let her go. I have never loved anyone else. I used to believe my father has never loved anyone else but my mother. But after seeing him here I realise that is a fake history. In Erasmus and no doubt in many others who have left this earth, he shared a love every bit as profound as his love for family, without debasing that familial love. I want to emulate my father. I want to extend my range. I want to love half a dozen people and feel their love reciprocated. So I have to let you go, Geena. And that is all right. That is what will be.

PART FIVE

'If a contemporary man went into the past he would not be seen.'

— GEORGE KUBLER

CITIES ON THE RIVER

Two heavily built white guys are in the mixed sauna. They aren't City boys, bankers, stockbrokers, evidenced by the way they talk, in rapidly delivered broken monotones, and by other things too. The older of the two keeps shaking a bottle of Olbas oil onto the coals, filling the room with camphor and menthol vapours. He says to the other, 'I've had this flu two weeks now, this'll kill it.'

His companion adds, 'You come down with that on Saturday, didn't you?'

'It's been dragging me down for three days, this is the place to kill it. Germs can't survive heat.'

'Anything over seventy degrees.'

'Well, sixty-seven degrees, seventy degrees, and they all get killed. You won't get nothing coming in here alive leaving the same way.'

'It's burning my fucking eyebrows off that Olbas.' He slaps a hand on his head, tearing sweat off his eyebrows, his face like a lampshade in the foggy doon.

'Six, say six. Six thirty, you know that time, you got to be there.'

'Six thirty,' the other repeats.

'No, six thirty's too late. Six, around six he shuts up shop and goes. You can put your car in the lock-up and leg it over there. I'll give you a photo. So you'll know what he looks like. He's got a young girl behind the counter. Really pretty. Model as good as, size twelve.'

'What's he done?'

'She's married to him and he's doing all this stuff, raising ten grand on her house and forging her signature. The family want you to whack him, no question, but don't do that.'

'At six . . .'

'Yeah, at six just go there and familiarise yourself. It cost me ten grand to get a divorce. My wife another fifteen. That's twenty-five grand. This woman don't want any of that, with two kids, and you stay talking to one another after. Don't break anything. I'll give you a photo.'

The two men get up and leave us the sauna to ourselves.

'Who the hell were they?' I ask. 'I thought this was meant to be exclusive. Chi-chi.'

'Private detectives?' Natasha opines.

'Maybe they come in here to score,' Geena suggests.

'Maybe,' says Natasha. 'I'm sure some do.'

'When I was in the gym,' Geena adds, 'those two guys kept looking at my tits through my T-shirt.'

Half an hour ago we had all been in the gym; Natasha and me on the bikes, Geena on the rowing machine in front of us, watching *Neighbours* on the TV. Dance rhythms of the Chemical Brothers shimmered over us. One day in the distant future archaeologists are going to dig up the remains of some health club like this and deduce that our time was a bleak time in the evolution of civilization, when people rode bicycles and got nowhere, rowed without a drop of water passing beneath.

From the gym we went for a swim. As you can't read when you swim and you can't talk when you dive, I've never been naturally inclined towards pools. But for Geena it was just what the doctor ordered. She still gets pains in her chest, dizzy spells and sleepiness – the symptoms of post-concussion syndrome, which a little light aerobic exercise helps to cure. You have to keep the body in shape to save the mind from shipwrecking. I kept her under surveillance as she stroked up and down our pre-booked lane, struggling to inhale.

Natasha's body has had a lot of time and effort spent on it at this health club, which shows in her leg and arm muscles. She has a body that attracts the male eye, and yet I still feel no desire for her.

'I can understand coming here to score,' I continue with the theme, 'because the exercise sure doesn't do anything for me.'

Geena bursts out laughing.

'What's so funny?' I ask.

'I was remembering your infant school sports day, your sun hat falling off in the middle of a race. When you stopped to pick it up all the kids stopped running. They didn't want to leave their buddy behind.' She laughs more. 'Their fathers went crazy. They were shouting: Run! Run! *Win! Win!* All of them insurance salesmen, actuaries. They just don't get it, do they?' She continues to laugh, a beautiful sound, something I've missed for too long.

'I can't remember any of that.'

'Then ask me, I'm four years older.' Geena gets up off the bench in the wrap of a white towel. 'See you in the shower.'

Natasha and I linger in the sauna for a while longer. Neither of us seems particularly keen to head the charge outside and face the world. We watch the egg timer run out of sand. Menthol and camphor vapours stick in our throats.

Finally Natasha asks, 'Does she still have no memory of Cape Town?'

'No.'

'That is so strange.'

'Her neurologist calls it dissociative fugue. A fugue is associated with epilepsy.'

'Is it epilepsy she's got?'

'Who knows. But Stein thinks the bump on her head, the fracture, repointed the brickwork.'

In the men's changing rooms I shower for ten minutes then blowdry my hair. I look at my reflection in the mirror. I have aged, I've definitely aged. What makes us age this fast, apart from guilt? My actions in Cape Town had been duplicitous. My motives were not so pure. I think of Hannah twice-losing her daughter. I worry that Geena has returned to a life less spectacular than the one she might have made for herself out there. But then maybe not. What future can there be for whites in South Africa, even good whites? I think a lot of things that I cannot resolve. I think fate is only a fiction.

We leave Natasha's private gym in Blackfriars and cross the river to get something to eat and drink in the Oxo Tower. From one exclusive City hangout to another, both of them on Natasha. Health clubs, Harley Street doctors, Wimpole Street dentists . . . Natasha's world will always be a long way removed from my NHS existence. It may be pleasant to experience once in a while, but more frequent than that and I'd feel too far removed from the rest of the world, more existential than I am now.

While we wait for a table we sit on the sixth-floor terrace in the freezing night air and drink margaritas. Geena still glows from her workout as she points down to the river flowing below.

'Why are cities in the northern hemisphere built on rivers and in the southern hemisphere on the sea?'

'Something to do with trade routes?' I suggest. The salt on the edge of my glass stings my mouth.

We wait for Geena to say more, more about the southern hemisphere, but she switches the subject to London. 'This programme I was watching, it said London's being abandoned. People are leaving in droves for the country. But I can't see the queue from here, can you?'

'No I can't.'

'I'm getting frustrated with TV,' Geena announces. 'It keeps giving out false information.'

At 11 p.m. I clock on for work. The night shift in hospital is the worst time, not my time at all. It is the world turned upside down, and for some it is the end of the world. Too often you find yourself in close proximity to strangers whose meandering rattled cries in the dark are intimacies you do not want to share. More patients die in the night than in the day, followed by the sound of the duty sister's feet shuffling across the rubber floor and the sound of screens being drawn around the bed. Moments later, little red lights at the nurses' station illuminate the same duty sister's eyes as she whispers sex-talk down the telephone to her lover back home. Nursing is erotic because the job entails a lot of touching, of both the living and the dead.

The night may not be my time but it is rush-hour for the priests. Priests are good souls, but leave their clients feeling heartbroken and guilty, and that's not so good; while nurses offer chemical solicitude out of the hand, without judgement or penalty.

Thank God for the pharmacy, I say.

Thank God for nurses too, for Nurse Dalrymple in particular, who saw me in the canteen reading the same author as her (Isaac Bashevis Singer) and invited me to join her for lunch. Within minutes she seemed familiar to me, as if I'd known her all my life. The countenance of a nurse is the more memorable because our desire to be numbered is reflected in her eyes. I number. I do matter to Nurse Sheena Dalrymple from the Firth of Forth, a dealer in care at an institution that was built out of profits from the Slave Trade.

How long it will last I don't know. How long can any relationship last that has been founded on fiction?

What if we had children? If I number in her eyes now, what would happen to our love once it is eclipsed by the love of those children? That's when everything goes wrong in a marriage. I think my parents were able to tough out their marriage precisely because Geena was adopted. There was a struggle in the raising of her and it was a struggle overcome.

Men love women but I'm not so sure they love mothers.

But I am getting ahead of myself, planning my hypothetical future with her in mind. That way madness lies. In the meantime at least Sheena has enabled me to break free of my shackles to Geena (even though I keep calling her by my sister's name).

1066 COUNTRY

Geena can't remember her South African odyssey. Ernie Sisulu, Joel Sugarman and Hannah Charles, Kenno Willmot and his parents have all been washed out of her mind. But she does remember Erasmus vaguely. Erasmus was the last South African she saw, who came with us to the airport and gave her a Xhosa dress. He was tearful saying goodbye to Dad and it was the most he could do to shake his hand. I promised to send him some good novels from England. As we were walking through passport control, I looked back to wave but Erasmus had already gone. In his place I spotted the same old Boer with the metal plates in his head and legs who we'd encountered on the train from Langa. He was engaging tourists at the check-in with his stories of survival. I saw him take some woman's hand and place it to his jaw, like he did with me. He was waving his aluminium crutch around in the air like a baton, taking gratuities in the other hand. As good a metaphor as any for South Africa to take back home with me.

On my parents' fortieth wedding anniversary we all go down to Hastings-on-sea to celebrate. Geena sits next to my mother on

243

the train, wearing her Xhosa dress. Handmade from black damask the bodice is embossed with fynbos and the skirt embroidered with buttons and finished with red and yellow trim. The headpiece that comes with it keeps slipping off her hair. She gives up and places it on the table. My mother and father can't seem to stop smiling.

In the adjacent seats Natasha can't stop smiling either. Surrounding her are her children, Richard and Amanda, aged eight and ten, listening to story tapes on their Walkmans and crumbling crisps into their beakers of Coke. To anyone who cares about such images, she might appear to be too adoring after ten years of being mother; too fresh and eager. Like the fathers in Maternity she imprints her loving smile on their memory cells, making her biological claim a bit late in the day.

We pass through Sussex with little to say. As we are approaching Hastings Natasha's kids remove their earphones and Geena leans across the aisle to tell them that John Baird invented television here.

We all know something about Baird. Natasha recalls his experiments with a flickering Maltese Cross projected on a screen, which I know he referred to as 'seeing by wireless'. My mother thinks his father was a Presbyterian minister and Dad adds that his wife was the South African pianist Margaret Albu.

From the train station we stroll down to the seaside, through the narrow alleyways of the Old Town. Against the wind Geena keeps holding down her skirt, as Mum and Dad show the children the clinker-built, bow-fronted sixteenth century houses that charmed such luminaries as Charles Lamb, David Garrick, Rudyard Kipling and J.M.W. Turner.

At the seafront, the Elizabethan dry-netting houses are still there at the Stade, and some of the shops I remember as a kid: the Magnetic Therapy Clinic, Pie, Mash and Liquor Palace, Arthur Green's Gentlemen's Outfitter. Many of the arcades are new to us: Delboy's Gifts, Deluxe Leisure Centre, Playdium. The

Georgian crescents look pretty forlorn and the racks of cheap hotels tatty.

We have only ever been here in summer, and at this time of year, out of season, Hastings looks ghosted, chilled through by cold winds upon which travels the voice of a bingo caller, with all the stress of a muezzin. As we walk down the promenade crowds of teenagers emerge from the School of English above Steve's Tackle & Bait shop, run across the road and start making international calls from a row of phone boxes. We hear many languages: French, Italian, Spanish, Polish, Russian. The only common denominator is the fish and chips, steaming in paper in the hand. An Italian girl drifts past shooting video footage of her friends, the architecture of Hastings in the background. I hear her mumble into the microphone of her digital camera: 'This is England. I love very much the England.'

My parents choose the venue for their anniversary tea, the same Greek Cypriot's café where we used to go twenty years ago. We order cod and chips (×3), rock and chips (×1), children's portions (×2) and baked jam roll and custard all round. Mum and Geena drink shandy; Double Diamond for Dad and me. Natasha is tempted by the wine list: Aphrodite, Sauternes, Panteleimon, but settles for a Cinzano, her first alcoholic drink in three years. The tomato ketchup is cut with vinegar but otherwise full marks to the Regal Café.

We finish the meal with cups of tea and listen in to four large women speaking in baritone voices at the next table. When one of them leans across and compliments Geena on her African dress I realise they aren't women at all, but transvestites. They ask if we are on holiday and it seems simpler just to say yes.

Outside the Regal, seagulls hover at low altitudes. Then one gull followed by another drop to the ground like stones, twitching and rolling in the road. I hear a pop from above. I look up and see, in the window above the Royal Albion pub, two boys firing air rifles at the birds.

To escape this stain on our celebrations we cross the road to the pier. But the pier boardwalk swarms with early night drunks and parents at the end of their patience with children demanding their last pound of flesh, riding out the final reserves of the day on the dodgem cars and the mini-dipper. At high tide several trawlers beach straight onto the shingle as a jaundice-yellow band of mist hangs above the sea. Everywhere the air stinks of rotten fish. We pay thirty pence a head to enter the pier and escape the boardwalk confusion.

We leave Natasha in the games deck, where Richard and Amanda play the penny slots, and stroll along to the ballroom. Mum wants to see if the old Victorian music hall has changed at all. But apart from a white muslin cloth draped from the low ceiling and Marshall PA speakers stacked up on the stage, it hasn't changed much. A rumba class is just letting out.

As we are standing inside, two African men carrying odd musical instruments climb on stage. An engineer turns on the microphones for a sound check. At the sight of these musicians my father and mother begin to talk to each other in earnest. Like they used to do. I break it up, demanding an audience. Without taking his eyes off the musicians Dad explains to us that their instruments are called koras. Twenty-two strings in two parallel planes attached to a wooden neck are anchored to a split gourd covered with cow's hide. A long time ago, Dad says, he and Mum attended a kora recital in District Six. The musician had travelled all the way from Mali and was called a *jali*.

He is excitable explaining their music. The history of the West African people is an oral one, and the province of the *jali*, whose songs are the equivalent of Viking or Arthurian legends; epic narrations about families lost to slavery, whole tribes wiped out in colonial wars. If a man commissioned a *jali*

246

to sing something contemporary he'd begin with the eleventh century and work forward.

Dad asks Mum if she can remember the name of the *jali* who they saw in District Six. 'Bansang,' she says without missing a beat. 'His last name was Bansang. And he was seventy-three years old.'

'That's right,' Dad says and takes it from there. Bansang was the last living *jali* to play a rare Malian tradition. When he died so would that tradition. As there were no recordings, each concert he gave was sacred. That concert in District Six in which he sang in Arabic, French and Mandinka could have been his last.

'When an old *jali* like that dies,' my father says, 'a whole library is burned down.'

And now, in the Hastings pier ballroom the two musicians sit cross-legged on the stage and start to pluck their koras with their thumbs. The crisp aged tone is underwhelming, but is as pure as the trees and hide the koras were torn from. What I marvel at most is how such a fragile instrument has survived at all – the internicide, genocide and bloody struggles for power, nationhood and identity. The kora is emblematic of this history and yet independent of it, giving its own statement of harmony – and in England to boot.

A woman dressed in a gown printed with fire finches and parrots joins the two kora players. She fills the ballroom with her voice. We don't know what she is singing about but it makes Geena cry. She isn't embarrassed but she is confused as to why this female singer with no shake, no vibrato at all, can make her weep.

My father says something quite fine to her. He puts his arm around her shoulder and says: 'When people speak there's no way of knowing if it's true or not. But when a singer sings the truth, you know because a secret world is unmasked, that you recognise as your own. That is why you are crying.'

'I can see them all,' she says through her tears. 'Joel and Hannah. Ernie and Kubasni.'

For a very uncomfortable few seconds we await the fallout. But the fallout is not forthcoming. Geena is aware, but safely aware. The recent past drifts in on a magic carpet of song. The fugue has ended. The circle has been squared.

We stay listening for a while to this woman's strong unaffected voice hovering just above the acoustic level of the medieval instruments. And we all feel something of the same; the same possibilities for recovering love which once was believed irretrievable.

We leave the ballroom to go find Natasha. She is already out on the pier deck with her children, their arms hanging over the rusting iron rail, watching the last of the trawlers return from the fishing grounds. We line up beside them as these boats travel past without pitch or toss across a sea so calm that it seems to have some of the qualities of air, with neither swell running nor surface tension.

ACKNOWLEDGEMENTS

Thanks are due to the friends and colleagues who helped me midwife this novel: John Tague, Jon Cook, Benita Parry, Richard Beswick, Antonia Hodgson, Derek Johns – faithful readers all; for their youthful counsel: Rebecca Jones, Anna MacKinnon, Ben Cattermole; for their hospitality while in South Africa: André Wiesner, Stephen Watson, Carol Campbell, Miki Flockemann, Robin Gaylord, Chris Roper, Fatima Dike; for sending me to South Africa in the first instance: Jonathan Barker at the British Council.

I have drawn information from the following texts: *Robben Island: the Politics of Rock and Sand* (University of Cape Town, 1992) by Nigel Penn, Harriet Deacon, Neville Alexander *et al*; *My Traitor's Heart* (The Bodley Head, 1990) by Rian Malan; *The Burden of Memory, The Muse of Forgiveness* (Oxford University Press, 1999) by Wole Soyinka, whose closing image inspired my own.